Someone <u>could</u> be hiding in the woods.

The thought terrified her. She hastened on, tripped over a maple root and fell into a thicket of brambles.

But her dog was so near that she could now see his pale-yellow shape, wriggling, leaping, unable to reach her because he was tied. She got up, clutching the raincoat around her, and went cautiously to him.

Yes, he was tied. Tied securely, too, with a rope knotted firmly around his collar . . .

A cloud of smothering blackness came down over her head. Her dog barked frantically. Arms were around her throat; at least they felt like arms, she thought wildly, but they were, in fact the sleeves of the raincoat she had casually flung over her shoulders. The blackness over her face was the stifling hood of the coat.

But the coat alone could not do what those sleeves and hood were doing. She had, literally, no air. She was tearing at the sleeves, the whole world turning dizzily. She could barely hear her dog. Then she couldn't hear anything . . .

Also by
MIGNON G. EBERHART

Another Man's Murder

Hunt with the Hounds

Murder in Waiting

Postmark Murder

Unidentified Woman

Witness at Large

Wolf in Man's Clothing

Published by
WARNER BOOKS

MIGNON G. EBERHART

FAMILY AFFAIR

WARNER BOOKS

A Warner Communications Company

The characters and events in this novel are entirely fictional; however, the author is grateful to Aunt Nelle, Cousin Constance, Cousin Richard and Nephew Bill for being themselves and thus inadvertently supplying factual and close-at-hand views of some distinguished worlds.

WARNER BOOKS EDITION

This Warner Books Edition is published by arrangement with Random House, Inc., 201 East 50 Street, New York, N. Y. 10022

Warner Books, Inc.
666 Fifth Avenue
New York, N.Y. 10103

Ⓦ A Warner Communications Company

Printed in the United States of America

First Warner Books Printing: November, 1984

10 9 8 7 6 5 4 3 2 1

One

Lights glittered below them and out across the myriad runways where the big birds swooped gently down and other big birds soared upward into the blue night. The truly exceptional one was waiting, looking like a vast bird of prey, its tremendous beak ready to swoop across the dark Atlantic. The windows in the dining room were large and offered a wide view, but must have been soundproofed, for they heard very little of the enormous engines coming and going. Small white trucks skittered like bugs here and there, busily carrying food. Fitz ordered a martini for each of them.

Sarah said slowly, "How long have you known about this?"

Fitz leaned toward her. "Since I was told to take Bill's place."

"You didn't tell me."

"I couldn't. Orders. Nothing over the phone. Nothing of the reason for my going to Ligunia. But I had to see you. I had to tell you."

"That's why you sounded—oh, so different when you talked to me."

"I had to say only that Bill was in the hospital and I was to take his place."

"How long will you be there?"

"I don't know."

"But—we had planned our marriage for next month." She tried to laugh, but it was not a success. "Always a good plan to tell a girl she's being jilted."

"Sarah, don't be an idiot."

"Where is Bill Hicks?"

"At the Walter Reed Hospital. They think he'll be all right—eventually. They don't say when."

The martinis came. Sarah turned her glass with fingers almost as cold as the glass. "So you don't want to marry me!"

"I do! But not now"—Fitz put a warm strong hand over Sarah's, taking it away from the cold glass—"when I can't let you come with me."

She waited for a long moment, thinking hard. "I could get my immunization shots and a place on a later plane and meet you—wherever you say."

"For God's sake, I've been thinking of nothing else. The fact is—there are complications. Bill isn't just ill, he was shot."

"Shot! Fitz—"

"Don't look like that. No war is breaking out—not just now, at any rate."

"But—how did it happen? What—?"

Fitz shrugged. "In the usual way of these senseless attacks. It seems he had just walked out of the consulate compound and was going through a sort of park, and he was shot. Somebody could have been waiting for him. But nobody is certain of anything, yet."

"Fitz! You *can't* go there—"

"Now, Sarah. I have to go."

"What did they do?"

"A clerk at the consulate happened to be not far behind him. He heard the shot—or shots. Actually, he said there were several of them. Anyway, he rushed up, got Bill to the consulate and a doctor, and then home. He'll be all right. One shot got him in the leg. It may have been someone simply trying to scare him or— Oh, nobody can guess ahead of time what motivates these affairs. Anyway, he's going to be all right.''

"But—but, Fitz! You said over the phone that you were to take over his post temporarily. I thought you meant—well, a week or two."

He nodded. "It's a great thing for me. My first chance. I've been at the Ligunia desk ever since emerging from the Foreign Service Institute. I was afraid I'd be stuck there forever. Sarah, this only means that we may have to postpone our marriage. It *is* a temporary assignment for me. I'll almost certainly be sent back as soon as they decide upon a more experienced man. Or when Bill is able to return. And then—''

"Didn't they catch whoever it was that shot him?"

"No. Of course, they're investigating, but they don't have much to go on because there has never been any terrorist activity in Ligunia. It could have been one of those freak isolated things. Happens now all over the world." He finished his martini and ordered two more.

"I don't want you to go!" She tilted up her own glass.

"I have to. Where would your father be if he had refused any post he was given?"

"I know." Her father had survived many a street mob, more than one convulsion of local political situations.

Fitz, his dark eyes troubled, essayed a joke. "I'll be faithful to you until this is settled or I get sent some other place."

She rallied to the extent of a tight grin. "Leave you to the attractions of the Ligunian beauties—or more likely, those pretty and smart clerks and typists in the Embassy."

"None as pretty as you," he said shortly.

Two more martinis came.

She pleated her napkin nervously. "I don't care—I'm

coming too, as soon as I can get my shots. I was only—only shocked at first, Fitz.''

"I tell you, I can't let you come now. Not until I'm sure it's perfectly safe."

She sipped thoughtfully for a moment, then said, "It's never safer than after lightning strikes? That is—Oh, Fitz, I can't believe he was really shot!"

Fitz said seriously, "I promise you I won't stroll in the park or anywhere. Luckily, the consulate is right in the middle of town. Now, we've all heard of people being shot or even kidnapped while they were entering or leaving a car, or— But I went over the whole thing with the man in the department. He was very matter-of-fact and straightforward. He had to—well, warn me. Told me I would receive protection. But he said there is no political beehive stirring in Ligunia. Actually, it has been as peaceful a post as anybody could find—up to now."

"Then there is—there might be danger to you."

"No! I'll be protected. I told you that. But just now the department is working on the possibility that there might be some undercurrent of, say, a terrorist movement. Anything."

"They can't protect you every moment."

"I can look out for myself."

She thought that over. "I suppose every Foreign Service officer has said that to himself."

He turned and turned a fork beside his plate. "Probably. But please, Sarah, understand. It's my job. And I can't take you anyplace where there is the slightest possibility of danger. But they've got the whole Service working on it. They'll clear this up. Then you can come, or I'll be sent home. And we can marry. Please, Sarah . . ."

She finished her drink too fast, but she felt she needed it. All prepared for her wedding within the next month and now told that it couldn't take place for—well, how long?

They were both silent, but it was a packed, thoughtful silence. Both looked down at the planes and lights and people below, absently. Clearly, Fitz was troubled. Well, she was troubled too. It was true that the wedding arrangements were not so fixed that they could not be postponed. When Fitz had telephoned her, hurriedly, saying only that he had a sudden assignment to Ligunia and asked her to meet him at the airport so they could make plans, she had thought only of plans for their marriage. However, knowing that he might be given some foreign assignment at any moment, she had already made sure that her passport was in order. She even had a list of the immunizations any foreign assignment would require. Now everything was different.

Or was it?

The dinner he had ordered came; they leaned back in their chairs to permit its serving, both still thoughtfully silent, so there was only the silvery tinkle of china and silver and the distant sound of engines being started down below them. One plane took off into the evening sky.

When the waitress had gone, Sarah said, "But I'm coming, anyway. We can be married somewhere."

He looked out the window. Dusk was gathering in blue shadows under the wings of the big bird. Turning back to her, he said, "Sarah, my darling, I do want you. And I don't know what else I can say to stop you." His dark-gray eyes lit up. He had the strong, yet lean Favor face, rather high cheekbones and forehead, a firm mouth and chin, dark hair, peaked dark eyebrows.

Actually, they looked somewhat alike. The Favor strain was strong. Sarah's eyes were blue, but her hair was almost black and curled smoothly back from her face; she knew she had the Favor smile, with at least some of its charm, because Corinna had told her so; Corinna believed in developing feminine vanity in a girl.

She said now, firmly, "I've made up my mind. You'd better eat your dinner."

"There'll be food on the plane." He looked at his watch.

"I'll get all the shots—and clothes. I must get more dresses. What kind of things will I need?"

He seemed startled. "Why, really, I don't know. That is—No, don't buy dresses. Not now."

"Fitz! This will be my wedding. And I suppose we'll have to give dinners and all that."

Frowning, he looked at her and said, "Well, sometimes—perhaps. There are always visiting firemen. But they don't expect a junior wife to be a fashion model. Remember, now, I'm only a temporary chargé d'affaires. Don't think I'm leaping into the diplomatic—"

"But they did choose you to take Bill Hicks' place. It's a big thing for you."

"If I don't make a botch of it! If Norm hadn't been on his vacation, hunting somewhere in the wilds of Maine, they'd have sent him. He's senior to me."

"By only a few months."

"But senior just the same." He took her hand and turned the engagement ring on it thoughtfully. "I'll do my best. Keep the family flag flying!"

It was a safe change of subject, which both quickly welcomed. Time, Sarah thought; a little time and he'll see it my way. "Fitz, we do have an odd kind of family. Corinna figured out our exact degree of relationship."

"Kind of her," Fitz said dryly. "I looked it up before I had the sense to ask you to marry me. Had to be sure it was legal. Fact is, our cousinship is so remote that it can't be said to have a drop of blood relationship. So it's perfectly legal."

"I don't really care whether it's legal or not. Oh, yes I do, of course. We only call ourselves cousins for convenience."

He said thoughtfully, "Corinna has welded us all into a clan. No doubt of that. She has a very strong character."

"She has been good to us."

"She's a lonely woman. But I've always thought she

needed a kind of reason for working as hard as she does. We provide that reason."

She had never considered that. She said slowly, "That could be true. She's very generous with the money she earns."

He eyed her seriously, almost as if warning her. "Don't forget that below that pretty, helpless little lady she shows the world, there's actually a woman of steel."

"I wish she had made a better job of welding Forte," she said absently.

Fitz gave her a quick look. "What's Forte been doing?"

"Oh, just being Forte. I pushed him out of my taxi—"

"You what?"

"Oh, it doesn't matter. The taxi I took to the train. I was just leaving this afternoon when Forte stopped the taxi and said he was going with me."

"So you pushed him out?" His eyes gleamed, laughing.

"Oh, yes. That is, the taxi driver helped. Forte had the door open and was about to get in, and the driver started up and went around that sharp curve quite fast at the same time I pushed Forte. He'd been drinking."

"Was he hurt?"

"Oh, no. I looked back and he was picking himself up."

Fitz grinned. "Well, good for you."

But Forte and his antics simply didn't matter right now. She said, "I suppose you don't really know when you can come home. Or I can go to Ligunia."

"Sarah, listen." He covered her hand with his, then turned her hand over, looked at the lines of the palm, and said soberly, "There are two things I have to ask you to promise me. First, no one is to know the truth of what happened to Bill Hicks. The second one is—well, it's harder. You are not to try to phone me."

"Fitz? Why?"

"Orders," he said shortly. "But I mean it. No matter

what happens. You see, it's this way. I'm to carry on Bill's job. But to outsiders it has to be a secret."

"You can't mean—Why, nobody can think you are Bill Hicks?"

"No, but the people who might be the source of . . . of any trouble must not know anything about my taking Bill's place."

"But that's impossible! Everybody will know."

He shook his head. "No. Steps have been taken. Only the immediate consular staff will know. And if there is a leak there . . ." He shrugged.

"But, Fitz, this means you're being sent there as a target. Bait for another attack!"

"Not necessarily. Oh, I'll grant you it isn't the kind of place I had hoped for my first assignment. But up to now, Ligunia has been a peaceable, honest, reliable little country. We hope to retain friendly relations. This attack upon Bill just might be the first act of a rising problem, which we—and the Ligunians—must deal with. But the entire investigation must be one of those very quiet—well, secret oparations."

Her thoughts careened wildly. "You can't pretend to be Bill Hicks."

"All I have to do is use his signature on papers that routinely come to his desk. I have a batch in this briefcase. Only the very closest of the consular staff will see me until—well, until we can get things straightened out."

"But suppose somebody takes a shot at you?"

"That won't happen. If it *should* happen, however, they'll see to it that you know where I am and how I am. I insisted on that. They were most considerate in the department."

"Considerate! Sending you to take the place of somebody they must think was deliberately shot—"

"Sarah!" His voice was firm. "You must see it my way. I must have your promise."

"Fitz—"

"Do you promise me? Solemnly? On your dear and—oh, darling, your loved word. I want to hear you say it."

"Of course. Of course I promise."

"You do realize that this is a very serious matter."

"Yes, I realize that. I'll stick to it. But I don't want you to go too—soon."

"And you will. Or I'll be sent back." At last a little smile touched his lips. "I am making you promise, Sarah, as soberly as I will take your promise to be my wife—to have and to hold from this day forward . . ."

He didn't continue with "till death do us part." A feeling of superstitious fear quivered like an arrow above her. Tears stung her eyes. "Yes, Fitz, I have promised. But in the meantime I can write to you. Can't I?"

His face cleared. "Of course. And I'll write to you, You understand that you'll have to send your letters to Washington,"

"Will anybody in the department read them?"

"No! No reason to. My letters to you can come through the department pouch."

"Oh—all right," She had almost always had letters from her father in that way.

Someone spoke imperatively over the public address system, and both Sarah and Fitz listened intently.

"Well, here we go." Fitz touched his lips with his napkin.

"I do wish I could go with you now. But I'm coming soon!"

Fitz motioned for the check. "As soon as I can let you. Sarah, you'll not forget your promise."

"I'll remember. Hurry up, you'll miss the plane. I'll go to the gate with you."

"No. I have other plans. Here's your coat," he said, rising, and held it out to her. He slung his own coat over his arm, and placed the slim leather briefcase, which he had held on his lap during their meal, on the table barely long enough to assist her with her coat. Her eyes must have widened looking at it, for he said, "I told you. Blank forms—those used most frequently. Signed by Bill. That is never to be divulged. Here, take my arm."

They were on the escalator. There were other people, presumably passengers, all with a definitely affluent look, but then, the S.S.T. was an expensive means of transit. There was another mixture of public address announcements and voices from behind and below her. Fitz said, "Here we are. But you're not going to the gate. I can't stand long farewells."

"You don't want me to stand there at the gate watching you leave—"

"Don't fuss. I can afford it this time."

"It" proved to be a long shiny car with uniformed chauffeur, an expensive hired car. The chauffeur opened the door. Fitz said to him, "Now, take care of Miss Favor. You have the directions—"

"Oh, yes, sir. The consulate made me repeat them."

"Good. Now then—" He took her hard in his arms and said, his lips against her face, "I love you so." Then he kissed her and turned abruptly away.

She sat in the car and watched as he went swiftly back into the terminal, hurrying toward the great plane, his topcoat and briefcase swinging.

The chauffeur waited discreetly until Fitz's tall figure had disappeared. Then he closed the door beside Sarah and went around to the driver's seat.

Fitz had been right, if extravagant, in hiring the car. Going back home by way of bus, train, taxi was tiresome. It was far easier to slip out across the Island, across the Whitestone Bridge, with the lights of the city sparkling magically at the left, on to the Henry Hudson Parkway and on and on north, through the autumn twilight, toward the Favor house.

It was not possible to dismiss the facts Fitz had told her. Strange and dreadful things had been happening almost all over the world. Her father had said sadly, on his latest visit home, that things had changed. Nowadays there was rarely such a thing as international laws about diplomatic immunity; that is, he amended, the laws still existed, but their observance had in too many instances declined or completely ceased.

The Favors were known for their Foreign Service connections, and Charles Favor, Sarah's father, was a senior and much respected diplomat. She had enough knowledge of the facets of his career to accept a mandate of discretion and silence. It looks reasonably easy, he had said, and sometimes it is; other times it is like walking on the very edge of a cliff, with disaster waiting at every footstep.

Now Fitz had asked for her silence about the dangerous details of his assignment. It was clearly her duty to keep her promise, and it might be difficult only with Corinna. She was generous, she was fair, she was kind, but she was also, as Fitz had said, steel-like in her guardianship of the little brood of assorted relatives she had collected almost like a magpie who collects various objects and nests them together. Especially, Sarah reflected rather traitorously, if those objects have the smallest glitter. Sarah herself did not glitter; but some of the clan did.

Corinna had, in truth, made a family and a lively one. But Corinna's sharp eyes and ears had to be placated.

At length she decided she would simply tell Corinna that she and Fitz had decided to postpone their wedding for a time. The whole family knew that Fitz was being sent to Ligunia; there was no reason to try to conceal that; she had told them all, proudly, the instant Fitz had you telephoned the news to her. At that time, of course, he had not told her the full truth of the assignment. Tears came to her eyes as she thought of Fitz's words—"to have and to hold from this day forward."

Lights came toward them constantly, lights from other cars, traveling at a steady speed near them. Sarah felt for an odd moment as if she were in the midst of something she knew nothing about and had no control over, simply speeding along through the night, along with everyone else.

She shook herself out of that curiously fateful impression as the car drew up to a tollgate, paused for a second or two, and went on. She decided not to think of Bill Hicks or any possible danger in the hitherto peaceful and proud little country of Ligunia. She would wait till she heard from Fitz.

She roused and leaned forward. "Right here, right again, then left—"

"Thank you, madam."

Rosart would be at home. Fanny would be vocalizing— no, at this time she would be getting dinner. She hoped that she would not see Forte, who would still be furious; he had managed to shoot a viciously mean glance at her over his silky little mustache as he picked himself up in the road and started dusting off his always natty, yet somehow rather seedy, clothes.

Corinna had gone to some kind of literary gathering in New York. There was no telling when she would return, since her views of literary do's (her word) were changeable— perhaps, Sarah thought meanly but honestly, depending upon the amount of attention Corinna herself got; not everybody liked the novels she wrote.

A smell of burning leaves grew stronger. Gus, of course, paid no attention to any law but his own; he had always burned his leaves in the autumn, and no matter if the present law forbade it, he would continue to do so. Corinna, indeed the whole family, was inclined to take the position that Gus was an old family retainer, a view that would have shocked Gus to the core. No family retainer, not he. Yet he had accepted the one-time chauffeur's rooms over the garage without demur, giving up the cottage he had used until Rosart took it over. He worked for the Favors when he felt like it, sandwiching in the hours at the Favor place between the times he spent among the neighborhood estates. Very few people, now, could afford, or could find, a full-time gardener. It was lucky that Fanny had learned to cook. Sarah herself was adept at putting dishes and silver (knives, too, over Corinna's protests) in the electric dishwasher. Rosart or Gus were roped in for heavy work. Lately, sometimes, Rosart prepared his own meals in the little kitchen of the cottage, which he had rigged up with stove, refrigerator, cupboards.

However, since Forte's most recent return home a week ago, when he had moved into the cottage, Rosart had taken his meals at the big house—he had to get away from Forte, he had said almost savagely. Forte was drinking heavily and becoming more and more obnoxious, which was regrettable on all counts—but particularly because he was in fact the only one of the brood who had a claim upon Corinna. He was her stepson, a reminder of her one and only very brief marriage; she had even changed his name to one of her own choosing, Forte Favor.

He was also the only one who depended entirely upon Corinna for money. Sarah's father sent a check every month. Fitz owned the house they lived in. Norm contributed what money he could; Fanny turned over every cent she made to Corinna, who either used it for Fanny or invested it suitably.

Yes, Corinna had welded together what amounted to a family of her own.

Sarah sniffed at the drifting odor of burning leaves and wondered where she would be in October of the next year. The world was wide and the moves of the consular service and the State Department were, to her, mysterious. Fitz was by now out over the Atlantic. She turned the modest sapphire and diamond engagement ring on her hand proudly. She had scarcely believed it when Fitz, the hero of her childhood days, had returned from his first months of consular training and had, she thought, really noticed her for the first time. Then, quickly, happily—almost magically—they were engaged to be married, and she was going to spend her life with Fitz. It wouldn't be all roses, nothing ever was—but roses or thorns, that was what she wanted.

She roused to the fact that the limousine must turn into what everyone still called, simply but with a kind of respect, the Favor place, and spoke to the chauffeur again. "Near here on your right. There isn't a sign, just a graveled road."

And what a nuisance that gravel was; the driveway had once been dignified and neat, coated with bluestone, but since it was on a slope, every winter the snows washed the bluestone down, so plain gravel was substituted, but that also washed down. The road was now rather bare, full of ruts, and the hedges had grown perilously near it.

"Ah," said the chauffeur with perceptible relief. "There is the door, isn't it, madam?"

Lights were shining from the library windows, the so-called library; nobody ever bothered any more with the ancient, dusty books lining the walls, but everyone liked the deep old lounge chairs and wide writing table. And they liked to gather near the fireplace—usually full of the ashes which, Corinna said serenely, helped start the next fire.

The chauffeur removed himself from the driver's seat, came around so the lights of the car fell briefly upon him, and opened the door for Sarah just as she had put out her hand to open it herself and hop down. Dear me, she thought, I must remember to be dignified. "Thank you," she said to him. Then, uncertainly, she fumbled at her handbag, but the chauffeur guessed her intentions and touched his cap. "No, thank you, madam. Your husband saw to that."

Husband, Fitz. Her heart warmed. She thanked the chauffeur again and knew that he watched politely until she had gone up the three steps to the terrace and opened the wide door. Then he slid back into the car, which glided smoothly away.

She held the door for a moment, looking at it in the stream of light from the hall; it was a beautiful door, and one of her childhood tasks had been to keep the teakwood panels waxed and satin-smooth. The eagle knocker looked over the correct shoulder aloofly. She thrust the door back and saw the great vase of bronze chrysanthemums on a nearby table. Corinna insisted upon flowers in the house, even in winter; she said loftily that they added ambience. Corinna was adept at picking up a current word or phrase; she had considered hype, psych-up and vibes rather vulgar; scam was a favorite for a while but difficult to work into casual conversation. Perhaps her swift adoption of current words or phrases partially explained her undoubted success as a writer.

Something was wrong with the house.

Sarah listened and heard only Fanny practicing in the distant playroom, once filled on rainy days by the Favor young, now used by Fanny for working. It was a very remote and oddly blurred song, almost as if she were singing with an orchestra accompaniment, which was impossible. It was, however, remotely identifiable as "The Bell Song." And Fanny sounded flat. Really, Fanny ought not try that song, Sarah thought; she was certainly not a coloratura. After all, Corinna had seen to it that all the young Favors had some knowledge of music.

Sarah shook her head, and then stood there quietly for so long that even her heart seemed to pause. Something *was* wrong with the house.

Still she heard only the blurred faraway song. It wasn't like Fanny to strain her voice. She was an excellent mezzo-soprano and very sensible about the use of her voice. Actually, Sarah thought irrelevantly, she wouldn't even sleep with open windows, which shocked Corinna, but Fanny persisted in believing that the night air might affect her throat. She got plenty of fresh air, however, for she took conscientious and long walks, deep-breathing the whole way, Corinna had commented crossly.

Obviously, Fanny wasn't cooking, so that drifting odor in the air couldn't be from the kitchen. Chrysanthemums smelled very unpleasant when they had been in a vase too long, but these were fresh and, at their worst, would not be like that faint whiff of smell. There were as yet no fires lighted, and besides, the apple wood they usually burned was faintly aromatic. This particular scent was somehow not pleasant. She went slowly up the stairs and along the broad hall; here there was no unusual and oddly disquieting odor.

Somewhat reassured, Sarah entered her own room, dropped her handbag and coat on a chair and went to the mirror. Her dark hair was ruffled, but she was rather pleased with her reflection. She was no beauty, as Fanny was (with her grandly heroic size), but her deep-set blue eyes were sparkling, her Favor features more delicately feminine. Yes, she was rather pleased with the girl in the mirror. Even her mouth looked—well, frankly, it looked as if it had been kissed and had enjoyed it. She laughed softly at her own thoughts and was brushing up her hair when the sound came—loud, shocking and terribly identifiable. It was a gunshot.

Two

She stood so still, she might have been frozen in that attitude, brush in hand.

The remote tinkle back in the old playroom continued remorselessly.

There had been no further sound at all. No voices, nothing. But it had been, it had to have been, a gunshot, and near enough to crash through the silence of the autumn evening. At last, after what seemed a long time and was probably at the most a minute, she ran back along the hall, whirled around the newel post and ran down the stairs.

There was nothing to be frightened about, she told herself, nothing. Perhaps someone had shot at—oh, a marauding woodchuck, something.

But the shot had been near, as if in the house. That could not be. The hall was the same, nothing different. She passed the open door of the library; there was nothing there and nobody.

Yet such a sound must be explained, she told herself almost in so many words.

It was explained. The door to the long living room was open and there was a light on a table near the fireplace. A long sofa crossed the room at the other end, and behind it she saw a man's feet at a very odd angle.

She had no recollection of moving, but she must have done so, for suddenly she was leaning over the sofa and looking at Forte.

He was turned to one side, in a curiously crumpled position; his checked jacket had fallen open. The light there was dim; he lay in the shadow of the big sofa with its yellow chintz cover. She said, over and over, "Forte . . . Forte . . ."

There was a patch of dark red on what she could see of a white turtleneck sweater. His ferrety face was half buried against the rug. His dark hair was smooth as satin. Oh, yes, she said to herself, not believing, it is Forte and he's dead and I heard the shot that killed him.

She couldn't touch him. She was suddenly out of breath. She stumbled to the long French windows on the west side of the room, flung them open and screamed once, then she made herself take deep breaths of the fresh air. She must call a doctor. Hadn't Fanny heard the shot? Where was Rosart? The cottage was near enough for him to hear a gunshot.

She had to do something; she couldn't simply stand there gulping for air and trying not to be dizzy.

But Forte was dead. He had been shot. There was that spreading dark stain on his white sweater.

"Did you scream?" She whirled around.

It was Norm Marsham, standing in the doorway. "What on earth is the matter? I thought I heard—"

Sarah motioned toward the sofa. He must have been shocked by something in her face, for he ran, thumping heavily over the rug toward the sofa, leaned over, said, *"It can't be—"* and went around the sofa so he could lean over Forte.

She had to sit down. She groped for a chair. Norm straightened up, but still stared fixedly down at Forte. "He's dead."

"Norm . . . I can't . . . the room is going around . . ."

He gave her a quick glance and came to her. The Favor strain was strong in Norm, too: dark hair, peaked dark eyebrows, a rather swarthy complexion. He was somewhat stocky and not as tall as Fitz, but they could have been brothers instead of distant cousins. He put a hand on her shoulder. "Lean over. Put your head down. Here—" He pushed her head downward gently. Gradually the fog that had come from nowhere cleared away. But she still felt sick.

"I'm all right," she said. "I'm all right, Norm."

He let her lift her head, looked down at her soberly and said, unbelievably, "Sarah, you shouldn't have shot him. You could have got rid of him somehow, no matter how obnoxious he was when he was drinking. Dear Sarah, you didn't have to shoot him."

The sense of it got through the lingering traces of fog and nausea. "Shoot him! I didn't! I just came from seeing Fitz at the airport. He's been unexpectedly posted to Ligunia."

"Yes, I know," said Norm. "I checked in with the office just before I started back from Maine, and they told me all about it."

"When the car brought me home, nobody was around. I was upstairs in my room when I heard the shot—"

"Now listen, Sarah. I'll back you up, whatever you say. But what did you do with the gun?"

"I never saw a gun—I don't know anything about it! Why—why, I wouldn't have shot him. I wouldn't shoot anybody. I heard the sound of a shot. I didn't even know that it came from this room."

Norm hesitated, as though thinking carefully, then said in an oddly troubled way, as if debating with himself, "All right. I believe you."

"But truly, Norm, I don't know anything about a gun. I don't know who— Good heavens, Norm!"

"What's the matter?" Rosart was in the doorway, eating

chocolate cake. His enormous black beard surrounded the piece of cake as he bit into it. "Norm, listen! I just found all your hunting stuff on the front porch of the cottage. You can't stay with me. No room there. You'll have to stay here in the big house—somewhere." He eyed them, munching, swallowed hard and said, "You both look— What's going on here?"

"Forte," Norm began and then simply put out his hand, pointing toward the sofa.

Rosart stared, frowning, puzzled, moved toward the sofa, gave them another puzzled look and peered over it. He stood there, a big bulk of a man, darkly Favorish in his looks, very strong and muscular.

Sarah had never seen a man faint. Rosart nearly did, for he tottered, dropped the sticky cake on the rug (Corinna wouldn't like that, she thought wildly), then dropped himself into the sofa and stared at Norm. "He looks dead."

"He is dead." Norm left Sarah and started toward Rosart. "He must have died very quickly."

Rosart said, in a numb way, "I suppose he did it himself. Drinking. We had a quarrel about that this morning. I had to throw him out. I couldn't get a line written while he was staying with me. But our quarrels were never—" He gulped, his beard moving up and down. "He was one of us just the same. He needn't have killed himself!"

"Yes, I know. We've got to call the doctor—"

"He can't do anything for him," Rosard said dully.

"Yes, I know," Norm repeated. "But that's what we must do. The doctor and the police. Right away."

Rosart's dark eyes glittered above his great beard. "Police? But a suicide . . ."

There was a pause. Then Norm said, "The gun isn't there."

"The gun!" Rosart surged up from the sofa and leaned over the back of it again, his corduroy slacks looking enormous, his shoulders invincible. He looked like the college football player he had once been. He had stayed on at the university until he earned a doctor's degree and then had turned all his attention to his poetry—but he still jogged, he claimed, at least five miles a day. That or something kept him in almost formidable physical condition.

Finally he shoved himself back to face Norm and Sarah. "I don't see any gun. He must have got rid of it somehow."

"I think he died at once," Norm said.

Rosart said slowly, thinking it out, "But then, if he didn't shoot himself . . ."

Norm nodded. "So you see we really must report to the police. Now, don't object, Rosart. If it isn't suicide . . ."

"It's got to be suicide."

"But if there's no gun . . ."

Sarah shook her head. "All I know is that I heard a gunshot. I came down. He was there—"

"Dead already?"

"Yes. I could see that. I—oh, Rosart, Norm is right. We've got to report it!"

"If it isn't suicide . . ." Rosart's face cleared. "Accident! Of course. He got hold of a gun somewhere and was cleaning it—or maybe just looking at it and it went off and—He had been drinking. Still smells of gin," Rosart added, with a shudder of distaste.

He was right; Sarah had smelled it when she leaned over Forte for only that instant or two. The lingering odor of gin, however, seemed to have been dissipated by the fresh air coming in the windows—along with the oddly acrid whiff of that smell which Sarah had noted as she entered the house, and which, recalling it now, she felt strangely certain she had recognized and yet could not identify.

"We told you. There is no gun," Norm said heavily.

For a long moment they were quiet, as though there was nothing more to say—yet it was not quite silent in the big room with its good if worn Persian rugs, its huge fireplace, its deep chairs, and an occasional milky-white ring from a glass put down, almost certainly by Forte with his usual lack of respect, on the various tables. It was not quite silent, for there was something like a whisper coming from somewhere, and it was the hushed whisper of a dreadful word.

Rosart sprang to his feet. "But I'm being given the Renichen Award! Tomorrow!"

There was another silence, this time one of too-clear understanding but also shock. "But, Rosart—" Sarah began, and he interrupted, "It's a very great honor for me. I can't go there and make an acceptance speech, and all the time—Well, say it, you both think this is murder."

So the word came out in Rosart's shocked yet angered voice. He had often been angered by Forte; all of them had been. This, he seemed almost to shout, this is too much— Forte again!

The Renichen Award was highly prized; it was given, after long consideration, only to really good poets. Yes, it was a great honor. And knowing something of the Board which made the decision about presenting the award, Sarah understood Rosart's frustrated fury. He said, "Every poet in the world wants that award. I couldn't believe they were giving it to me. I'm so young and— I've been out in the woods practicing my speech all afternoon. It's to be tomorrow noon. At the university. *I can't give it up!*" He stood up straight, squared his big shoulders and said, "I won't give it up! We are not going to call the police. At least"—he weakened a little—"not right now. Not until—"

"Until when?" Norm asked. "Oh, Rosart, I do realize what this means. But we cannot break the law."

There was a flurry of footsteps in the hall and Fanny came to the door. Sarah realized that the dim sounds of music had, sometime ago, stopped. Fanny had apparently not heard the gunshot or Sarah's scream. She seemed upset only by the cake she saw at Rosart's feet. "You took a piece of my cake! I made it for our dinner. You got into the kitchen and—" She stopped and looked fixedly at Rosart. Then very slowly she turned her light-blue eyes to

Sarah and Norm. Somebody must have made a motion, for she strode (but gracefully, every muscle in harmony) to the end of the sofa, stared down, put back her long blond hair and whirled around toward them. "Who did it? He's dead, isn't he? Who killed him?"

Norm and Rosart began to tell it. Suicide. Accident. Suicide. Accident. And then, the fatal words from Norm. No gun. Murder. Police.

"Police!" Fanny strode away from the sofa, reached a table and planted her hands upon it. "You can't. I won't let you. Don't you realize I'm to sing Amneris this winter? It's my big chance. You can't get the police. The newspapers! They—you can ruin my whole life!"

"But, Fanny—" Norm began.

Fanny swerved her big eyes toward him; she had a remarkably firm chin. "I won't have it."

"But an opera singer—Nothing like this—I mean nothing can be of such importance. I mean"—Norm was beginning to be flustered—"people don't feel upset if an opera singer gets newspaper publicity—"

"Publicity about a murder? In the house where she lives? In her own family? Are you out of your head, Norm! You've got to be very careful and discreet now. A lover—nobody minds that. But you can't get personally involved in murder."

"But—but it's your private life—"

"Only if it stays private," said Fanny firmly.

"But I tell you—" Norm began just as Gus loomed up in the doorway.

Gus's underlip stuck out when he was displeased. It stuck out now. His strong gray hair stuck up belligerently. He gave a tug at his constantly sliding, baggy khaki pants. "Who left Fitz's gun out there on the lawn?"

He waved the gun, a revolver, and it glittered as it caught the light from the lamp at Sarah's elbow.

After a moment Sarah whispered, *"Fitz's* gun?"

No one paid the slightest attention to her. Rosart and

Norm both leaped over to Gus, who, however, held the gun away from them. Gus was furious. "Nobody had any right using Fitz's gun! He left it with me to take care of! This and a shotgun and his two rifles. This gun has been fired not long ago. I can smell it on the barrel—" He stopped and looked around. "What's the matter with all of you?"

It began again. Forte. Over there. Behind the sofa. Suicide. Accident.

Fanny stood at the table. Norm and Rosart followed Gus, who, as the others had gone, leaned over, then moved around the sofa and squatted down so only his gray head could be seen. Finally he rose, his craggy face suddenly old. He still had the gun clutched in one hand. "Who did it?"

Suicide. Accident. Fanny cut through it. "They think it's murder! They want to call the police."

Gus came back around the long sofa, walking rather unsteadily. He was certainly no longer young. He was also, certainly, deeply shocked. He had never liked Forte, but he had known him for years, as he had known the assembled group of Favor youth. He came to a chair and sank down in it, staring at the rug. "I don't like this," he said finally. Then he got to his feet again and looked angrily at Fanny. "Why don't you get a sheet or something! Isn't decent leaving him like that. Go on!" He almost yelled. "Get something!"

Fanny blinked, shoved her hands in the pockets of a big apron she had fastened over her blue jeans, and stunned into compliance, left the room. They could all hear her footsteps on the stairs. "Now then, you." Gus turned around to give them a searching, still angry glare. "Come on. Not decent to stand around here and talk, with Forte—" He didn't finish, but tramped across the wide hall and into the library. Norm, Sarah and Rosart followed him obediently, as they always had.

"Now then," Gus said, "This needs thinking about."

"See here, Gus." Norm had recovered somewhat from the old-time respect they had all given Gus, who had so often acted as Corinna's surrogate. "There's no use trying to think for ourselves or—or do anything. We've got to call the police. Now!"

"Yes," Sarah said. "And a doctor."

"Doctor can't do anything. Too late for that. What I want to know is which of you took Fitz's gun?"

Norm shook his head. Rosart sagged down into a chair, shoved his sturdy legs out, stared at some very dirty sneakers and said, in his beard, "I didn't even know that Fitz had left his guns for you to see to."

"But you knew he had guns." Gus stood in the middle of the room, eyeing Rosart as keenly as a prosecuting counsel.

"Sure." Rosart hitched his sweater comfortably up from his big wrists. "Always shooting things, Fitz was."

"Things?" Norm said quietly. "You mean—"

Rosart shot him a glowering look. "I mean things. Living things."

Norm sighed. "You mean he went on hunting trips. So do I. I got back here, dumped my junk on your doorstep, and then I heard somebody—Sarah—scream. I ran to the house. If you're trying to imply that Fitz shot—well, shot people, he didn't. Anyway," he added firmly, "according to Sarah, he's on the plane this minute. Sarah has been with him—haven't you, Sarah? You did see him leave?"

She nodded. "Yes. I didn't actually see the plane leave— But he couldn't have shot Forte—he had no earthly reason to. I heard the shot. I was in my room. I had just gotten home. It was quiet except for Fanny singing, away off in the playroom. I could almost have heard a leaf fall—"

"No," Rosart mumbled. "Too many leaves falling just now."

"That doesn't matter! It was very quiet. I heard a

gunshot and listened and then came back downstairs and—then I saw Forte's feet—'' She choked there.

Norm said, "Obviously Fitz couldn't have shot him."

Rosart, still studying his long legs, said, "No right to shoot innocent birds and little animals. Big animals, for that matter. Gus"—he looked up—"has the deer season opened?"

"No," Gus said with finality.

Sarah said miserably, "The windows were closed. I opened them."

Gus nodded. "I noticed as I passed them. No gunshot through them."

Rosart said heavily, "I hate hunting. It's not fair. Not right—"

"All right," Norm said soothingly. "We know your feelings, Rosart."

Fanny was coming back down the stairs; her footsteps seemed heavy as she went toward the living room. Sarah looked around and knew they were all visualizing the same thing: they could see her bend and cover Forte. Poor, weedy, malicious Forte.

Fanny left the living room and they could hear her marching heavily again along the hall toward the dining room.

Gus rubbed his thick shock of gray hair. "This is going to upset Mrs. Favor." Despite their long association, Gus always called Corinna Mrs. Favor, never Miss or Madam.

Sarah had dropped into a chair again, mainly because her knees were not dependable. "Gus, we mustn't wait like this! We must call the police. I'll go now and use the phone. Unless— Norm?"

"I'll call them."

"No," said Gus and unexpectedly moved so his thick and sturdy body was between Norm and the door. "You're not going to do anything till Mrs. Favor comes home. It's her house."

Sarah gathered herself together. "No." Her voice was

rather shaky, but there was a note of firmness in it. "It's Fitz's house and he'd want us to act according to the law."

Rosart lifted quick eyes, peering at her with a suggestion of triumph from the thickets of his black beard. "Fitz's house. Sure. And Fitz has his first big chance. And you're going to marry him. Do you want to wreck his career before he even gets started?"

"But . . . but Fitz . . ."

"Listen! A diplomat's wife has got to be like . . . like Caesar's wife. Believe me. Murder, newspapers—and Fitz's own gun. Do you think the department is going to approve of him after a mess like that? Well, do you?"

She moistened her suddenly dry lips; this was a completely unexpected argument and it had its authority and force. "Fitz would say . . . act according to the law," she said, but weakly.

Gus frowned. "You can't decide for him, Miss Sarah. Not right to decide anything like that for Fitz. Means too much to him. To you, too, if you take a second look at things. Right now you're upset—"

"Oh, stop that!" she cried. "I *know* what we ought to do. Fitz would say report it—now! We've talked and waited too long already."

"Here's Mrs. Favor," said Gus loudly and moved toward the hall. Fanny came in, and he ducked to one side to avoid her and a tray of glasses and bottles in her hands.

Fanny said, "Look where you're going, Gus," and put the tray down on the writing table, flat upon the morning newspapers. "You'd better have a drink, all of you. Think more clearly. I don't approve of drinking as a rule, but— here—" She splashed a good slug of whiskey into a glass and held it toward Sarah.

Rosart drew himself partially upright. "I don't drink. Never drink. You know that, Fanny. Does you no good either—"

"Oh, Rosart!" Fanny's voice was very deep but uneven.

"Everybody needs a drink now and then. Corinna says so. But of course, Forte overdid it."

"Yes," said Rosart. "Poor old Forte! If he wasn't an example—"

"Don't talk like that!" Fanny handed him a glass. "Now behave like a civilized person—as usually you are not."

There was a rush of cool air, a flurry of movement in the hall as the wide front door opened and Corinna's voice was heard. "I missed the train! Had to get a rental car all the way out here. Lord, I'm tired. Some fool asked that Lowton woman about her new book, and she told them. For forty minutes. A word or two of apology would have been quite enough."

Gus muttered something. Corinna's voice sharpened. "What's the matter? What's wrong? Where is everybody?"

Gus must have made some gesture, for she appeared in the doorway, pretty, smart, with her neat little figure and her snow-white hair and arched black eyebrows. She shot a swift glance around, saw the glasses and bottles, and said, "Good idea! I'll take one of those. You can't guess what I've been through this afternoon. That Lowton woman—"

Norm cut in. "We heard you, Corinna. Something serious has happened."

"Something very bad," Fanny said gloomily.

Three

Corinna took the glass Fanny handed her and looked around at all of them, seeming to single out each one for piercing inquiry. She had always done that, and with remarkably accurate results. She had acted as an aunt and also as a very active guardian, even to Norm and Fitz, who had come under her dominion only when they were close to university age.

Finally she chose the tall winged chair, sat down, adjusted her pretty ankles in their pretty shoes, tipped her pretty face to sip at the drink with her pretty lips, and said, "May as well come out with it. What have you been up to now?"

As if we might be sent to bed without our suppers, Sarah thought in one corner of her mind. "Corinna, it really is very serious—"

Rosart broke in. "Forte has been shot with Fitz's gun. He's in the living room."

"Forte was— Oh, now, really!"

"Corinna, you must listen."

"I did listen. You said Fitz had shot at Forte. He can't have. Fitz isn't here."

"Corinna! Listen!" They all spoke at once.

Corinna lifted arched black eyebrows. "You can't mean—What on earth—Forte!"

All of them were losing their oddly induced attitude of bad children caught in some mischief and about to be disciplined.

"Somebody's got to explain to her." Sarah heard herself speaking unsteadily. "The point is we've got to call the police."

"Police!" Corinna sat upright. "Why?"

"I'll tell her," said Norm, and did. It was the same ugly progression of suggestions again: suicide, accident—murder.

Corinna, now alert to the tip of every white curl, listened, seemed to weigh every word, sipped her drink, then put down her glass. Her vivacious face was suddenly as still and white as marble. At last she removed her trim green suit jacket and said, distantly, "Just be quiet for a moment, will you?"

Rosart would not be quiet. "If Sarah calls the police the whole thing will be in the papers just when I'm about to get the Renichen Award, and Fanny is going to make her debut in *Aida,* and Fitz is off to his first big job—and you know how things are in the diplomatic service—"

"Consular," said Corinna absently. "That is, unless Fitz had an unusually swift promotion."

"Same thing," Rosart said. "And it wouldn't help Norm's career either. Incidentally, Corinna, isn't your new book about to come out? What about *your* image?"

Corinna eyed him rather stonily for a long, very thoughtful moment. "Not good," she said finally and reached for her glass again.

Norm came to stand before her defiantly. "Oh now, see here, Corinna. Nothing about all this can possibly hurt your book."

"I said image," Rosart interjected, and Corinna nodded as if taking up a challenge.

"You don't understand, Norm. My books are . . . are so

clean, you see. No nonsense about sex and violence.
Nothing that has what was once called shock value. But all
the same, people do buy them, thank God, and just now—
Heavenly days, Norm! Publication date is next week. All
this in the newspapers and—No, Norm, I can't have it.
Rosart is quite right." She now looked rather relieved,
almost as if Rosart had offered her a needed excuse—but
an excuse.

There was a pause. Sarah happened to look at Gus in
time to see him exchange a look with—she followed his
glance—Rosart.

Norm said at last, with an edge to his voice, "Then
what do you suggest we do about it?"

Corinna brushed her white curls upward in a distracted
gesture. She had suffered from Forte's activities but had
continued to supply him with money because of her sense
of responsibility. "I don't know," she said blankly. "We'll
have to think of something."

Norm seemed to be holding in his temper with an effort.
"Well, what might we think of? It *is* murder, Corinna. It
simply can't be anything else."

"Well—" she said stonily. "But we don't have to let
anybody know about it right away. Do we?"

"Yes, we do," Sarah said.

Corinna didn't even look at her.

Norm was angry. "Look here, Corinna. You don't seem
to understand. Murder has got to be reported to the police.
At once—"

"Not at once." Corinna's face cleared just slightly.

She's got some notion, Sarah thought.

"What do you mean?" Norm demanded.

Rosart moved gracefully, his big body as lithe as a ballet
dancer's, out into the hall.

Corinna said carefully, "We can report it at any time,
can't we? You say nothing could be done for him. No
doctor. By the way, why didn't you call a doctor?"

"We knew it was no use. A doctor couldn't do anything."

"He could give a . . . a death certificate. Or something," Corinna said vaguely. But she was not at all vague about some plan which Sarah was sure had entered her fertile mind. "We can report his—the accident—"

"Murder," Norm said.

"Whatever it was doesn't have to be . . . be known right now. It can wait."

"Wait for what?" Norm was really angry and spoke sharply.

Corinna glanced at Fanny. "May I have another drink, Fanny dear?"

"Go on! Wait for what?"

"Now really, Norm, don't hustle me!"

"Corinna, you aren't living in one of your novels. Don't make up some fancy idea, something out of one of your own books. This is real. This happened. Here. Now!"

Corinna took the glass Fanny handed her, full again and rather dark. "Thank you, Fanny. Now really, Norm, I know the difference between fact and fiction."

"You don't act like it. All right, go on, how do you propose to keep—well, it has got to be murder—keep that a secret until just possibly you get ready to report it? And how are you going to explain the delay when the police doctors figure out the time Forte really died?"

Clearly, Corinna was playing for time. "I think that will work itself out," she said and sipped. "I told you not to hurry me, Norm."

"I'm not hurrying you." Norm, as if goaded beyond control, shoved his hands in his pockets and glowered at Corinna.

Probably he was searching out convincing arguments, Sarah thought as she rose and held on to the back of the chair. "I'm going to phone now."

"Yes," Norm cried. "Yes—"

"Wait!" Corinna's quicksilver mind was working at top speed, but her pretty face was still very white. She gave Sarah one piercing glance, then swerved the full brilliance of her dark eyes around the small circle and said, again, "Wait! You *must* think of Fitz and his career. And Rosart! That award. To be given tomorrow. Darlings—" Her face was imploring; she put down her glass so she could hold out small and white hands toward them. "Please—*please* listen to me. I only ask you to wait. If Forte is . . . is gone, then why open such a dreadful investigation. Newspapers, reporters! The damage to Fitz's career, Sarah! The damage to Rosart's, and possibly yours too, Norm. And as for Fanny, she's got her first big role—a really big one—and this publicity would do her no good. Oh, Norm—Sarah, you can't be so cruel."

Fanny suddenly sat down on the sofa, and as suddenly burst into sobs.

Norm hesitated, eyed her and said, "Now, now, Fanny. You didn't like Forte all that much."

"But I did! I loved him. And he loved me! Oh, Forte, Forte!"

"Oh, dear me," Sarah said under her breath, knowing that Fanny's barometer was set for dramatics.

An odd flicker of something like satisfaction crossed Corinna's face. "There, there, Fanny. Many opera stars have had tragedy in their private lives. It may deepen your art!"

Norm turned to Sarah. "We've got to take things into our own hands."

"*No!*" Corinna said. Rosart had come quietly back into the room. He gave Corinna the faintest nod. Corinna's eyelids drooped once. She said, rather breathlessly but firmly, "We are all very upset about this dreadful thing. We are in a state of shock, and we can't decide anything sensible right now. So I suggest—"

Norm broke in. "Now, Corinna, we *know* what must be done."

He started for the door, but this time Rosart's stalwart body blocked the way to the telephone. "No, you don't.

Corinna is right. We've got to think things over and then decide—''

"Good God!" Norm stared at him. "You do realize that this would make everyone of you—me, too—an accessory after the fact."

There was a pause. Fanny sobbed but in an absent way, as if she were trying to listen at the same time.

Finally Corinna said, "What do you mean, Norm dear?"

"You know," said Norm, biting off the words. "It means that every one of us is criminally liable for not reporting murder."

Corinna thought for a second or two, then rose. "I think I'll go and freshen up. Is dinner ready, Fanny?"

Fanny gave a gulp and took her hands from her eyes. "It's been ready. I've got it in the warming oven. Everything will be spoiled if we don't eat soon."

Corinna emptied her glass unhurriedly, picked up her jacket and walked out of the room.

Rosart gave Norm and Sarah an enigmatic dark glance and slouched, this time with no grace at all, out into the hall.

Norm sat down with an air of collapse. "Sarah, are we the only sane people in this family?"

"Now is our chance. Shall I phone, or will you?"

"You really don't want to, do you?"

"No! But I know what Fitz—''

"Wait a minute." Norm leaned forward, elbows on his knees, staring at the rug. "Wait just a—I don't know. This might hurt Fitz. His gun. And his fiancée. You didn't touch that gun that Gus found, did you, Sarah?"

"No! What are you getting at, Norm? I told you! *I* didn't shoot Forte. I'd never think of such a thing."

"I know. I know but . . . but maybe they are right. Fanny—''

"Fanny cried, but—''

"Did you see any tears in her eyes?" Norm asked skeptically. "Eventually," Norm said slowly, "eventually, when the discovery of Forte's death is known and reported, Fanny could invent a beautiful myth about the tragedy of an opera singer's young love. Corinna caught on right away.''

"But, Norm, just now, moments after Forte was killed like that? They *couldn't* either of them have been thinking of a possible story of tragic romance!''

"For Fanny's career? Of course, it could be that Fanny only decided to help Corinna by creating a diversion. Oh, I don't know. Perhaps they're right. By the time they do whatever they may intend— But what are they planning? I expect they don't quite know themselves. They do understand one another. Gus understood. Rosart understood. Anyway, by that time—''

Sarah said flatly, "Now you've gone out of your head, too.''

"I think I'm beginning to see a little more clearly. Corinna is devoted to you—to all of us, really. But you did find Forte. It was Fitz's gun. If Forte, drunk, had made himself objectionable—and Forte could have, you know. Suppose all that—''

She was as cold as if she had been plunged into an icy stream—and a treacherous one. "I did not shoot Forte. All I did was push him out of my taxi.''

Norm sprang up. "You *what?*''

"Oh, it was nothing. He knew—everybody knew that Fitz was leaving and that I was going to meet him. He tried to go with me. He wouldn't get out of the way. He had opened the door and I . . . I just pushed. By then, the taxi was going around that curve by the mailbox.''

"But, Sarah, suppose there are bruises—a bruise—anything to indicate that he had a quarrel with you?''

"We didn't quarrel! He was only being obnoxious and—'' A frightened notion struck her. "Norm, nobody could say that I shot him just because of that! He wasn't hurt. He got up and started to dust off his clothes.''

Norm said slowly, "Maybe we'd better give this some

thought. If Forte told anyone about that—or if he has a bruise that can't be explained and they find out—Did the taxi man see all this?''

''There wasn't much to see! But yes, he saw and heard, and I think he went around that curve so fast to help get rid of Forte.''

Norm shoved his hands over his hair. ''Which taxi man was it? Old McConnell? Or some new man?''

''Not McConnel. A young fellow. New, I suppose. I had never seen him before, that I remember.''

Norm gave a kind of groan. ''*He'd* remember the moment he heard about Forte.''

Sarah clutched a chair back. ''But I know I didn't hurt Forte. Oh, he didn't like it. He gave me one of those mean looks and—''

''Did anyone else see this?''

''No. That is—no, I don't think so. I didn't really notice.''

Norm walked across the room, stared out the window, then turned to face her. ''All right. Now then, Sarah. You went on to the airport, met Fitz, came home and found Forte was shot. Tell me just what you did from the time you left the airport.''

''Why, I . . . I came out here. Fitz had hired a car for me. When I got to the house, there was the gunshot—''

''The minute you arrived?''

''No, no! I told you I was upstairs when I heard the shot. It sounded so near that I ran downstairs.'' She tried to remember even the smallest convincing fact, and then thought with dismay, Do I have to convince Norm that I didn't kill Forte? Norm, everybody? Just because I pushed him out of the taxi? Just because I was in the house and found him? That's preposterous. ''There was a kind of smell like—It wasn't leaves burning, but—''

''When was this?''

''When I opened the front door and came into the hall.''

''What was it? Cigarettes?''

"Oh, I don't *know*! Certainly not cigarettes. I only remember being a little bothered by it, nothing important. I went on upstairs to my room and heard the gunshot—"

"Were the windows closed?"

"My bedroom windows?" She thought back. "No. I remember the breeze. But the French windows in the living room were closed, I told you that—at least I tried to while Gus was talking. After I saw Forte, I felt a little dizzy and sick and I thought I must have fresh air, so I opened the windows and . . . and screamed, and then you came in—and really, Norm, that's all I know. But I did not shoot Forte!"

"Oh, I believe you. I'm only wondering how we can prove that to the police. I expect we can, eventually. The truth does come out. But months of investigation—I'm not sure. I may be wrong about this. I can't advise you. You'll have to decide for yourself."

After a moment she found her voice. "Nobody would ever believe I killed Forte!"

"It might be a good thing for you to get Fitz's ideas about this. It does affect him, you know. They're right about that."

"But he's on the Concorde. I can't reach him. Not now."

"You can phone him later."

Yes, she thought; I'll do that. But immediately she thought, No, I can't! I promised Fitz.

Her throat tightened, painfully, and she wouldn't, she mustn't, let anybody, even Norm, know what she had promised or why. "I . . . I don't think I can."

His dark eyebrows lifted. "Why on earth not?"

She groped for an excuse—and found one, although it had little force. "It'll be in the early morning when he arrives."

"Doesn't matter." He paused and added, "But maybe . . ."

"Maybe?"

"Maybe it wouldn't do Fitz any good to rouse somebody in the consulate with an urgent message for Fitz when he arrives. News gets around. No use in spreading it until—'' He shrugged. He went very quietly to the door and listened. In a moment he said over his shoulder, "What do you think Corinna has done? She didn't go upstairs at all. There's not a sound from there. I'll bet she slipped outside to talk to Gus. I'd love to know what they've all done.''

"What *have* they done?''

He shrugged. "Whatever it is, I'm sure it's something that would keep the police away until they're ready to let Forte's murder be known.'' He said thoughtfully, "Certainly the easiest way out would simply be to give the impression that Forte has slipped away on one of his usual trips. Nobody ever knew just where he went or what he did, for that matter,'' he added grimly. "Forte only turned up when he needed money, anyway. Oh, I know *de mortuis* and all that. But people don't change just because—''

"Stop it, Norm!''

"I have no idea what the family is planning specifically, but anything is possible when crackpots get together.''

"They aren't crackpots.''

"Prove it,'' said Norm. "Corinna—Fanny—all of them.''

Fanny called from the dining room in her resonant voice, "Dinner!''

Norm turned to Sarah. "I don't know what to do. That is, I do know and so do the rest of them, but they prefer to wait for a more convenient time. Oh, well, Sarah dear, why don't you come on to dinner even if you can't eat?''

"I had dinner with Fitz before he left.''

He went off down the hall toward the dining room. A faint but enticing fragrance of food drifted into the room.

At least it would have been enticing at another time. She made herself rise and cross the room. From the hall she could hear the mumble of voices, noting how very positively and clearly Corinna's high voice predominated. So wherever she had gone, she had returned.

She trudged up the stairs which she had hurried down earlier, scarcely knowing what she was doing after the sound of the shot.

There was the same wide hall and the room which had been hers since she was a child. She felt rather as if she were walking without motion, floating in a kind of numb current. Once she reached her room, she closed the door firmly behind her, as if by that gesture she could shut out the family downstairs, and leaned against it. She simply did not believe that Forte had died; she did not believe that Forte had been shot; she did not believe the crosscurrents of individual reactions to his death; she did not believe the way Corinna, Fanny, Rosart—even Gus—were behaving. She could not believe any of it.

But it had happened.

Accessories after the fact.

She had to talk to Fitz. She would telephone the consulate in Paris. She would leave a message for him; she wouldn't say anything about Forte, she would only ask that he telephone home.

He could not have anticipated anything like this when he asked for promise not to get in touch with him except by letter—and the diplomatic pouch. That would take days, she didn't know how long. She needed his advice at once. It was his house. It was murder.

Would time—not too much, perhaps a few days—really be against the law?

Yes, it would. No question of that. Worse for Fitz, in the end, than if the police came now, at once.

Or would it be worse?

She ached to talk to Fitz, only long enough perhaps to ask him what should be done.

But she knew what he would say, she thought again: Call the police. Report this dreadful thing. Murder.

And yet . . . and yet she had promised him. There were certainly reasons which she could only surmise behind his urgent request. Because her father had been in the Foreign Service so long, she had gained some idea of the webs of diplomacy, investigation and quiet action behind the patient, steady services of the whole department.

Keep her promise to Fitz? Or break it and take what would come?

It was really Fitz's province to advise her, but she couldn't, yet, break her promise to him.

That seemed, just then, a clear mandate. But, she thought, I am too shocked, too horrified, too thoroughly shaken—and, yes, frightened—to make any sensible decisions just now.

With a vague feeling of trying to come to her senses, she took off the red dress she had worn so happily to see Fitz off, and picked up the extravagantly purchased matching lightweight coat. She hung coat and dress carefully in the wide closet and took out a comfortably shabby blue woolen dressing gown.

She looked around the room, identifying everything in it as if by so doing, she might enforce reality. It, too, was shabby in a way, but she loved it: the dulling white paint, the fireplace, where now—since Rosart consented to cut wood only rarely—there was seldom a fire. The chaise lounge was worn, its pillows faded in blues and pinks. The wallpaper, too, was faded into some unidentifiable flower pattern, which, she had thought in her childhood, must have been intended to be apple blossoms. There was still a cool breeze from the windows.

Two people she knew had been shot recently. Forte had been shot, and died. Bill Hicks had been shot, and lived.

There could be no possible connection between the two. There was no significance in what could only be a tragic coincidence.

She leaned her elbows on her knees and told herself over and over again, Coincidence. Nothing more. Forte simply had nothing at all to do with Ligunia or Bill Hicks.

At least she could write to Fitz. Across the room stood

her writing desk, where she had once composed school themes and struggled over Caesar's Commentaries. All this summer she had been completely absorbed with Fitz's plans, Fitz's letters—mainly Fitz's telephone calls.

A sudden, searing thought flashed through Sarah's mind.

Nobody, *nobody* had actually said: All right, it looks as if Forte was murdered. So *who* could have murdered him?

Four

She was suddenly on her feet, pacing the room, trying to order her mind to do some cool and analytic thinking.

There were several people who might possibly have been deceived, hurt or threatened in some way by Forte.

There were very few people who could have known of Fitz's gun, in Gus's care.

There was nobody who would shoot at Bill Hicks and then come to America and murder Forte.

When the police were notified, there would be an autopsy; the bullet would be removed—and might prove not to have been fired from Fitz's gun, in spite of the fact that Gus had come in, flourishing it, having found it, he said, on the lawn and claiming that it had recently been fired.

It struck her forcibly and frighteningly that murder requires a certain intimacy. Only somebody who knew and felt he had to get rid of Forte could have shot him. Yet his murderer *had* to be some outsider, someone, she had to admit, who had known that Fitz had left his guns in Gus's care, but some outsider. Nobody in the family could have killed Forte.

Nevertheless, automatically, she went over the short list of the people she knew who had been close to Forte. First, well, take Corinna. Corinna had been in the city, listening to her rival author, under the gaze of many eyes.

Fanny had been in the distant playroom, singing, recklessly, "The Bell Song"; Sarah had heard it.

Rosart said he had been in the woods, working on his speech. Hadn't he? But at least part of the time he had been in the kitchen, coolly cutting himself a piece of chocolate cake. Gus, she supposed, had been—where? Raking leaves probably. Or illegally burning them somewhere.

Norm had returned from his hunting trip, left his gear at Rosart's cottage, and come running to the house when she screamed.

Only Fanny and Corinna had what might be called an alibi. Sarah had read enough about crimes and trials in the newspapers to think in factual terms. *She* had no alibi.

Norm had no real alibi either, unless he could prove that one of his hunting party had left him at the driveway with only time to dump his bags, guns, boots, whatever, at Rosart's door, before he heard Sarah's scream.

Rosart had no alibi but a piece of chocolate cake.

Was that suspicious? Oh, no. Rosart had shown no apparent grief for Forte, but with the threat to one of Rosart's greatest ambitions being realized the next day— No, he wouldn't have shot Forte. And he hated violence. In spite of his fury with Forte's drinking and irritating presence, he wouldn't have killed.

Yes, she thought, after pacing and pacing the worn rug—then who? An outsider. It had to be an outsider, someone Forte had injured—and that could include a rather large number of people.

She sat down again on the chaise longue. She wished she dared telephone her father; almost automatically she put that wish aside. There were too many telephones, too many possible listening devices that could publicize a murder in his family; she knew that.

Suddenly and dreadfully another shock crashed its way into her realization: nobody had grieved for Forte.

She thought back over the childhood that Forte and Rosart and she had shared. Fitz had not been constantly at home; he had been away in school, and then, after graduation, had trained for the consular service. He had been just enough older than the others to seem very adult.

Norm had arrived, also when about to attend university. His mother was some Favor connection in Australia—a collateral branch, Corinna had said, and impoverished; she had made him welcome and spent money certainly freely for him.

Sarah knew that her own father, Charles Favor, had made an impression on Fitz and Norm during his many visits to the Favor house. They had been, of necessity, brief visits, all too likely to be interrupted by some immediate demands from the State Department. Yet there had been opportunity for both Fitz and Norm to learn about the Foreign Service. He had warned them, saying that any beginner was likely to be the third secretary to the third secretary of the secretary to clean the basement. It was said jokingly, but there was an underlying truth relating to an arduous, sometimes slow, always exacting carer. At any rate, both Fitz and Norm had chosen to train for the consular service, and they hoped that just possibly, sometime, they might be in the State Department.

She thought longingly again of her father, who, it had seemed to her, always knew a wise and quiet way of making hard decisions, and then made herself again consider the all-too-short list of the family in the Favor house.

Fanny was the only one of them whom Corinna had practically kidnapped and forced to study. Corinna had happened to visit Fanny's home, on one of her many flying trips here and there, and she had heard Fanny sing. Nobody could withstand Corinna when she was determined. She had schemed to get Fanny to New York; she had a tiny *pied-à-terre* in the city and Fanny had used it while she was studying. Corinna had made Fanny study and study and study, and she had been right.

The six of them had created a kind of family of their own; certainly they provided a nucleus for Corinna's true gift of guardianship.

Corinna was a born Favor. She and Sarah's father were related in some distant way, too. She had been christened Cora, not Corinna. She had married early and briefly a man whom Sarah had never seen; his name was something or other Briggs, and he was Forte's father. Nobody knew or cared whether Mr. Briggs had vanished by way of death, divorce—or simply because he wished to. And nobody asked. When Corinna started to write, she sensibly decided that Corinna Favor was a better name for an author than Cora Briggs. And Sarah did know that Corinna had taken over the management of the house when Fitz's mother had died—and, some years later, his father.

She could not quite trace the workings of Corinna's mind; no one knew how or even if she had discovered latent poetic genius in Rosart; but there was no doubt that Corinna had encouraged his ability. If he was not truly a genius, he was certainly already, at twenty-seven, a poet to be reckoned with.

Forte had been a failure. Yet he had been one of them.

Glimpses of Forte through the years flashed across her memory like a reel of film run too swiftly. Yet there was always his thin, rather ratty face, the ugly little gleam in his eyes, and oddly, his reedy legs, running hard to escape condign punishment from the other Favors after he had accomplished some particularly spiteful trick. Forte had never been a lovable boy, and he had changed very little. He had grown older; he had developed a habit of natty dressing, and acquired a small black mustache about which he was very vain. It did not disguise the sly smile with which he greeted them on any and all occasions. When he made a visit home, Sarah had simply avoided him whenever she could. During his recent stay he had foisted himself upon Rosart, knowing that there was a vacant bedroom in Rosart's cottage.

But she remembered too well that short scene when she'd last seen him alive. Forte, stopping the taxi, opening the door, leaning in and saying, "Off to meet Fitz? Our hero! I'm coming too. Don't try to stop me—"

She didn't want Forte. He was crawling into the taxi when the driver started up and drove around the curve, and in sheer exasperation she had shoved Forte and the odors of gin and hair tonic out of the car and onto the road, slamming the door behind him.

Was he or was he not rubbing his face when she had the swift glimpse of him picking himself up from the road? She could remember only the malicious glance he had sent after her when she looked back from the taxi, an ugly glance that seemed to promise revenge.

Perhaps, as Norm had suggested, a bruise would still show—sometime. There was no use just then in trying to surmise when.

She had been too angry, too quick to act—and yet she had felt no hesitation and no twinge of remorse; she had scarcely thought of it until Forte's name came up in her talk with Fitz.

Nothing could be done about it now.

Sarah remembered, though, with a kind of chill, how she had hoped that she would not see Forte when she returned to the house. Well, she had seen him—too late.

A series of excited barks came to a stop outside her door. Frantic yet purposeful assaults were made upon the door, and since Solly was very smart, and had learned to work at a doorknob in a certain way which would release the catch, the door burst back and a large, lanky, yellowish figure flung itself upon her. She automatically braced herself, and Solly thrust big dirty paws on her shoulders, gave her face some licks with a delighted tongue, then dashed in wild circles around the room, uttering cries easily translated to: "Where have you been? Why did you go away? When did you get back?"

"Where have *you* been?" she said crossly, interpreting his canine remarks but eyeing the burrs caught in his coat. "Chasing rabbits, huh?" Then a pungent scent came in waves from the dog's gyrations. "No! A skunk! Again! Oh, Solly, how could you!"

His name, properly registered at the American Kennel Club, was Beau Soleil; he had a sunny yellow coat (when clean) and a sunny disposition (unless crossed). Naturally, this elegant name had become Solly. The theory in the Favor family was that Solly's mother, herself a fine French poodle, had had an *affaire de coeur* with a deer. Solly was taller and longer than a standard poodle, and more agile and swift in leaping hither and yon than any dog Sarah had ever known. He was hyper, Corinna had said with a flicker of interest; she liked people or dogs to be something unusual, even if not exactly desirable.

Aware of a slight rustle, Sarah looked past the dog. Corinna was entering. She had changed to a pale-pink long taffeta robe—not precisely a negligee, it was a cross between that and a dinner dress. Corinna affected these garments, and indeed they were becoming. She had them made from imported Italian silk by a small and exclusive firm in New York, and never changed the pattern from one year to the next. They displayed her figure most charmingly and were always, since Corinna was almost pathologically neat, spotless.

Now she spoke sharply to the dog: "Down! Down! Don't touch me—"

Even Solly was affected by an order from Corinna. He stood still.

Corinna sniffed. "Skunk!"

"Yes, I know. I'll see to it."

"See that you do." Corinna sat down with dignity, arranged her flowing skirt, crossed one elegant knee over the other, swung a dainty foot, clad in an equally dainty pink slipper, and said astutely, "Surely you aren't thinking of phoning the police just now, my dear. And I truly don't think it would be a good idea to try to phone Fitz."

Corinna did not know, of course, the reason why, even after Sarah knew he must have arrived in Paris, she could not try to telephone Fitz. She wished she had not promised him; yet how could she have refused?

Corinna's calm, however, roused a kind of rebellion in Sarah. "Forte was murdered. The police——"

"An accident," said Corinna.

"Whatever it was, we should report it." But she couldn't do that yet; it had to be Fitz's decision, and she could only write to him, tell him——and wait until he replied.

"But, my dear child, we will report it."

"When?"

Corinna sighed. "When I——we have had a little time to think."

"But you simply can't break the law this way!"

"Who will know the difference? It was probably a deer hunter, anyway. He obviously killed Forte by accident. Your father would never forgive me if you insisted on publicity——police——just now."

"He'd say it was right."

"No, he'd not say that. I know your father."

Something in Corinna's lowered eyelids, her suddenly hesitant pink lips suggested to Sarah an absurdly new notion. "You like my father," she said unexpectedly.

Corinna hesitated, then lifted velvety dark eyes, which to Sarah's astonishment shone with tears. "I thought *you'd* have guessed long ago. Why do you suppose I took you in and acted as your guardian?"

Stunned astonishment caught Sarah. "But . . . my father . . . nobody ever said . . ."

"Good heavens! I've been in love with your father since you were——oh, two or three years old."

Sarah simply stared at Corinna.

Corinna's pretty lips managed to smile, amused. "Oh,

yes. We promised one another to wait. It's been a long wait, but perhaps . . . However, you can't say I haven't kept up this place for Fitz . . .''

"Oh, yes. You have done that," Sarah said weakly.

"Of course, your father helps. Your checks. You know all that.

"I never dreamed . . .''

"You weren't thinking. Where do you suppose— Oh, never mind, I'm going now. Do be sensible, darling.''

She airily extracted a lacy handkerchief from a recess in her billowing taffeta skirt. Yet for only a second, an old and lonely and frightened woman looked out from her lovely eyes. Then she shook her head, waved a kiss at Sarah, and at the door, turned back. "By the way, you didn't take Forte's pulse, did you?''

"Why, no, I never thought of it—''

She was gone, closing the door gently but firmly after her.

Take Forte's pulse? So what did this mean? There was no need to try to take his pulse, no need to send for a doctor. All of them had realized that.

How many of the Favors knew of what must have been for Corinna a long and very strong alliance with Sarah's father! She couldn't see now how she could have been so blind. Yet—yet Corinna had taken her in when Charles Favor was sent to some impossible post; and when Charles came on his visits to her, Sarah, hadn't those visits been very frequent, even if brief? But the notion of a romance— no, more than that, a long and deeply serious love affair— had never once occurred to her.

She loved them both.

Solly rose and stretched. "Oh, you do smell," Sarah said crossly. "Come on, then—''

He leaped ahead of her down the stairs, skunk smell in his wake. In the kitchen Fanny was stacking dishes in the dishwasher. She gave Sarah a stern gaze. "That dog needs a wash.''

"Oh, I know! Where's some tomato juice?"

"In that cupboard."

Sarah opened the cupboard and took out a bottle of tomato juice. Solly knew perfectly well what was coming. He whirled around and started for the door to the dining room. Sarah, on to his evasive tactics, snatched him back by his collar.

She dragged him into the big, old-fashioned laundry. "Come help me boost him into the tub, Fanny."

Fanny sighed, then dried her large but unusually beautiful and expressive hands. "I suppose Corinna talked you out of phoning your father," she said. She went on without waiting for an answer. "I thought she would. She's been in love with him for ages."

Sarah's breath went out of her. "How did you know? I never dreamed of it."

Together they pushed a now-resigned Solly into a tub. Fanny opened the tomato-juice bottle. "Why do you think Corinna took all those trips?"

"She always said for collecting material for her writing. Seeing foreign publishers."

"She went to meet your father. Always someplace he could reach quickly and where they would not be known. It's been going on for years. You mean you didn't guess until now? Or did she tell you? But really, I can't see why they didn't marry. And I can't see why they had to make such a secret of it. Nobody cares now about anybody's love affairs. Although," she added thoughtfully, "I have a feeling that Forte guessed too. Yes, I think he did. And Forte wouldn't be above a spot of blackmail, you know."

Five

Sarah poured tomato juice over Solly, who gave an anguished moan. Finally she said, "He couldn't have."

"Couldn't have blackmailed Corinna? Oh, but he could. She wouldn't want it to be widely known that she was having an affair with your father. Come to that, he wouldn't have liked it, either. They are both—well, vulnerable."

"I simply don't believe that Forte would do that."

"Forte," said Fanny calmly, "would do anything he took a notion to do. Especially if it was likely to bring him money."

"But you said—why, Fanny, you said Forte was in love with you. Or you were in love with him. Anyway, you cried. Or," she added frankly, "tried to cry."

Fanny was entirely cool. "It only struck me that—oh, opera singers are supposed to have some kind of romance in their lives. More interesting if it's past and tragic. It just occurred to me, all at once. Corinna, of course, saw through it and agreed. She's very shrewd."

"How could you invent such a lie—and so fast! Here, hold still, Solly."

Solly shivered pathetically to engage her sympathy.

"My God," Norm said behind them. "What are you doing to that dog?"

"It's only tomato juice," Fanny said.

"But—what—" Norm came to stand beside them, eyeing the tomato-drenched Solly with horror.

"Skunk," Sarah said tersely.

As Norm watched, Fanny gripped Solly with one hand, then reached up with the other to grasp the box of soap powder on a shelf. Fanny's hands, Sarah had often thought, were a true musician's hands: not slim and delicate, which some people thought showed artistic gifts, but strong and blunt-fingered, with sternly governed muscles. A musician, a surgeon, almost all artists had of necessity strong and adept hands. And even though Fanny did not use the piano except to accompany herself rather sketchily for practice, her hands were beautifully controlled.

Fanny dashed a shower of soap powder over Solly and said, "I'll get his towel," and started for the pantry closet, leaving the washing and rinsing for Sarah.

"Do you mean that all that red . . ." Norm said blankly.

"I told you. He's been chasing a skunk and got too close."

"I'm relieved." Norm still stared at the change from a reddish-pink dog to a pale yellow. "It looked really dreadful there for a minute."

"It's the only remedy." She took the huge and ancient beach towel Fanny returned with and started drying Solly, who escaped with one of his deerlike leaps onto the floor, the towel trailing after him, and dashed for the front of the house, pausing at intervals to shake vigorously before galloping on. Sarah sighed. He would end up, as always, on her bed leaving a huge damp spot.

Fanny went into the kitchen. Sarah started to follow Solly, but Norm said, "Wait, Sarah. Corinna has been talking to you, hasn't she? She's really been working on you, I'll bet."

"Didn't she talk to you?"

"Yes."

"You let her influence you."

Norm gave her a fleeting but understanding grin. "So did you."

Corinna had not influenced her. The promise to Fitz was the reason for her decision. But she said, "What's going to happen? I mean—if we just go on the way she wants us to?"

"About Forte? I would say that when she thinks the time is right, Forte will be found in the woods somewhere—obviously shot accidentally by some hunter getting a jump on the deer season."

"Did she ask if you had felt for a pulse?"

Norm shot her a swift glance. "Why, yes. Yes, she did."

"But you knew he was dead. Gus and Rosart and Fanny—all of them knew it. There's no question about that."

"Are you going to phone Fitz tonight?"

"No. Not . . . not tonight." But I'll write to him, she thought.

"Or your father?"

"No." She wondered briefly what kind of letters came to Corinna with the checks her father sent for her support. Again the knowledge of the long-time love affair between Corinna and her father shocked her, not by its seeming disregard of connections but by the fact of its existence without even a suspicion on her part. It was still—it would be for some time, she knew—a difficult piece of knowledge for her to accept. However, now was not the time to think of it.

Norm shoved his hands through his thick black hair. "Sarah, you do realize how wrong all this is. We shouldn't even have touched the body. The police ought to have seen it, just as you—I mean we—found it."

"It's too late for that."

"I don't know. It would be better for all of us even now

if we called the police and reported the whole thing as we know it.''

''Well, call them if you think that.''

''You don't agree.''

''I don't know!'' she cried, feeling harassed. ''I just don't know, Norm. If only Fitz or my father—''

''You know what either one would say.''

''Oh, yes, I know. But, Norm, let's wait till morning. Perhaps all of us need time to think—''

''Morning will make it no better. I tell you, it's a felony or something. We are all accessories after the fact, and that is no light matter.''

''I'm too tired, Norm,'' she said honestly. ''I can't seem to think.''

''I'm right. You know I am.'' Then he said abruptly, ''Goodnight, Sarah.''

She went slowly to her room. Solly had reached his haven and was rolling luxuriously on the middle of the bed. Anticipating disapproval on Sarah's part, he got down reluctantly.

She closed the door and went to her little writing desk. So, now. Write to Fitz; describe the whole dreadful situation. Tell him that a quick decision had had to be made. That all of them had been deeply shocked. And that had led them to make the wrong decision.

But then she sat, looking at nothing, thinking of all the serious problems her letter could evoke.

She had absorbed, first from her father, then from Fitz and Norm, a close-at-hand view of a strange era. Her father called it the temperature of the times and said it was both feverish and apparently infectious. Hijackings, kidnappings, assassinations. Even the clerks and typists for foreign consulates or embassies were very closely observed. ''It's like living with a ticking bomb,'' her father had said, ''or walking on the edge of a dangerous abyss.'' One never knew what a day would bring about—such as the shooting of Bill Hicks.

Such as Fitz's being ordered to go to Legunia, trying to act the part of Bill Hicks so carefully that only a few of the closest of the consulate staff knew the truth.

Yes, there had been many, too many, tragic events among Foreign Service officers, who quite often were not told all the sound and logical reasons for their orders.

Fitz might know more than he could tell her, in spite of his seeming frankness. She understood that. She took a pen and some paper and began to write quickly. "Dear Fitz: I must tell you about all this. I don't know what to do—"

There she stopped. Fitz had said, Send your letters to Washington, and had assured her that they would not be seen by anyone but him. But perhaps he was wrong. She could envision some chilly factotum reading her letter casually, then reading it again with horror and instantly reporting it to someone in the next higher rank.

She wasn't sure of anything. Rosart's words echoed in her mind: she had to be "like Caesar's wife."

The wife of a Foreign Service officer ought never to commit a shockingly illegal act.

She tore up that beginning, thought for a long time, and started again in veiled terms. "Dear Fitz: There is something I'd like your advice about. As soon as you receive this letter—"

When would that be? How many days would pass before she could receive a reply from Fitz? It seemed to her just then, tired and really frightened at the prospect, that every day, every hour that passed increased her own, and the family's, guilt in concealing so grave a crime.

After a long time she tore up that one too. She'd rest, even sleep, perhaps.

Once in bed, though, with the light turned off and Solly sprawled contentedly on the chaise longue, she began to think again of Corinna. Steel, Fitz had said, below that helpless little-woman façade.

Corinna had been firm with all of them; yet she had

provided all the young Favors with indulgences they might not have had otherwise. Sarah's father's checks might not have gone so far as a place in Corinna's box at the opera and the splendid dinners Sarah shared with the other young Favors beforehand at one of the fine restaurants in the city.

Corinna had quietly engaged language tutors for Fitz and Norm during their vacations. Sarah was permitted to sit in on the strenuous studies which were mandates for Fitz and Norm. Norm was good at German and Russian, Fitz at German and French, but there would be other languages certainly. The trick, Sarah's father had said once, was to listen; everyone in the Foreign Service in any capacity acquired a greatly increased value if he developed a gift for languages. Charles Favor had himself paid for Sarah's education and for her tiny car. But Corinna had been earning remarkable amounts of money ever since Sarah had come to live in the Favor house, and Corinna enjoyed spending some of it—some of it, for although she could splurge beautifully on luxuries, she kept a tight little fist on what she thought were needless expenditures such as servants, which had become almost an obsolete race, anyway.

Now Sarah wondered how she could have been so abysmally blind to the facts. Her father, she supposed, received an income commensurate with his present status. But it hadn't always been like that. Luckily, Corinna's writing had started off with a whiz and kept on whizzing.

Corinna's prematurely white hair suggested a greater age than in fact was true, and was as lovely as it was deceiving. Together with her jet-black eyebrows and long black lashes, she looked quite dramatic in press photographs. She had kept her youthful, graceful figure, in spite of long sedentary hours at the typewriter—lodged in a back bedroom which she had converted to a study, with only a telephone, desk, one lounge chair and a line of business-like steel filing cabinets. Nobody ever bothered Corinna during her fixed working hours; they knew better.

One always had to come back to the fact that while Corinna had probably earned a great deal of money for as long as Sarah had known her, she also spent a great deal of it for her chosen family of young Favors.

Sarah had been so young when her father had brought her to Corinna to care for, she only remembered liking Corinna, the lovely big house, the wide stretch of woodland behind it where Corinna always had the big Christmas tree cut so it seemed especially a family tree. Forte and Rosart were already there, big boys, it had seemed to Sarah then, at least seven and eight; later she must have begun to question (not with much interest, it was true) how the young Favors had come to live with Corinna. Sarah had, as children do, merely accepted the fact that there they were—Forte and Rosart; Fitz at school, Norm arriving and then also away at school, both coming home for vacations. Then Fanny had come, it had seemed to Sarah, out of the blue.

Corinna had seemed just sufficiently old enough to justify the authority of an aunt. And she had welcomed all of them. They were truly her family and she loved them, helped them, spent her own money generously on them— but demanded instant obedience even from Fitz and Norm when they were at the university, each studying hard for the Foreign Service. Fanny's parents were still alive and thriving, and, Sarah eventually learned, had disapproved of Fanny's studies; indeed, they had disapproved so strongly that there had been a battle of sorts between them and Corinna's sending of Christmas greetings to every possible branch of the Favor family was an established custom, none was received from Fanny's parents in return. Fanny did not seem affected; Fanny knew she could sing and was going to sing, and Corinna knew it, too.

Rosart's parents had died in some sort of accident; it was so far back that if indeed Sarah had ever known what kind of accident, she had forgotten now.

Fitz had inherited the house and a moderate amount of

money; and certainly with the consent of any trustees Fitz's parents had appointed to assume their son's care, Corinna had taken over. She was Fitz's closest relative; also, she had paid most of the expenses of the house.

Sarah's thoughts came back to the present. The nagging and ugly question of Forte's death could not be ignored for long. If a deer hunter had not accidently shot Forte, then who had?

There were not many people in the house or near it when she had heard the shot. She went over the very short litany again. Fanny was singing; Rosart said he was practicing his speech in the woods; Norm had barely returned from his hunting trip; Gus—Sarah felt that Gus was telling the truth when he said he was raking leaves, and indeed there was no possible reason for him to kill Forte. And Corinna was not even near the place.

In a way, the Favor young had been very close. Yet that night there had been no real grief for Forte, and that alone was tragic. The plain fact was that even in his childhood Forte had been a very unloved and unloving boy. A sneak, Rosart had once said angrily, is always a sneak—and a liar.

Another deeply shocking fact was Gus, coming into the house, carrying a gun which Fitz had left in his care.

Was it possible that a deer hunter had found the gun and used it?

The answer to that was, simply, no. A far more likely hypothesis was that Forte himself had nosed around, discovered Fitz's guns and removed the revolver.

But then—well, then what?

There was the faintest sound somewhere. She wondered absently who was prowling about at that time of night. There was only herself, Corinna and Fanny in the big rambling house!

With a prick of alarm she sat up, listened, and was suddenly sure that the third step from the top of the stairs had creaked, as it always did unless one stepped upon it very carefully, close to the wall. It had, however, only begun its normal creak. Someone who knew the house would have known that and swiftly stopped it.

Fanny, of course. Sarah moved, though, and switched on her bedside lamp. Solly was sitting straight up, tall and pale yellow, ears slightly perked. So he had heard it, too.

Six

"Fanny!" Sarah called.

There was no sound from the hall or from the stairs.

It had to be Fanny or Corinna.

Either one would have replied.

No getting around it, the three women were alone in a house that murder had entered.

Solly sighed and flopped down in the cushions of the chaise longue again.

So then there was nothing to alarm anybody.

Solly, in his peculiar way, was a good watchdog—due in part to the fact that he enjoyed barking; he was incurably vociferous.

Also, he liked all the members of the family—except Forte, who had teased him as a puppy until Sarah herself had caught him at it and flung herself at thin, weedy Forte in such rage that he had fled. Actually fled, for she was then about eighteen, Solly only a few weeks old, a gift from her father and her own treasured possession, and Forte knew that not only Rosart and Fanny but Corinna whom he had good reason to respect, would also have fallen upon him. He had fled, literally, to New York and

Greenwich Village, where some friend—or at least some acquaintance; unlucky Forte had had few friends—had given him refuge for a time. From there, Forte had drifted, as she remembered it, to San Francisco—where Corinna, resigned to Forte's shortcomings, had in the end sent him sums of money and for a time found jobs for him. These never lasted. Forte had wandered about—where? She couldn't remember. He had made short visits to the house during the past few years, only sufficiently long to attempt to induce one or the other of them to finance some scheme he had in mind, that imprudent person knowing full well that the money was being wasted but at least it might insure Forte's absence until he ran short again.

All the same, Forte hadn't deserved murder.

But he certainly must have made enemies in his helter-skelter, possibly dishonest, almost certainly ill-advised, to put it politely, way of living.

The police would have insisted upon an autopsy; they would have made sure that the bullet that killed Forte had, or had not, come from Fitz's gun.

In the morning some reasonable course might suggest itself. Eventually, wearily, she slept. But the next morning things were worse rather than better, for another potent argument for secrecy about Forte's murder arrived. It came by taxi, as a matter of fact.

Fanny and Sarah were in the kitchen, Fanny munching crisp fall apples; Sarah, feeling that she really could not move a muscle, had managed to let Solly out and been led to the kitchen by the odor of coffee.

Fanny looked up from the apple that she was demolishing with her strong white teeth. "Pancake batter ready to put on the griddle."

"Pancakes! Oof!"

"You don't have to eat them. I took up Corinna's tray."

Sarah poured herself a cup of coffee. "Good of you," she mumbled.

"Good for my lungs. Have an apple."

"In a minute." Sarah sank down at the other end of the huge wooden table, white from Fanny's stalwart scrubbing.

Fanny eyed her. "You look as if you haven't slept."

"Oh, I slept." Sarah sipped her coffee. "Fanny, why were you running around the house late last night?"

"Wasn't," said Fanny, biting into another apple.

"I heard you! I think." She wasn't sure of anything just then.

"Not me. Corinna maybe. Look here, you decided not to call the police last night. That was very sensible."

"Sensible! Good God, Fanny!"

"Needn't swear," said Fanny, chewing briskly.

The doorbell pealed sharply, pealed again, then kept on ringing as if at the determined pressure of a thumb.

Fanny leaped to her feet, her blue eyes wide. "Reporters! Or police! Oh, Sarah, how could you—"

The doorbell stopped. The front door was apparently flung so wide and impatiently open that it struck the wall with a thud. A feminine voice, high and happy, called, "Rosart! Rosart, I'm here!"

Fanny stared at Sarah, and Sarah met her stunned gaze with her own, equally stunned. The feminine voice came rapidly nearer and also the sound of feet thumping merrily along the hall. "I'll bet you are still eating breakfast, you lazy hound," said the voice and a girl came into the kitchen doorway and stopped, staring in her turn.

She was perhaps twenty, certainly near Sarah's age. She was a very pretty girl, dressed in woolen skirt and coat and a bright green sweater. Her eyes were dancing and excited, her long light-brown hair flung around her shoulders. She stopped staring and said, "You must be Fanny! And you're Sarah!"

Fanny recovered her usual poise. "And who are you?"

"Why, I . . ." The girl advanced lightly as a dancer toward the table, dropped a rather heavily laden tote bag on it and said happily, "Didn't Rosart tell you about me? I've come to spend the winter with him."

Fanny was the first to recover, doubtless a result of her stage training in control. "I didn't—we didn't know that Rosart had married."

"Oh, we're not married," the girl said blithely. "May I have an apple, please?"

Fanny's mouth opened and stayed open. Fanny was remarkably shockable in spite of her theater experience.

Sarah said weakly, "But you did say you intend to spend the winter with him."

"Oh, of course. I'd have come yesterday but I couldn't get away from home. My father and mother had to take a later plane, so I had to wait until I was sure they were gone. They don't like poets, especially with beards."

Again Fanny reassembled her usual calm. "Your father and mother do not know that you are here to . . . to see Rosart?"

"Certainly not!" the girl said and surveyed the apple in her hand rather cautiously. "I suppose these have been washed."

"Yes!" Fanny said, like an explosion. Fanny was fantastically clean about everything in the kitchen.

Sarah said, still weakly, "But you said Rosart . . ."

The girl giggled. "Didn't he tell you?" She bit into the apple.

"But Rosart . . . but you . . ."

"Oh, I was—that is, he called me his roommate. At that summer school where he taught. You know."

Fanny said, "Blenners. How did you—That's a very respectable school!"

"Why, yes. We're respectable too, and don't you forget it!"

There was a moment's silence except for hearty apple-crunching on the girl's part.

Sarah said at last, "You might tell us your name."

"Oh, sorry. How very impolite of me. I'm Nancy Butterling. Silly name, of course. I mean Butterling. Can't help that."

Fanny made a motion to rise, and sank down again, clearly at a loss, which was unusual with Fanny.

Sarah, feeling backed into a corner, said feebly, "I'd better call Rosart."

But Miss—oh, decidedly Miss—Butterling stopped crunching, lifted her pretty face, dashed some hair back over her shoulder and cried in ecstatic tones, "Here he is! Oh, Rosart! It's been so long."

Rosart came rushing in from the back entry. Another man his size would have galloped across to the girl; he sped lightly and swiftly, and gathered Nancy into his arms in, Sarah felt, a suitably bearlike hug. Nancy had leaped to meet him. Fanny's face was so thunderstruck that Sarah had to restrain a gasp of laughter.

"All right!" She checked the laughter. "Rosart, what is all this?"

Rosart eyed her over Nancy's head, snuggled into one of his vast shoulders. "It's Nancy," he said as if that explained everything. He amended it. "I mean *she* is Nancy."

Sarah swallowed. "We know that. What I mean is—"

"Oh, she's come to spend the winter with me. Her father and mother are on their way to—" He broke off. "They did leave, didn't they?"

The brown head nodded up and down.

"That's good. I wouldn't like to have your father after me with a gun." He looked at Sarah and Fanny in an explanatory way. "You see, her father is from the South. Takes a dim view of anything modern."

Fanny exploded again, rising to do so and standing with her hands planted firmly on the table. "If you mean living in sin is modern, Rosart—"

"What is all this?" Corinna asked from the doorway. Probably she had paused in the hall to listen. Corinna was never too delicate about eavesdropping. Her voice was soft yet, curiously, it broke into the rather confused exchange as keenly as a knife through butter. Or Butterling, Sarah thought wildly.

Nancy turned from Rosart's arms to stare at Corinna with one happy blue eye.

Corinna was all dignity—not a hair out of place. She wore a neat white blouse and tweed skirt, and had a yellow sweater draped over her shoulders. She might have been clothed in robes of state.

Rosart, however, was not at all affected by her icy demeanor. He replied, "She's my girl friend. Nancy, this is my . . . that is . . . Miss Corinna."

The girl turned around in Rosart's arms and actually, in spite of his embrace, contrived to suggest what must have been intended as a proper bow.

"I've heard so much about you," she said politely.

Corinna looked a little grim. "I'm afraid I have never heard of you. Really, Rosart—"

"Oh, its all right, Corinna. She was the roommate I must have told you about—"

"You didn't," said Corinna.

Rosart was not in the least abashed. "She was. All the time at that summer school where I taught the appreciation of great poets."

"That does not seem to be all that you taught. Or were taught—" Corinna began icily just as Fanny recovered some kind of awareness and said, "I wouldn't if I were you, Corinna."

"Wouldn't—Oh," said Corinna.

Fanny nodded, mumbled something about glass houses, and finished, "—that's what I mean."

Rosart looked merely puzzled. Sarah, after an instant's bewilderment, recognized the meaning of Fanny's surprisingly impudent but appropriate warning, which was simply that Corinna was in no position to throw stones when she herself lived in a glass house.

Rosart said cheerfully, "Bring your baggage, Nannie Pie? I'll get it. Why didn't you let me know you couldn't come until I've been expecting you all week. Now I'll shoot Norm and his junk out of my cottage."

They were, inconceivably, walking into the hall together, arms twined around each other.

Fanns sat down again. "That's why Rosart had the cottage all fixed up. Refrigerator and cookstove and all . . ."

Nancy's voice floated back. "I had to get here in time for your big day, darling. Have you got your speech ready?"

Corinna's pretty features set. "I suppose that means she intends to go to the award ceremony. No doubt explaining to all and sundry her . . . her position, if you can call it that in Rosart's life."

"I suppose we could ask her to be discreet about it," Sarah said dubiously.

Corinna said, in a hushed voice, as if she couldn't believe it, "Nannie Pie!"

Sarah considered it. "Nothing wrong with that."

"She seems to have come from a good family," Corinna said.

"They would have fits," Fanny said trenchantly. "I'll cook breakfast. Norm will be along soon. I'm starving."

Corinna said, "The award ceremony is at twelve. Then lunch with the trustees and honored guests. We'll take the big car."

Sarah jerked around from the stove. "You mean you're all going to the award, just as if Forte—"

"Certainly," Corinna broke in, her dark eyes stern. "We can't spoil Rosart's big day."

It was, suddenly, a last straw for Sarah. "No," she said. "We can't go."

Corinna, for another dreadful second, looked old and drawn, but determined.

Sarah said, "Dear Corinna, you must see! No matter what it does to us—"

"And to that girl," Fanny said as she put sausages in a pan. "If it's in the papers, if the police come and drag Rosart away from the award ceremony, and of course that girl, it will all come out in the papers! She'll never live it down.''

"Please, Corinna. Please see it my way—I mean the way it is—'' Sarah began.

"It's been over twelve hours,'' Fanny said flatly. "We'll be in trouble enough no matter when the police do something about it.''

Sarah gave a despairing look at Corinna, who was simply sitting, frozen, lovely—and scared.

"All right,'' Sarah said miserably. "We'll go. But it's all wrong.''

"Eat your breakfast,'' said Fanny, putting a plate down before her.

Sarah picked at the food while Corinna and Fanny talked, unbelievably and coolly, about the rehearsals for *Aïda*.

Sarah knew she must, at least, make another attempt to get a letter off to Fitz. She hurried to her room and wrote quickly, not trying to disguise anything. If some clerk in the department wanted to read it, then let it be read. She wished she had the courage to defy everybody—and her own forebodings—and go straight to the police. If she told them everything—But no—not yet.

She took a sweater and ran downstairs. Fanny and Corinna were still in the kitchen, talking; Fanny's always melodious voice floated out.

It was a crisply cool, blue-and-gold fall day. Her own little car stood out near the garage.

Gus had probably gotten it out for her at some time. She always left the keys in the car; everything around the Favor place had been safe—up to the previous night.

She didn't see Gus, she didn't see Rosart and his Nannie Pie. She thought of waiting for Norm, wherever he was, but with an instinct for acting before her resolution could fade, she got into the car. Solly sprang in before her, edged past the wheel and settled down on the seat, poking his nose forward. "Oh, all right,'' Sarah told him resignedly.

The car started promptly; she knew that she had enough gas for the run into the tiny village. It was only what Fanny had called a wide place in the road; but besides the post office, a handful of stores and two filling stations, there was what professed to be a police station, with a chief of police, Captain Wood, and four or five policemen whose main duty was to nail speeders. As far as Sarah knew, there had never been so much as a break-in around the village. Guiltily, she thought that the police station ought to be her destination.

Bedford, a short distance away, was much larger and the main source of supplies, doctors, utility offices for the entire neighborhood.

She took Brook Hill Road, the narrow and graveled short-cut.

Solly stuck his head out the open window, allowing the breeze to ruffle his ears and watching in the event of a daring rabbit. Solly had clearly paid no attention to any hunter or other outsider the day before.

She tightened her hands on the wheel as the narrow road grew even narrower. The gravel began to slide a little under the wheels.

Suddenly she realized that it was sliding too much and that the car was going too fast. She always took this treacherous bit of road cautiously, for it swooped down a hill and then turned abruptly across a narrow bridge over rocks and a little stream. It was a very tricky turn—oh, very, she told herself as she gently worked the brake. Not too hard; don't go into a skid or— No, no, not too hard.

Gravel flew.

The brake wouldn't even check her speed. She was going faster and faster, and she could see the curve and the narrow wooden bridge ahead.

Frantically she reached over and flung open the door beside Solly. She could brace herself, perhaps. But Solly—

"Jump! Get out! Quick—"

She was going to crash! She couldn't stop the car.

Solly crouched low and hung on. Jump out of a moving car? No fool he!

"Solly!" She must have screamed it as she clung to the wheel and tried to control the car.

She couldn't check the speed. But the wheel did obey— slowly, slowly—There!

The planks of the bridge creaked and sped past.

The road sloped the smallest grade upward. Ten feet farther on she managed to stop the car, even guiding it to a narrow shoulder.

She sat back, shaking.

Seven

Solly finally sat up and, she thought absently, sighed.

She couldn't move; she couldn't speak.

"That," she told Solly at last, "was a very narrow squeak." Her voice shook.

She was shaking now, too, trembling and half sick; she had never had such moments of terror in her life. Moments? Seconds only.

Well, it was over. She hadn't crashed down into the rocks or the little stream which flowed along quietly below.

She must have automatically turned off the ignition. It was very quiet save for her own sobbing breaths. Solly suddenly stood up and looked back, and then she heard another car, coming very slowly, very cautiously down the hill. It drew up beside her—the ancient rattletrap which Fitz, Norm and Rosart had shared for years. "What the hell were you doing?" Norm shouted furiously.

She let out her breath, put her arms on the wheel and her face in her arms. She heard Norm get out of the car and slam the door. "Good God, Sarah! You had me scared! What possessed you to come down that hill at such a speed?"

"I didn't!"

"Well, you've not hurt, are you? Or anything—" He opened the door on Solly's side. "Look at me. What's wrong?"

"The car . . . the brakes. I don't know . . ." Her voice still shook.

"The brakes . . ." He went around to the engine, lifted the hood, looked down blankly while Sarah sat up and wiped her forehead.

"The brakes . . ."

"Yes, I know. That is," Norm said glumly, "I don't know. The only thing I know about a car is to keep the tires up and get gas and oil. But—No, I can't see anything wrong. Where were you going, anyway?"

"To the post office."

"Oh. Writing to Fitz."

"Yes."

He came back to lean on the open door of the car. "Good for you. At least it's a step in the right direction. If we had any sense, we'd go straight to the police station."

"Did Corinna send you to stop me?"

"No. That is, she did send me after you to tell you that you ought to get the first of your shots. She phoned the doctor in Bedford."

"How does she know what shots I'm to take?"

He shrugged. "Oh, you know Corinna. She thinks of everything. Said if you intended to join Fitz in Ligunia— or travel anywhere after your marriage—then you must have all sorts of immunization. She gave me this list. My God, I'm glad you didn't crack up just now. Has your car ever pulled anything like this before?"

"No. I'll have to get it to the garage. But first, this letter to Fitz."

"Good. Okay, Solly, get in." Solly leaped happily to the back of the old car. Sarah, still feeling rather weak, crawled in beside Norm, who said, "Honestly, Sarah, Corinna is not so dumb. In fact, she's a very, very smart little lady, saw far more than I did last night. She doesn't really give a hoot about what Rosart called her image. She just snatched at it as an excuse.''

"She does care—"

"About her sales, yes. That's sensible. But not one of her fans would care if she—oh, knocked out Forte herself.''

"Norm!''

"Well, no. I suppose that would be going too far. But she is in the clear about Forte. That's not the point. She's afraid of what Forte might have got himself involved in.''

"Forte!'' She stared at him. "Involved in what?''

"Well, we are kind of a Foreign Service family, everyone knows that. With your father and Fitz and me always talking about it, nothing more natural than that some of it would rub off on Forte—give him some ideas of his own, especially if he thought there was something in it for him. That's what Corinna thought, and I wasn't smart enough to guess right away.''

"Norm, you can't mean spying? Oh, really—''

"No, I don't think Forte was what one could properly call a spy. Mainly because I can't think of anything he'd be in a position to spy about. But he could have gotten into something that would reflect discreditably upon Fitz and your father—and yes, upon me, although in a minor way.''

"Something,'' she said slowly. "You mean—concerning some foreign country?''

"Yes,'' Norm said. "Forte never had any scruples about ways to get money. We all know that. We were ashamed, but because he was a part of the family, we all tried in whatever way we could to shield him—to give him a little help when we could. But this could have been something big.''

She thought it over. "How *would* Forte get involved in something big?''

"I don't know. Any way. Heavens, he could have overheard something. Got in with people who represent the wrong group—''

"You still mean a spy. Or an enemy agent."

"No," Norm said slowly, "I'm not sure about that. I'm not even sure that he was up to anything disreputable or really important. But Corinna was so quick, so smart. She instantly saw that possibility. People," Norm said, "aren't killed just for the fun of it. Not as a rule. There must be a damn good reason. So he may have been, as I say, involved in a dangerous way. No, you needn't look at me like that. You see, the climate for all our embassies is, at the moment, not precisely an easy one. If it should come out that Forte happened to be participating in some kind of anti-American activity, for instance, it would be in the papers. In fact," he said grimly, "your father just could be recalled."

"Oh, no!"

Norm shrugged "Perhaps not recalled. He's been in the Service so long. They might merely send him to some unimportant little post. But Fitz is just beginning. Chargé d'affaires, even on a temporary basis, is a big thing for him. In short, a scandal of that nature would be very bad for your father and could just about finish Fitz. No matter how conclusively they could prove to have had nothing to do with any scheming on Forte's part, the mud would stay there. No, Corinna just thought faster than I did. Or," he said with cousinly candor, "you."

"It still seems impossible to me," Sarah replied. "And I'm going to mail this letter to Fitz. Then I may as well start my shots. We'll have to send the garage man for my car." She looked back. Her own car was perched safely on the shoulder of the road; anybody coming over the hill would see it.

"It's no conclusion," Norm continued. "But, for now—yes, I think Corinna was just quicker than the rest of us."

"No, it's not conclusive. Nothing is proved," Sarah said, "but our own involvement. If it comes to getting involved, you said it last night: accessories after the fact."

He had put the car in wheezing motion. "Depends upon what the facts are."

"Norm," she said, "How can you—how can anybody—find out what, if anything, Forte was doing?"

"I don't know. We'll have to play it by ear. Maybe if we go at it the right way, we can find out."

"No good," Sarah said sadly but realistically.

"Maybe we're all wrong."

"Norm, when will they report—I mean Forte. . ."

He glanced at her. "I told you before. My guess is that Gus will eventually discover him—somewhere in the woods—shot, obviously, by an illegal deer hunter. But it's only my guess. Corinna knows I wasn't in favor of the whole thing, so she won't tell me."

"It seems barbarous."

"Not as barbarous as what could happen if his murder got into the papers just now. That is—always *if* he was involved in any kind of agreements or activities with any enemy agents, terrorists, or anybody even touching upon foreign affairs. Oh, Sarah, this is all nebulous. It's only because Forte was Forte that it occurred to Corinna. And at last to me. I was slow on the uptake."

"Here's the doctor's office," said Sarah.

"I know. Go ahead. I'll wait." He stopped the car and she got out. The post office was in the same block. She dropped her letter into the slot and felt as if part of a burden had lifted from her shoulders. She went on to the doctor's office.

The nurse opened the door for her, and rattled crisply in her white uniform as she told Sarah that the doctor had had to leave but that Mrs. Favor had telephoned about the shots and she could give them. Then she led Sarah into the adjoining room, where a shining needle was ready, rolled up Sarah's sweater sleeve, dabbed, told her cheerfully that it might hurt a little and said goodbye just as cheerfully afterward.

When Sarah came out to the street again, Norm, his

black Favor eyebrows drawn together, was still at the wheel of the car; Solly—his head out the window—was exchanging dissenting views with a spaniel who had wandered up.

"I'm glad you got that letter off. But it would have been better to phone Fitz."

"Not yet."

"All right, but—" Abruptly, he changed the subject. "I called the garage. Did it hurt?"

"No. A prick, that's all."

He gave her a long, oddly serious look. "You wouldn't say a word if it hurt like blazes. Not you."

"Why, Norm! Heavens! I'm not brave."

"You suit me," he said, half under his breath, getting the car into gear.

She opened her mouth to say something, glanced at his unrevealing profile, decided she was reading far too much into his few words, and closed her lips firmly.

But Norm said presently, "You didn't even guess."

"Guess—" Sarah began.

"How I feel about you. Now, don't say a word. Just— That's the way it's been—well, always, I think. But Fitz got ahead of me and— No, don't talk, Sarah. Just call me a stand-in for Fitz. I can see you're happy. So forget I ever said a word. I wouldn't have if that car of yours careening down the road hadn't given me such a scare. Now, really forget it."

"But—"

She was astonished by Norm's few words and what they seemed to imply; Norm had never shown by the faintest hint that he liked her more than in a cousinly, friendly way.

And yet— She reviewed swiftly, somewhere in her consciousness, Norm's entry into the household and the years she had known him. She had realized, in a remote way, that his parents had had no money; she had guessed at some time that Corinna was, in fact, financing his school expenses—only guessed, because Corinna would never have mentioned it. Norm had never, in all those years, showed the slightest favoritism for her, Sarah. Yet he had always been there, reliable and sturdy, a part of her life.

Instinct told her not to make the slightest gesture that would indicate any understanding of his reaction following her near-accident.

Norm's face was again just Norm's face, strongly Favor, attractive, but only the Norm whom she had known for years. He was saying, "Now then, what about Forte? There's no proof that I know of that he could have been engaged in anything at all that concerned foreign interests. But there's the room he used in Rosart's cottage. I slept there last night. Rosart booted me out this morning."

"Booted—"

"Listen, when Rosart tells you to get out, you get out. Unless you want your neck broken. But last night I stayed in the room Forte had been using. It's barely possible that I can find something there to show just where he was and what he was doing before he came back here this summer. Some possible indication of what he was involved in. That is, always *if* he was involved in some skulduggery. Knowing Forte . . ." He sighed, told Solly to keep down and said slowly, "Perhaps we're wrong. Yet I'm sure Corinna was afraid that Forte's murder might prove to be extremely disastrous in its consequences to your father and Fitz."

"You, too."

Norm considered that, rounding the curve into the main and better road toward home, thus avoiding Brook Hill. He said parenthetically, "The garage will see about your car. We'd better take the main road. They'll all be waiting for us."

"Norm, we can't go to watch this ceremony. We can't— just as if Forte hadn't been killed."

He waited for a long moment before he replied. "I think we must. You see, no matter what happens eventually, we have all concealed the knowledge of his murder. So there we are. In for a penny, in for a pound. Can't do anything about that now. I tell you, we'll have to play it by ear.''

"Who would shoot Forte? If he was involved in something connected with a foreign country and shouldn't have been, then who—''

"Haven't you heard of the old double cross?'' He asked absently, watching the road.

She fumbled her way through to his meaning. "Somebody who was working with him? Wanted to stop him or—what?''

"Oh, I don't *know* what I mean. I'll have to try to find out what—if anything—Forte was planning. It's barely possible that Corinna had a notion about it. She was remarkably quick. She leaped at that nonsense about her image.''

"Rosart started that.''

"I suppose it is possible that Rosart had the same idea about Forte. How long had Forte been here this time?''

"Only about a week. You know how he came and went, and nobody— At least, I never knew where. Oh, it seems dreadful now, but really, I don't think anybody cared what he was doing. We just—just said to ourselves, That's Forte.''

He drove on, slowly. "In any event, we're already in for some trouble.''

She thought while the old car rattled and jolted along the road. At last she said, "It's got to be somebody from outside. There are so few people at the Favor house—''

He turned a blank face to her. *"What!"*

"Well, I had to think of that! Didn't you at first? You actually accused me! And he *was* killed in the house. But one of us didn't—wouldn't have shot him. Besides, Gus was probably raking leaves. You were just returning from your hunting trip. Corinna was at that literary party and then being brought home. Fitz was on a plane. I was on my way home. Rosart says he was in the woods practicing his speech.''

"He wasn't at the cottage when I got there. I didn't go

in. I just dumped my traps at the door and made for the main house. I was hungry. Then you screamed. What about Fanny if you're considering family alibis? Not a very nice thought.''

''Fanny wouldn't have killed Forte. And she was singing. I heard her.''

''When?''

''When I got home and went into the hall. She was back in the piano room, singing. I just remembered something— there was a strange smell in the hall when I got home. Something I think I know but can't— Norm, we're almost home. What are we going to do?''

He swung the rattling car around into the overgrown driveway. ''Try to get as much information as you can from Corinna. Maybe she doesn't really know anything— she may simply have sensed danger in anything that concerned Forte. She has supplied him with money, I'm sure. None of the rest of us could give him much. Corinna's the wealthy one. If Forte had a chance to blackmail anybody, he'd have to choose someone with money.''

''But you don't think his murder was due to his trying to blackmail anybody, do you?''

''I don't *know* what it was due to! I only know that'' —he braked the car; Corinna's big automobile, shining brilliantly from Gus's polishing, was drawn up at the steps of the terrace—''that we're in trouble any way you look at it.'' He gave his brake a thrust which sent Solly flying up against Sarah's shoulders. She opened the door for the dog, who leaped out.

She said suddenly, ''Why do you think Corinna asked me if I had felt Forte's pulse?''

He grinned without humor. ''I can't imagine she was thinking that possibly we could be induced to admit that Forte wasn't dead at all and that he had simply gone off on one of his usual departures. Never saying where he was going or what he intended to do. Come on, there she is. And Fanny, too.''

Sarah said, ''If it were only a deer hunter! But, Norm, who would know that Fitz had left his guns in Gus's care?''

''Gus,'' he said. ''Even Forte himself. Come on. They're waiting for us.''

''Hurry up,'' Corinna called them firmly. ''It's time to leave for the award ceremony.''

Norm said, ''Half a second. I'll put on something decent,'' and ran into the house, jerking his sweater off over his head as he went.

''You, too, Sarah. You can't go like that. Now hurry!''

Corinna was dressed elegantly, even glamorously, in a beige dress, silky black broadtail jacket, black gloves and handsome, neat black pumps. Fanny, although as always seeming bigger than life, looked dignified and elegant in a dark-blue suit which flattered her splendidly Junoesque figure. Gus was hovering in the background, looking pleased about the whole affair: the car shining after his labors, the whole family about to engage in a formal and creditable enterprise!

''I said hurry, Sarah!'' Corinna adjusted pearls at her throat. ''Oh, here's Rosart. And Nannie Pie,'' she added smoothly.

Solly gave a startled yelp and backed into Sarah, who had to clutch at Corinna's car to keep her balance. Not that she could blame Solly, for what appeared to be an enormous black bear was walking in stately fashion along the path from the cottage. He had the whiskers on his face and Nannie Pie clinging to his arm which identified him as Rosart. He wore a full black gown, with velvet bands around the flowing sleeves; he wore his doctoral hood, fastened at the throat and dangling majestically down his back. He wore a mortarboard with its tassel swishing over his eyes. Sarah, taken aback, said irreverently, ''Masquerade?''

Rosart did look a little abashed behind his beard. He said sheepishly, "They asked me to wear it. It's the university, you know." Rosart always said simply "the" university, as if his were the only one. "I can't remember which side the tassel goes." He gave a jerk to his mortarboard.

"It doesn't matter," Nannie Pie said, her face glowing. "Doesn't he look great!" she said proudly to Corinna.

Solly recovered to the extent of advancing rather cautiously toward Rosart, but a vehement odor of mothballs from the black gown checked his advance.

"*Sarah*!" said Corinna in a way which Sarah knew so well that she ran into the house and up the stairs. To Corinna, it was mandatory that all of them join on this great day.

Sarah got into the red dress and coat, quickly examined herself in the long mirror and decided she was pleased at what she saw. She seized gloves and her handbag. She met Norm at the top of the stairs; he had also changed swiftly, and was in such conventional banker's gray and discreet tie that, she thought, he could have presented himself at any meeting of the Foreign Office provided, of course, that it was not a more formal affair requiring striped pants and dark coat.

Neither spoke as they hurried down the stairs and out to the car, where Corinna and Fanny sat in stately fashion in the back seat; Nannie Pie perched, like a polite child, on a jump seat; Rosart sat in the front seat; obviously, Norm was to get behind the wheel. Gus gave them a proud kind of gesture as they moved away and Solly watched sadly, left behind.

As they left the house, Fanny, the stalwart conventional, muttered, "Not one of us is wearing black."

"Sh," Corinna hissed so sharply that Nannie Pie gave her an inquiring look.

"Rosart is," Sarah said, repressing a slightly hysterical giggle as the odor of mothballs from his collegiate gown wafted through the car. Rosart was aware of it, and said apologetically, "I told you. They asked me to wear one. I rented this at the College Shop. Sorry about the camphor smell."

Corinna and Fanny opened windows. The fresh, clear autumn breeze swept away the lingering scent.

It was only about a ninety-minute drive to "the" university where the award was to be presented.

Nobody could have dreamed of violence of any sort, let alone murder, in connection with the decorous, indeed rather impressive, appearance of the Favor family, seated together in the very front row of the auditorium where the ceremony was being held. Corinna was particularly sparkling, her chin high, her eyes bright. Fanny was massive, blond and handsome in her well-tailored skirt and jacket; Norm could have walked into the most distinguished gathering without causing a lifted eyebrow; and Nannie Pie was so obviously well-bred and her beaming and pretty face so obviously happy that Rosart's own face seemed proud as he glanced down at all of them before he took his place behind a microphone and began his speech.

Perhaps Corinna was right, Sarah thought wearily; perhaps Norm was right.

She heard only a few words of Rosart's speech, but she gathered that it was properly erudite and also properly modest; the applause and the groups that gathered to speak to him afterward were evidence of that. The luncheon that followed in the house of the president of the university was perfect too. There was wine—extremely good wine, Sarah discovered as she lifted her glass for the first toast; the food had been provided by the best caterer in the vicinity. The president's wife seemed flattered to be spoken to at length by Corinna, and told Fanny she couldn't wait to hear her sing Amneris. Various scholarly gentlemen were present also, and all of them praised Rosart sincerely. Surely Rosart's usually resonant voice shook a little with his thanks.

Rosart took the wheel as they started home again. They paused briefly at the College Shop, where Rosart returned his rented gown and mortarboard; he always kept the doctoral hood proudly folded away in cellophane. Then they went on. As they drove away from the tiny main street rental shop and the campus with its shrubs and trees, its red brick and ivied buildings, the vivid scarlet and gold and orange leaves that still clung to the trees, Corinna leaned back and sighed.

They had turned into the driveway of the long white Favor house, green-shuttered, ivy and wisteria still clinging to the lattices around the windows, when Corinna said, "You all did very well. Nobody could have guessed anything was wrong." All at once, she looked tired and bleak. "I talked to your father, Sarah, last night."

"Oh," Sarah said, and remembered. "That was you on the stairs—using the hall phone."

Corinna shot her a stern glance, which also contained, just for an instant, a flash of humor. "Not at all. I used the phone in my room, of course. I also used our code word. It means: serious! We must meet. I don't know," Corinna said reflectively, "that I have used it since you had measles and such a fever. The code word—"

"It's Sarah," said Rosart over his shoulder.

"You really are intuitive, Rosart. The point is," Corinna continued, "I'll meet Charles in Rome day after tomorrow. This is too serious. I can't take the entire responsibility, and really, I don't know what is right to do."

Nannie Pie turned a puzzled face back toward Corinna; clearly, Rosart had told her nothing of Forte.

Corinna leaned suddenly forward. "Who is that?" she said sharply.

Sarah's little blue car was parked at one side of the driveway. Andy, the mechanic, stood beside it, smoking.

"It's Andy from the garage, with my car. He must have fixed it." Sarah got out.

Solly bounded from somewhere and greeted her as

extravantly as if she had been away for months. Norm was out of the car, too, walking with her.

Andy removed his cigarette. "I'm sorry about this, Miss Favor. But I have to tell you myself. Your car's been tampered with. Somebody—"

"What are you talking about?" Norm demanded.

"Her car," Andy said. "Somebody's been at the brake. I'll show you. Want to see, Miss Favor? It was no accident."

Eight

For a dizzy moment Sarah could almost feel again the sliding gravel, the runaway speed of her usually obedient little car.

She did hear Norm speak to the others; he kept his voice under complete control, although he must have felt her own shock. "It's all right. Andy fixed Sarah's car."

The little group around the step divided, Corinna and Fanny going up the steps and into the house. Rosart, clad remarkably in a conservative suit that had been underneath his academic robe, departed cottage-ward, Nannie Pie with him. He would return now to jeans and a turtleneck sweater.

Sarah forced herself back to the nightmare world Andy had suggested and met his eyes. "If you ask me, Miss Favor, somebody doesn't like you," he said bluntly. "And I can guess who."

"Oh, well, now——" Norm looked shocked. He was just Norm now, not the trained Foreign Service officer, collected and in quiet control. "You'd better show me, Andy."

Andy's green, very observant eyes, set in his angular Yankee face, blinked a little from the smoke of his cigarette;

he shook his head. "Okay, Norm. I'll show you. But that cousin, or whatever he is—anyway, Forte is the only one of you that might do this kind of thing. He was always fooling around our garage, getting in the way. He's kind of mean, too. Or used to be."

Andy knew them all; many times he had patched up the old family car. He said, a glint in his eyes, "You ought to report this to the police. You should give Forte a scare. Could have killed somebody."

Sarah caught her breath. Now Norm's face showed nothing at all. Andy added, "I'll show you, Norm. Come around here—just under the car— It's easy."

Neither Fitz nor Norm had ever shown much interest in the car, only doing such things as checking the battery and making sure of anti-freeze in the winter, gasoline and oil whenever it was in use. Rosart had been interested in the mechanics of any engine, any car. He could probably have done some of its minor repairs.

But Andy was right about Forte; he had always had a passion for automobiles—he could have taken the old car apart if he chose and put it together again.

They couldn't of course, report anything to the police. Nobody would ever be able to question Forte.

The fact of murder had been, in a sense, retired for a few hours; naturally, it couldn't stay indefinitely in a sort of limbo. They had been moving and talking and living in a normal world, not the nightmare their world had so suddenly become. Self-control, Corinna might have called it, but it was really a kind of self-anesthetic. The nightmare lay just below the surface all of them seemed to be trying to maintain.

"I'm sure I can understand," Norm said.

Sarah simply stood still.

Unexpectedly she remembered again the slight sound in the night, which Corinna had disclaimed making. It had been merely the soft creak of a stair step, which ceased at once. Had whoever was on the stairs forgotten and then remembered the way that step creaked?

Solly had listened, his ears alert, then sighed and settled down, so whoever had stepped upon the creaky step had to be someone Solly knew and had no apprehension about.

Solly knew everybody in the family, and Gus, too, of course.

Norm and Andy were behind the car, half under it, muttering. After a few minutes, the two heads, Andy's red, Norm's black, emerged above the car. Norm had a streak of oil on his face. Andy hitched up his jeans and said, "It's all right now, Miss Favor. Perfectly repaired. But take my advice. Report it to the police."

He had called her Sarah when she was young; at some time Andy had decided that he must call her Miss Favor. She said weakly, "Thank you, Andy."

Andy's eyes were very intent. "Where do you leave your car, as a rule?"

"Why, usually in the garage. Not always. There's a kind of lean-to beside the garage. Of course, in winter, I always put it inside."

"Remember how you left it the last time you drove? I mean before this morning?"

She thought back. "I don't know. I think I must have left it outside in the back drive. It was there this morning—"

Andy said, "Oh, there's George from the garage."

Another car shot along the driveway, and George braked with a spattering of small gravel, leaned out and shouted, "Hurry up, Andy. Mr. Thompson is having a fit. His car won't start."

"All right." Andy gave his jeans another hitch and spoke to Sarah. "I really do mean what I said, Miss Favor."

The garage car whirled off down the drive. Sarah turned to Norm. "What was done? What was tampered with?"

Norm sighed. "I really can understand English. Most English. But not a mechanic's vocabulary."

The car the Favor boys used, and which for years Andy had contrived to keep in running order—barely, but running, came racketing along from the back drive. Rosart was still, astonishingly, clothed in a respectable suit and tie; Nannie Pie, face sparkling, sat beside him.

"See you," Rosart shouted and they rattled away, his beard waving.

Norm took a deep breath. Sarah said feebly. "Norm, do you think Forte could have tampered with that brake just . . . just to be mean?"

Norm said seriously, "Andy was very convincing. If your car was left out of the garage—"

"Anybody could get into the garage if he wanted to. It's never locked."

"Yes—I mean no. That is, yes, anybody could have got at your car either inside the garage or out. But I can't see why anybody except Forte would . . . would . . ."

"Try to"—she paused and made herself say it—"try to kill me. If it wasn't Forte, then who?"

Norm wiped his forehead and got a smear of black oil widely across it. "Makes no sense. I suppose Rosart could have done it, although I can't imagine why. But, see here, Sarah, do you know anything about Forte's murder that you haven't mentioned?"

"I heard the shot and found him. I told you."

He started toward the terrace. She walked along beside him, thinking, None of this is possible. It was one of those brilliant blue-and-gold days of late October. A few leaves shuffled crisply under their feet. The sun was nearly setting but was still warm; the old white house was completely itself, unchanged in any visible way. It could not be that murder had occurred anywhere within that tranquil and beautiful world.

There was a wide balustrade around the terrace, below which were box shrubs that sent up a pungent and rather ammonical aroma. Norm and Sarah sat down on the balustrade.

He put an arm around her. "Now, Sarah, brakes do sometimes just—fail!"

"You heard Andy."

"Yes. But, look here. Gus or Rosart might have done it unintentionally. Of course, Fanny wouldn't—"

"Fanny," said Sarah before she could stop herself, "knows about machinery. Some, anyway. She sees to the fuse box—both of them. Old-fashioned. Gus does also. I can't."

"And Corinna," Norm said, "wouldn't soil one of her pretty hands to delve into the interior of any car. Besides, she doesn't know anything at all about a car, except that she wants it to behave perfectly on all occasions. Reasonable," he said and sighed. "To tell the truth, the only person I can think of who just might purposely tamper with your car would have been Forte—if he took it into his head to hurt you. Revenge. Because you shoved him out of the taxi. That would be like Forte." Norm fell into deep thought, scuffing worriedly at a flagstone below a neatly polished back oxford.

She said slowly, "What is it, Norm? Is there something you don't want to tell me?"

He took a long breath. "You're the one who found him, you know, Sarah."

She sat up straight. "What on earth do you mean by that?"

"I mean—well, everybody knows—"

"Knows what?" she cried explosively.

"Well, you see, sometimes the police—sometimes they're suspicious about the person who claims to have found a murdered person. That's all I mean."

She jumped up. "Norm, you know I didn't—"

"Oh, Sarah, my darling—I mean, Sarah, *I know* you didn't shoot him! I was frightened when I found you in the room and Forte shot and—just for a second I was afraid he had made himself so troublesome that— But I know you didn't shoot him! I just— Well, all right, I don't like the fact that it was you who found him and that taxi driver just might remember that you shoved him out of the cab and—Sarah, believe me, we have to think of police investigation. I can't let them suggest that—well, I can't let them suspect you!''

Sarah faced the crowding shrubbery below and, more distantly, the trees. Already the dogwood were red, already the enormous golden maple, above what had once been a formal, carefully tended sunken garden, was a mass of brilliant yellow, so brilliant that it actually sent a warm glow all over her bedroom and the long living room—where Forte was shot.

A few notes of music drifted out the door of the house, open to the warm and sunny day.

'Ah! vieni, vieni amor mio . . .''

There was a pause, and then Fanny repeated it carefully, beautifully, *'Ah! vieni . . . vieni . . .''* This time she ventured a few more syllables. *''M'inebbria . . .''*

''She'll go on like that,'' Sarah said on a tangent, struck as she had been innumerable times by Fanny's resolve to achieve perfection in every note. ''She's really got a fine voice.''

''And she works,'' Norm said. ''Even I can hear that. Yes, Corinna was very good to all of us. She didn't miss a trick to turn out what she thought of as well-rounded people. And now this.''

''Norm, nobody can possibly think I killed Forte. Now listen.'' Sarah had what seemed to her a valuable idea. ''Rosart is out of the way, so you can really search his cottage. Anything Forte could have left there. You just might find''—she finished feebly—''something.''

Norm thought for a moment. Fanny, away in the playroom of the house, tried again, *'Ah! vieni . . . ah! vieni . . .''*

''She'll not stop until she's satisfied,'' Sarah sighed. ''But you can't help admiring her. Norm, could Corinna have guessed that I had written to Fitz about Forte?''

He shook his head. ''Perhaps. I don't know. She'd deny

anything like intuition. She'd call it common sense. But she does seem to know or make very accurate guesses as to what anybody she knows is about to do."

"She couldn't have kept me from mailing my letter."

"I only wish you would phone him."

Sarah backed down hurriedly. "No, I—no."

He gave her a puzzled look. She said, hurriedly again, "But I never once thought that Forte might have got himself—and the rest of us—into a miserable business like—"

"Like consorting with enemy agents? Or terrorists? Perhaps he didn't. Perhaps we're making something out of nothing." He rose. "All right. I'll get busy in Rosart's cottage as fast as I can. Not," he finished gloomily, "that I expect to turn up anything."

He walked down the steps and along the path to Rosart's cottage, the very epitome of the neatly dressed Foreign Service officer except for the remaining smear of oil on his forehead.

Sarah listened to Fanny, over and over again, the same few notes. Fanny was absorbed in learning, one phrase at a time, the exacting role of Amneris.

She thought vaguely of Fanny's truly good voice and, with a certain qualm, of the hour or two which always preceded Fanny's singing onstage. It was a time that demanded assistance from Sarah, but grim endurance from Fanny, who was a good cook, a hearty eater—and a victim of hideous nausea before the curtain went up.

Once she was on the stage, she sang with calm beauty.

Forte could have tampered with Sarah's car the previous day, while she was in town meeting Fitz. That kind of revenge would have pleased him. But then, why had Forte himself been murdered? The old double cross, Norm had suggested. What double cross?

A squirrel scampered across the lawn and Solly loped after it; the squirrel shot to a high branch on the tree and sat there, waving his tail and chattering. Solly sat down at the foot of the tree and uttered reciprocal threats.

Corinna apparently heard and came out on the terrace. "What on earth are you doing there? Dreaming?"

Dreaming! "No." She paused on the brink of telling Corinna about the brakes of her car, then, for no sensible reason, decided against it. Wait, she thought, until Norm has discovered something—either clearing Forte of any suspicion or actually involving him in ugly activities. But even that could, possibly, help answer only one question: What had kept Forte occupied for the most recent few months during which he had rarely been at home? Forte had been gone, she thought back, during most of the summer; he had made a short visit in June. He had left before Fitz came home for a few days and she and Fitz became engaged. A happy week, she thought now.

It must have been in September when Norm had come to gather up his hunting clothes and guns, and then left almost immediately. Corinna had been at home almost all summer; she had made one flying trip to Paris in August, but that was all. Probably, Sarah reflected swiftly, she had met Charles Favor.

Fanny had stayed home and worked resolutely. Rosart had taught at Blenners for most of the summer; when he came back, Forte had still been away, returning only a few days, about a week, she remembered, before his murder.

She herself had been at home most of the time. She had flown to Washington a few times when Fitz had asked her to come.

Beside her Corinna said unexpectedly, almost as if she had plucked the question out of the air, "I keep wondering what Forte was up to last summer. I mean, when he was away from here. Do you have any idea?"

"No."

Corinna sat down on the balustrade. "I thought he might have told you."

"I saw very little of Forte."

Corinna smiled faintly. "You mean you were thinking so hard about Fitz all that time that whenever Forte—or any of us, for that matter, spoke to you— Really, Sarah, sometimes I thought you were half asleep. I had to repeat, often, to get the slightest response from you. Ah, well, that's the way it is."

A softer expression came into Corinna's face; even her dark eyes seemed luminous and gentle. But then she turned abruptly to Sarah, shrugged as if forcing herself back to the present and said, "There is something else you really must think about. I haven't wanted to point it out to you but if—I mean when—we go to the police, you know what they are likely to say."

"They'll ask who murdered Forte."

Corinna shook her crisp white curls. "Naturally. But they will also ask if you did it."

"That's what Norm said!"

"You found him. There is only your story of how and when you found him."

"But it is the truth."

"Oh, I believe you. But sometimes an investigation into murder seems to fasten itself first upon the one who claims to have found the person murdered."

"Corinna!" Sarah could feel her whole body tense itself.

"I know, my dear. I promised your father that I would see to you, and I always have. Now that you know, I expect you disapprove of our relationship. But that's the way it is and has been since just after your mother died. We"—she lifted her pretty shoulders—"we simply fell in love. And we're been in love ever since."

"All those years . . ." Sarah said softly.

"All those years. From that time on. He hasn't changed. I haven't changed. And you're his daughter and I've got to protect you in every way I can."

Corinna, who could be as dramatic as Fanny when it suited her, was never sentimental. But now she looked off across the lawn to where Solly was still threatening at the foot of the tree, with the squirrel chattering away triumphantly above him, and said, "You are Charles's daughter. Because of that, you have been, from the first, like a daughter to me." She turned the full and compelling gaze of her beautiful eyes upon Sarah. "So you see, I cannot turn you over to the police. Not as the person who found Forte."

Away off in the house Fanny repeated the one phrase, *"Ah! vieni, vieni, amor mio . . ."*

Corinna said, more briskly, "All of you are dear to me. Forte—well, I had to care for him. Nobody wanted him. I was earning enough money and I felt sorry for him. Forte—yes, Forte was a failure to me and a sorrow. Fanny—I practically wrenched her from her parents because I knew she had that voice. Rosart needed a home and is a Favor. Fitz needed someone older to see to him. And I—yes, I needed a home. I made the arrangements to live in this house and take care of it and make a home for Fitz, too. You know all this. The same with Norm. Norm and Fitz are like, say, nephews, but loved nephews. And Fanny is truly like a niece. But you, Sarah—you are Charles's daughter."

Sarah put her hand over Corinna's small one.

"No use in talking any more about it. I'll see Charles and then we'll know what to do."

"I know what he'll say."

Corinna's eyes lost their soft and gentle look. "You mean report to the police? No, I really don't think that likely. You see, it's hard for me to say it, but—"

"I know what you don't want to say. You think Forte may have been doing something like—well, enemy activity?"

"Did Forte ever say or do anything that suggested that to you?"

"No."

"Yet when it occurred to you, it didn't seem impossible."

"That's the *real* reason you wouldn't let us go to the police."

Corinna eyed her steadily.

"I told you all that seemed necessary at the time. That is, of course, that both Charles and Fitz are in positions of some sensitivity. Good heavens, I'm surprised that you didn't think of that at once."

"There isn't anything around here to get or . . . or give information about."

"He could have caused trouble for your father. Really, I don't know the answer," she said bleakly, looking again cold and drawn.

Sarah said, "My father will know what to do."

"In the meantime, I'm thankful that you agree with me about reporting this. By the way, did you get your shot?"

"Yes." Thinking of the shot for the first time, she realized that there was a tiny itch beginning on her arm. She shrugged her shoulder to relieve it. "Oh, yes, I got that. Corinna, Norm thinks as you do about Forte. That is, he thinks it is a possibility. And he says you must have thought of that immediately. Did you?"

"Why, of course." Corinna looked blankly surprised. "What else? I could see that such a notion had not struck you, but given time, it would have inevitably occurred to you. You've heard talk of all the precautions any Foreign Service officer must take. Heavens, the entire embassy or consulate staff must be on the alert at all times. Charles says that with all the devices for hearing and watching . . ." She smiled a little. "He says if he wants to sneeze, he locks the door, pulls the shades, goes into the bathroom, turns the water on full, then sneezes. And the next day his opposite number will ask how his cold is."

Sarah said slowly, thoughtfully, "Yet all these years no one has known of your—" What word could she use? she wondered in instant panic. Corinna supplied it, again with a faint smile: "Liaison. Love affair. Call it anything you like. No, we've been very careful. Merely because it seemed indicated. Actually, that part of it has been a great bore." She sighed.

"Oh," said Sarah flatly.

Corinna made an impatient gesture. "Discretion. I still hate the word. Cautious phone calls. Careful arrival in any city. Discretion, discretion, secrecy, secrecy. Oh, God, yes, that part of it has been a bore. But"—the softer look came back into her face—"it's been worth it."

"Corinna," Sarah said suddenly. "I wonder—that is, did Forte ever have anything to do with his father?"

"His father?" Corinna rose as if jerked up by a strong arm. "Len Briggs? No!" She paused. "At least I don't believe so. I don't think he even knows where he is." She waited a moment, dark eyes narrow. "Sarah, do you think his father has been seeing Forte?"

"I haven't the least idea. But—"

"I know. Yes. His father would do anything for money. So would Forte. Like father, like son. Yes, it could be that he drew Forte into some sort of scheme."

"But his father wouldn't have shot Forte."

"His father," said Corinna, so calmly that it was curiously frightening, "would have done almost anything. But no, I don't think he would have shot Forte."

"Where is Forte's father?"

"Good heavens, I've been trying to find out where he is for years. You wondered why Charles and I hadn't married. Len Briggs is one reason. I can't find him to get a divorce."

"But if you can't find him—isn't desertion a reason for divorce? It's been twenty years—"

Nine

Corinna eyed her thoughtfully and nodded. "It was partly because of your father. All right, then. Here is my dull story. I married Len Briggs, who seemed to be a handsome, charming young widower with a little boy. A geologist, traveling the world—romantic. I was young, good heavens, I was so young and foolish. Indeed, I thought I loved Len Briggs. It didn't take long to discover what an idiot I had been. His first wife hadn't died—she too, had left him, and left Forte with him. I don't know or care what happened to her. I haven't heard of her since—oh, I don't even remember when."

"Didn't he—Mr. Briggs—object when you left him?"

Corinna laughed softly. "He wasn't there to object. He was off on one of his many trips. I was so young and silly, but I knew that I must simply leave, not make any fuss about it, so that's what I did. Forte was alone with me. He was such a little boy. I had to take him. Then later I had an attorney who did manage to nail Len down to something, so Len promised to take Forte. But then he disappeared. And," Corinna said with finality, "I haven't heard of or from him since. I've tried. Your father has tried to find him. He may be anywhere in the world. He may be dead long ago, and no way of proving it. So you see . . ." She sighed and turned toward the door. "We'll go along, as we have been, Charles and I, until—oh, until. That's all. Not a charming story. It's getting late and cold."

"But you had met my father before you left—"

"Yes. But barely met him. I think now that when I met him it was at a Favor family gathering. Aunt Cora's house in Palm Beach. She's gone now, many years. But yes, I had met your father and liked him. Perhaps it even entered my mind to wish that I had met him before he and your mother were married. And before I had made such a rash marriage. But that was all, Sarah. After your mother died, Charles and I met again, not purposely, another of those family meetings. Then we began to correspond. Then meet—intentionally. Yes. So he asked me to see to you. And I did try to, Sarah. Now, that's all of that. I'm going in." Her high heels made little taps on the flagstones.

It was colder; the sun's glow had gone; the golden maple tree was dimly yellow. Solly had tired of threats and lay full length at the foot of the tree, and the squirrel, probably tiring too, had gone on about his business. The sky was all at once deeply blue, almost dusk.

Suddenly Sarah ran after Corinna and into the house. Corinna was standing at the tall vase of chrysanthemums, her pretty nose wrinkled, Sarah said, "Did you like my mother?"

Corinna turned fully to her. "Why, yes. Nobody could help liking her. You're very like her in some ways. Blue eyes, for instance. The Favors always have dark eyes. But your dark hair and—well, my dear, your nose and rather marked cheekbones, all that is Favor. The Favor strain," she said rather complacently, "is a strong one. You and Norm and Fitz are all Favor. I flatter myself that no one could take me for anything but a Favor. Fanny looks like her mother—tall, blond, regular features. But she has the gift of work. That's Favor. Your mother . . ." She paused thoughtfully. "Probably I was a little jealous, just at first, only because she was such a beauty. Before I knew how—how much I wanted Charles. After that—no, I wasn't jealous. I only knew how lucky they were and—yes, that was good. You don't understand that now."

"I think I understand. It's so very much a part of you that—well, I don't know the word . . ."

"Whatever it is," Corinna said and smiled.

"What about Forte's mother?"

"My dear, I told you. I know she left Len Briggs, but that's all. She may be anywhere, she may be dead."

"Forte might have found her."

Corinna shook her head. "Not Forte. He knew she didn't care enough about him to take him with her."

"Poor Forte."

"Yes. But all the same, even as a young child nobody ever could trust Forte. And later he would really have done almost anything for money, except work for it. That's partly my fault. I knew the circumstances, you see. And I had taken him of my own will. I felt responsible for him."

"So you kept giving him money."

"What else could I do?"

"Did he . . ." How could she put it tactfully?

But Corinna guessed. "Did he try to blackmail me about Charles? No. He didn't know."

"Ah! vieni . . . vieni, amor mio . . ." sang Fanny off in the distance, almost as if she chose to remind Corinna of Charles.

Corinna touched the drooping yellow heads of the chrysanthemums. "Really, these ought to be removed. They're beginning to smell."

"I'll take them."

Clearly, Corinna had told all of her own private life that she intended to say, and it was indeed a great deal. Sarah grasped the vase, holding it away from her new red dress. The flowers did smell, and it reminded her of the curious and rather disquieting odor that had drifted through the hall when she had returned home—and Forte had been shot.

The memory of that little whiff of something she couldn't identify nagged slightly at her. But she shrugged it off. It could have been—oh, anything.

As she entered the kitchen, Fanny, off in the playroom, let something drop with a crash on the keys—probably one of her hands, crossly, for in a few minutes she arrived in the kitchen in a state of impatience.

"Honestly! My voice has dropped at least half a note! No, probably not that much. But if I miss my daily work, it does drop, you know. And that simply will not do!"

"It sounded all right to me," Sarah said comfortingly. She emptied the big vase of water and stuffed the faded flowers into an overflowing trash can.

"Oh, perhaps. I'm not sure. All this is really a little upsetting. I'll get dinner."

A little upsetting, Sarah thought with incredulity.

Fanny said, "I told Rosart to empty that trash, but he forgot. I'll have to remind him. Where is he?"

"I don't know. He and Nannie Pie went off somewhere. A long time ago," Sarah said—and realized that it hadn't been a long time, not really; it seemed a long time only because Andy and Norm and then Corinna had given her so much to think about.

Sarah rinsed the large vase, and Fanny began getting food from the refrigerator and saying some uncomplimentary things about Rosart, who, apparently, had robbed the refrigerator of steak, lettuce, endive and, indeed, almost everything that appeared to have appealed to him. "He ought to buy these things for himself and Nannie Pie," said Fanny angrily and thumped down potatoes, another steak, parsley, without which she refused to cook, and a dish of hamburger. "For Solly," she said.

Solly, however, did not arrive at the back door promptly with the sound of the refrigerator door, as was his custom.

Neither did the lure of broiling steak produce him. Not another skunk, Sarah hoped.

Norm came in; he had changed to his more customary slacks and sweater. He made drinks for them in the pantry, put them on a silver tray and was starting out toward the library when Sarah stopped him.

"Find anything?"

"I don't know yet. I looked in the room Forte had used, but it was all neat and cleaned up, and there were only some of Nannie Pie's clothes. You know Rosart. He's painfully tidy."

"Nannie Pie has got herself a good housekeeper," Sarah said shortly.

Norm did not so much as grin. "It was that way last night. Not a thing out of place. But Forte's suitcase and canvas bag were on the porch—Rosart must have put them there—and I've taken them up to my room. I'll have a look after dinner, but honestly, I don't see what he could have had that would give us any hint—" Norm stopped as Corinna called, "Norm, Sarah! I'm in the library. Fanny!"

"Yes, Corinna, I'm coming." Fanny arranged cheese and crackers and brought them and the little kitchen timer into the library with her. Corinna had changed; this time she wore a silvery gray taffeta housecoat; she had brushed up her white hair and was so perfectly cool and collected that Sarah almost doubted the conversation they had had out on the terrace. It had been what Fanny called a real heart-to-heart. Corinna gave not the slightest evidence of it.

Nobody knew where Rosart and Nannie Pie had gone; nobody questioned it. Solly still had not turned up for his handout.

The kitchen timer ticked so loudly that it seemed almost to insist upon reminding them of some great significance of the passage of time. Norm, Corinna and occasionally Fanny made some brief observation about Corinna's proposed trip to Rome. Had she packed? That was practical Fanny. No, she didn't need to pack until the last moment.

"Not Corinna," Norm said, teasing her but not very zestfully. "She's always prepared for anything—" His face changed. "I didn't mean that," he said hurriedly, making it worse, which was not like tactful Norm.

The timer gave forth an imperative ring and Fanny, a glass of sherry, which she did not permit herself as a rule, in her hand, hurried back to the kitchen. Norm poured a second drink for Corinna, and at Sarah's nod, a second one for her. Then he turned on the television. "Might as well hear all the bad news," he said not very cheerfully.

In fact, there was bad news. As the picture on the screen cleared, there were mingled shouts and sounds of jeering. Then they saw the picture all too clearly. A single-minded mob was storming some embassy—a very stately embassy. It was one which they all recognized from its photographs. Corinna sat forward.

Norm said, "My God, *look—look—*"

Two men, standing on a balcony above the shrieking mob, were turning away from the camera. One of them was Charles.

They vanished inside doors, which closed behind them. The mob yelled. The camera swerved to the street scene, full of screaming and gesticulating people.

An advertisement came on.

Sarah let out her breath.

After a moment Corinna righted the glass in her hand, which was dripping sherry over her skirt. Her face was as white and cold as a sheet of ice on a pale-gray lake. "This means that Charles will not be able to get to Rome," she said, her voice perfectly steady.

Fanny came back to the library door. "What's the matter? What—"

"Never mind, Fanny," Norm said. "Is dinner ready?"

"Steak," she said laconically. "I'll get you something to clean the sherry off your skirt, Corinna."

Corinna looked at the stain. "It doesn't matter." She seemed to call herself from a great distance. "Yes, of course. Dinner."

"It's steak," Fanny said again, looking puzzled but firm. "Broiled. It won't keep."

It was just right. The salad was crisp, the French dressing perfect, but nobody had an appetite, except Fanny.

The meal wound up with apples and oranges. "Give you your head, Fanny," Norm said, "And you'll make vegetarians of us."

"Not with steak," Fanny said, factual as always. "I've made coffee, by the way. Want it here or in the library?"

Nobody replied. Corinna swished silkily down the hall. Norm took the tray Fanny had prepared and Sarah followed him and the tiny clink of porcelain cups and saucers.

They were all subdued, for another news program was filling the air with the news account and pictures of Charles's embassy. A demonstration of any kind outside any embassy was not good to hear. Corinna listened, said nothing more and went upstairs.

Fanny sighed. "She hates that kind of thing. Well"—she looked at Sarah—"I'm sure you don't like it, either."

"Nobody does," Sarah said shortly. "She says it means that my father can't meet her in Rome."

"Oh." Fanny's hand hovered over the silver sugar bowl, but her better instinct prevailed; she took no sugar and said only, "Then he will manage to meet her somewhere later, I suppose."

"And in the meantime she means for us to go on keeping quiet about Forte." Norm held out his cup for more coffee.

"Can't do us any harm now," Fanny said tersely. "We're already in the soup."

Norm gave her a half-admiring and half-dubious look. "You may be right."

Fanny turned off the television and went toward the

kitchen with some of the empty cups. Sarah gathered up the silver service and the rest of the cups and was starting to follow her when Fanny called from the kitchen. "What's the matter with Solly?"

Sarah hurried to the kitchen, where Fanny was holding up Solly's dish of chopped meat. "Isn't he here?"

"No sign of him. And here's his dinner."

"He's hunting again," Sarah said resignedly.

"Maybe," said Fanny, "he's out somewhere in the woods. I thought I heard him."

"When?"

"Just as I came back to the kitchen. I'll put this in the refrigerator until he comes in."

"Oh, I can't stand another go with skunks!" Sarah started out the back door, and felt the chill of the fall night as she opened it. The tiny entry was in fact a small hall, which had once been the depository of roller skates, ice skates, hockey sticks, a big box for worn-down tennis balls and baseballs. Now there was only one baseball bat, looking deserted and lonely. On the wall there was a row of hooks from which dangled a motley collection of sweaters, jackets, coats that anyone might want before going to the garage, or to Rosart's cottage. Without looking, she flung around her a red raincoat, which, as a matter of fact, Fanny had once bought and later refused to wear after Rosart had said unkindly, but truthfully, that she looked like a balloon in it.

The night was really very cold; there was almost the nip of coming frost in the air. Lights from the kitchen windows made two rectangles on the grass. There was no light in Rosart's cottage, no light in the apartment over the barn. Gus always went to bed early.

She was sure then that she heard a distant but angry and demanding bark, as if Solly were locked in somewhere and didn't like it. The garage?

She went along the path toward the old barn, which had been turned into a garage by the simple process of enlarging the doors. Later there had been some discussion about installing an electrical device to open and close them, but it had been decided by Corinna that it was an unnecessary expense, involving as it would also the installation of all-new doors. The old ones were usually closed only in the winter, and then merely to keep what heat could be kept in the car engines. However, somehow Solly must have got himself into the garage, and someone, not realizing it, had closed him in.

But when she reached the garage the doors were open upon perfectly silent blackness, and Solly gave an anguished yell somewhere off in the woods.

The woods belonging to the Favor place were extensive. Fitz and Corinna had both resisted all offers to buy land, so there were still about eighty acres, largely of unimproved woodland: great maples, groups of silver-white birches with their V marks in sharp black, clusters of green firs, a stand of stately beech trees and thick undergrowths of laurels, rhododendrons and blackberry canes. It was a wilderness which had always been enticing to the young Favors and which Sarah would have expected to be able to find her way through swiftly and precisely.

This did not happen. She passed the garage and found what they called the brook path, which went through the woods and came out at a tiny rill, usually dry. There was a small bridge with a handrail; she groped for that in the thick darkness of the woods, found it, called, "Solly . . . Solly . . ." and heard the dog yelp again: Hurry up. Come and get me.

There were never traps in the woods. They were not allowed in any neighboring woods, either—although those were too distant for her to hear Solly if he had strayed that far. She hadn't actually walked in the woods since—oh, it must have been last spring, she thought vaguely. Yes, last spring she and Fitz had strolled along, pretending to hunt for the first trillium and violets.

Everything about the place reminded her of Fitz. She

loved the house, she loved the woods—and all of it seemed to her an enchanted realm because it was so closely associated with Fitz and her childhood—then growing into a young woman and, always, it seemed to her now, in love with Fitz. He loved the woods too. Probably in the long-distant future, after he had had a fine career in Foreign Service, they would come back to live the rest of their lives in the big house and, again, explore the woods together.

The brook path crossed the tiny bridge; several rather straggly paths extended from it deeper into the woods. It was now very dark, for besides the crowding trees, clouds had come up to cover the thin and rather chilly starlight. "Solly," she called again, and again there was another demanding yelp from him. She chose what seemed to be a direct way toward the sound, bumped painfully into a tree, rubbed her forehead and felt for the next tree, stumbling into a thorny shrub. She got to her feet, muttering words which Corinna would never have permitted her to say, and heard Solly—nearer now. She stopped to listen. The crisp leaves of autumn rattled softly somewhere near. Had someone else moved not far away? But now she could no longer hear the faint sound of leaves being trodden on.

She tried to assure herself that nobody would follow her into the woods. Certainly not without calling to her, letting her know. And now there was not a sound anywhere—until Solly gave another despairing, what's-the-matter-why-don't-you-hurry yelp. She stumbled on, and avoided another bump by touching the trees warily. Solly's barks were impatient but louder, so she was nearer—very close.

She couldn't see Solly but she could hear him. Everybody in the county could have heard him, she thought and tried to laugh at herself, and failed because suddenly she was sure that someone else had paused to listen to Solly.

Someone *could* be hiding in the woods. Maybe the someone who had shot Forte.

The thought terrified her. She hastened on, tripped over a maple root and fell into a thicket of brambles.

But Solly was so near that she could now see his pale-yellow shape, wriggling, leaping, unable to reach her because he was tied. She got up, clutching the raincoat around her, and went cautiously to him.

She got down on her knees and Solly pawed at her, nearly knocking her over. "Wait a minute—Keep still, Solly—wait—"

Yes, he was tied. Tied securely, too, with a rope knotted firmly around his collar.

"Hold still, Solly! I can't find the knot—"

A cloud of smothering blackness came down over her head. Solly barked frantically. Arms were around her throat; at least they felt like arms, she thought wildly, but they were, in fact, the sleeves of the raincoat she had casually flung over her shoulders. The blackness over her face was the stifling hood of the coat.

But the coat alone could not do what those sleeves and hood were doing. She had, literally, no air. Solly's barks suddenly seemed far away. She was tearing at the sleeves, the whole world turning dizzily. She could now barely hear Solly. She couldn't hear anything.

After a time—moments, seconds—the pressure on her throat was relieved!

She was lying flat in a bed of pine needles and gasping with thankfulness at the fresh cold air. Norm was leaning over her. "All right? All right?"

Somewhere a flashlight lit up a circle in which Solly, barking wildly, was straining to get near her.

The light came from the lanternlike flashlight which Gus—or anybody else who wanted it—used. It stood now on the ground, with the light shooting upward, but she could see the dog, and a glimpse of Gus, scowling and working at the rope tied to Solly's collar. Norm said, "Try sitting up, Sarah. Or should I give your lungs some help—you know, press under the ribs."

"No, no!" Fanny's exercises to encourage deep breathing, she remembered distantly. She sat up and pressed her own hands close under her ribs, but found she didn't need the pressure. She could breathe in the beautiful, wonderful air. She hadn't quite lost her senses—or had she?

Certainly she had felt very dizzy. Then blackness had submerged her. Gus said accusingly, out of the circle of light, "Somebody tied up this dog."

Sarah had heard that tone of voice before. Somebody else had said that—no, not quite that but something like it. Yes. Andy from the garage had said it. "Somebody doesn't like you."

Norm said, "It's all right, Sarah. You're perfectly safe. But what are you doing with that red thing?"

"It's Fanny's." Sarah's throat hurt so she spoke indistinctly. But her memory was far too clear. *Somebody doesn't like you*. And Andy had added "And I can guess who."

But it couldn't be Forte this time.

Ten

Gus, of course, knew his way through the woods. He went ahead, obligingly turning his big flashlight down so Norm and Sarah could follow him. Solly, subdued, walked soberly beside her, his cold nose at her hand as if to make sure she was there.

The flashlight jerked ahead. She could see Gus's khaki work pants in the circle of light. Norm's arm was around her, steadying her. She began to feel slightly—only slightly—like herself. She said at last, gasping, "Somebody tried to choke me!"

The flashlight gave a jerk, and she blinked as Gus shot the light straight in her face. "Who?" said Gus.

"I don't know! I don't know . . . I only heard . . ."

"What?" Norm said. "Go on, what did you hear?"

"I don't know! I thought—once I thought someone was either following me or walking through the woods along with me. Whoever it was seemed to stop when I stopped. I listened, and could hear the rustle of leaves, and then it stopped and—"

"All right." Norm steadied her. "We'll get you in the house. You're shivering."

She was cold. She was shaken and suddenly trembling. She said unevenly, "Please turn the light out of my eyes, Gus."

Gus moved the flashlight. Norm said, "Why did you happen along just then, Gus?"

There was a pause while Gus trudged on and they followed. Finally he said, "Heard the dog. Knew he was caught somewhere. The Simmons boys have set up a trap in their woods."

The Simmons woodland adjoined the Favor woods. "Oh, Gus!" Sarah cried. "Not a trap!"

Gus said gruffly, over his shoulder, "Not that kind. I mean, it's the kind the Humane Society lets people use. Doesn't hurt the animal, just pens him in. Thought Solly would be too big to edge into one of those traps. But even if he had, it wouldn't have hurt him." said Gus. "But he was tied up. I've got the rope. Far as that goes, how did you happen along, Norm?"

Norm said, "I was following Sarah. I was upstairs, happened to look out my window just as she passed in the light from the kitchen window. When I got downstairs and opened the door I thought I heard Solly. So I guessed what she was doing. But I didn't see anybody in the woods. I didn't even know you were there, Gus, until you turned on that light. By the way, did you find my guns? I left them at the foot of the stairway in the garage?"

"I found them."

"Clean them?"

"Of course," Gus replied in a what-did-you-expect tone. "Get any quail?"

"Not many."

They had reached the garage before Gus handed the flashlight to Norm, then said, "You take care of that dog, Miss Sarah. Not much to look at maybe, but a good watchdog."

In fact, Gus was devoted to Solly.

Norm took the flashlight. "Look here, Gus. I think I did

just—well, I think I heard somebody moving around. I was trying to avoid bumping into the trees, couldn't really see anything, but I knew that Sarah must be looking for Solly, so I tried to go in the direction of his barks. Then Solly began to yelp as if Sarah had reached him, and I got out from some pines and actually stumbled over her, there on the ground. I sort of felt for her and—I didn't hurt you, did I, Sarah?''

"No! I was so wrapped up in that coat— But no, I'm not hurt."

"I reached for you and felt the raincoat wrapped around you," said Norm rather unsteadily. "So I got that off."

Gus said, "Didn't you see who jumped at her, Norm?"

"No. That is, it seems to me now that there was something, something dark on the very edge of—I can't say my vision, because I couldn't see a damn thing. I just felt that somebody had moved, and maybe jumped away—I don't know. Solly was howling and I was trying to get Sarah out of the raincoat. Even if Mrs. Favor doesn't want the police here, I think I ought to report this."

"Right," said Gus bluntly. "But report only this. Needn't tell them anything about Forte. Just tell them somebody in the woods attacked Miss Sarah. They'll send men out to take a look."

"And suppose they find Forte," Norm said.

"They won't find Forte," said Gus and turned into the garage.

"All right," said Norm, his arm steadying Sarah, who as a matter of fact welcomed some support. "You're sure you aren't hurt."

"I'm scared!"

His arm tightened around her. "Sarah, how could you have gone out alone like that! Suppose—" He stopped abruptly.

She said, "I tell you I'm not hurt! Not really. You came in time."

"Why didn't you call me before you—Oh, Sarah—"

"I tell you it's all right. I mean I'm all right." But she was still frightened. Terrified would be a more exact word, she thought.

There were no lights in Rosart's cottage and the car was not under the big elm where he usually left it.

Lights streamed out from the kitchen, and Fanny stood in the doorway of the back entry. "What on earth?" she cried. "Where have you been? What are you doing with my old raincoat?"

Sarah took a deep breath as she went up the steps and into the house. Solly pushed against her and continued to keep his cold nose close to her hand.

Norm said, "Never mind now, Fanny. Get Sarah a drink—anything. I'll call the police—"

Fanny stared and started to scream, apparently thought better of it and put her hand over her mouth.

"Got to," said Norm. "There was somebody in the woods. Attacked Sarah."

"Attacked!" cried Fanny.

Sarah said, "Tried to strangle me." She sat down at the table and put her head down on her arms.

"What were you doing in the woods? This time of night—"

"Somebody had tied up Solly."

"So you went to get him. What a fool!"

"I know. I know. But I heard Solly, so I went and—"

"Then what happened?"

Norm's voice was heard, speaking at the hall telephone.

"Nothing," Sarah told her. "That is, somebody wound the sleeves of your red raincoat around me and and then Norm had followed me and Gus came too, and whoever it was got away."

"They'll find Forte," said Fanny after a moment.

"Gus says they won't. That's all, Fanny, really."

"You were wearing my red coat," Fanny said in deep thought. "Well, now that he's here, I'll get Solly's dinner." She opened the refrigerator door. Solly nudged closer to

Sarah. Fanny put the dish down. "Here you are, Solly. Dinner—"

Solly didn't move. Fanny said, "He doesn't seem hungry. I wonder who tied him up."

"Oh, I don't know! He wouldn't let anybody get near him, would he?" She wasn't sure just what were the limits Solly put upon strangers.

Fanny said, "Anybody with a piece of steak could have got near that dog. Near enough to tie him up— That reminds me—where's Rosart?"

Sarah made an effort to speak. "I don't know. The cottage is dark and his car is gone. Steak! You mean you think Rosart held his steak out for Solly and tied him to a tree and— Oh, no, Fanny!"

Fanny shrugged. Her heavy blond braids swung over her long woolen dressing gown. "I'm probably wrong. I was only thinking of the steak that was gone and Solly and— What about it, Norm?"

Norm was in the doorway. He walked over to Sarah and put a glass down on the table beside her. "Better drink that."

"Are the police coming?" Fanny asked. "Are you going to tell them about Forte?"

"Yes, they're sending a car. No, I'm not going to tell them about Forte. Down with that, Sarah."

Sarah gulped down some very strong whiskey. Choking and coughing, she stood up and saw Fanny lean over the refrigerator, disclosing dirty jeans and muddy sneakers below her dressing gown.

"Here are some steak scraps from dinner. Maybe he'll eat them, unless," said Fanny morosely, "he has already had steak."

"Solly sniffed, stretched out his long neck, finally accepted the bits of steak—but worriedly, casting glances at Sarah as he ate.

Probably, Sarah thought, Fanny had on jeans and sneakers because she had adopted Rosart's recipe for health and had been jogging. Certainly it had not been Fanny who had followed her out into the woods.

There was a slam and bang of the front door and feet running down the hall, light and swift feet which stopped at the doorway. Nannie Pie stood there, her usually rosy cheeks pale. She looked around the kitchen and said, "Where's Rosart?"

The aftermath of shock plus the very strong whiskey went to Sarah's head, and waves of returning dizziness caught her. But she heard Fanny say, "Isn't he with you?"

Nannie Pie seemed to want to sag against the door casing, but resolutely stiffened her spine. "He's not in the cottage?"

Sarah put her head down, but still heard Norm say, "No. What's wrong?"

Sarah lifted her head. Everything seemed dim, shadowy, but she could see the tears come into Nannie Pie's eyes. "He's gone, then. I knew it. I was afraid of it."

After a moment Fanny said, "You'd better sit down here and tell us what's the matter."

"Yes, I'd better. Thank you." Norm gave her a chair and she sat down, but still seemed to find it mandatory to keep her head up. "He couldn't stand matrimony. That's all. I knew he couldn't. I shouldn't have made him."

"Made him—" Fanny began and then looked down. Sarah and Norm looked, too. Nannie Pie's left hand bore a new and shiny wedding ring.

Fanny said flatly, "Oh. You were married today."

Nannie Pie nodded. Then she bristled a little, indignation flashing over her face with a pink wave of color. She glared at Fanny. "You don't think I'd live with a man if I didn't plan to marry him?" she cried. "I wouldn't think of such a thing!"

Quite right, Sarah thought vaguely. She put her chin in her hands in the hope of clearing her swimming head; there were too many problems for her, all at once.

Nannie Pie subsided a little, but she gave a kind of wail

and put her hands over her face. "He really didn't want to get married."

"Why not?" Fanny was practical.

"His poetry," Nannie Pie replied with a choked-off sob. "He was afraid that marriage and . . . and a domestic life . . ."

"God help us all," Fanny said devoutly. "Well, looks as if you changed his mind. That ring."

"But it didn't change his mind! Oh, he was kind and—why, he got our license last summer. Then he couldn't bring himself to undertake marriage. But he promised it for today. After he had got that damned award."

"Don't swear," Fanny said automatically, still frowning.

Nannie Pie put down her hands. Norm had poured whiskey for her, too, apparently, for he put a glass into one of her hands. Nannie Pie seemed vaguely aware of it, and said dimly, but very politely, as usual, "Thank you. We went to White Plains. And we were married in the church. I had made the appointment with the rector. And then we had dinner at some place, a big restaurant and . . . and then Rosart said he had to take the car to a garage for something or other and . . . and then . . ."

"He didn't come back," Sarah murmured in a dreamy way, wishing she had her hands around Rosart's sturdy neck; then she decided nothing mattered but the terror she had experienced. Yet her throat scarcely hurt. She touched it carefully with her hand. No pain now, really. Remotely she began to feel as if she had been the victim of some joke—ugly and terrifying, but only a clumsy kind of childish joke, the kind of thing Forte could have done and then stood back and laughed.

But Forte would never move again. She made herself listen to Nannie Pie.

"No! I waited and I waited, and I walked up and down until people began to look at me. In fact, one man . . ." Nannie Pie wavered, took a long breath and said. "But never mind that. Where *is* Rosart?"

"How did you get here?" Norm asked.

"Taxi, of course. Oh, the driver's waiting. I didn't have enough money."

"All right. I'll pay him." Norm went off into the hall.

Fanny turned around to the refrigerator again, whisked out lemons and took up the teakettle. "What all of you need is a good hot toddy. Not that I think much of this habit of drinking, drinking, drinking, but there are times..."

Nannie Pie drank quickly from the glass Norm had quietly put in her hand. A very unwelcome notion edged its way through Sarah's sense of shock. For all his bulk, Rosart could move as quietly as a Red Indian. There had been the barest rustle of leaves behind, near her somewhere, which had stopped at once when Sarah herself stopped. There had been bearlike strength in the hands that wound the empty sleeves of the raincoat around her and pulled so hard that she actually lost her senses; pressure like that, if sustained, *could* kill.

But Rosart? Oh, no, not Rosart.

Norm came back. "The police cars are coming. I think I saw one of them shooting up the driveway."

He was wrong. The front door slammed open against the wall and Rosart stalked in, eyes blazing at Nannie Pie. "Where have you been? I told you to wait. When I got back you weren't anywhere."

Nannie Pie was not the kind to forgive easily, or indeed to accept anything she regarded as an insult. Which was a good thing, Sarah thought hazily, especially when dealing with a Favor.

"I did wait!" she flared back at Rosart. "Waited and waited. So I decided you had run away and would never come back and——" She shot up to her feet, angry now, cheeks pink, blue eyes blazing. "That's what I'm going to do! I'm going to leave *now*! I'll never be treated like that again."

Rosart was taken aback; he literally seemed to shrink against the wall. "But, Nannie Pie——"

"Don't Nannie Pie me!" The girl turned to Fanny. "Can I stay here tonight? Then tomorrow I'll go home—" But then, at the words "go home" her voice choked a little. Rosart perceived it, and gathered her into his enormous embrace. "There, there, now. There, there."

"But where were you, Rosart?" Norm asked. Was there a touch of suspicion in his voice?

Sarah had leaned back, her eyes closed; now she opened them.

Rosart said over Nannie Pie's brown head, "Oh, you know that old car. The battery went down. Just gave up while we were having dinner. I had to hunt for a garage. Then it took forever to find a place open and get the right battery. Then I had them look at the carburetor, and that took time. But I thought Nannie Pie would have the sense just to stay in the restaurant where we had dinner—"

"But you are properly married, though?" Fanny obviously thought it sensible to nail it down.

"Oh, sure. You can't mean— Why, she's got the marriage certificate. Certainly we were married. We got our license last summer, but then I—well, never mind. We're married now. Come on, Nannie Pie, stop crying, for heaven's sake."

Corinna said from the doorway, "There are police cars at the door. There are men and lights down in the woods. What has been going on?"

Rosart turned to her, "We were married this afternoon— late."

"Really?" Corinna replied absently. "Why are policemen in the woods? Isn't anyone going to tell me? Did you report . . . Forte?"

Norm seemed to brace himself. "No, Corinna. But tonight there was somebody in the woods and he tried to strangle Sarah."

Corinna put her hands on a chair back. "You can't mean that!"

Sarah found the strength to speak. "But it was only—that is, I'm not hurt. Scared, but that's all.

"Who—"

"I don't know. Norm and Gus heard me. That is, Gus was looking for Solly. Norm followed me."

"Then who was it, Norm?" Corinna's delicate features seemed again carved from white marble.

"I don't know! We couldn't see him and we didn't try to find out. The first thing to do was get Sarah back to the house."

Rosart said coolly, "She must have tripped over something."

"No!" Sarah began, and then there was a mixture of sounds. Solly at a window, barking wildly at the cars and voices outside, and a clatter as Fanny adjusted the teakettle on the stove. Rosart cuddled Nannie Pie against his shoulder, and with complete detachment, as if nothing existed outside their own world, they turned away and went out into the hall. Sarah thought she heard Rosart say something about going home. (Rosart, who had stood out against domesticity, was going to love it. And Nannie Pie!) Through the tumult Sarah was barely aware of the front door opening with another slam against the wall, a murmur of voices—Rosart, Nannie Pie, and . . . No! It couldn't be!

But it was.

Fitz came running along the hall, his quick footsteps pounding. He burst into the room, surveyed them all with one fleeting look and came to Sarah. He pulled her up into his arms.

"Fitz!" said Corinna and sat down.

The teakettle began to whistle. Solly barked, bounced to Fitz, shoved against him, leaped at his face, and Sarah to her shame burst into tears.

Nannie Pie had been far more courageous. At least she had tried not to cry. Fanny snatched the kettle off the stove and its frenzied shriek stopped.

Fitz said, "What the hell has been going on here? There

are two police cars at the door. And Charles said I had to get back here as fast as I could.''

"Charles . . ." Corinna put out one hand toward Fitz.

"Sure. I had barely gotten to the consulate in Paris. There was a message to get in touch with Charles. He had to talk in careful, general terms, but I gathered it was an emergency and I was to return here. He couldn't leave—I was to tell you that, Corinna. Something has happened at his embassy."

"I know." Corinna's lips seemed stiff. "We saw. On television."

"Is it that bad?"

"Who knows about those things! But I knew then that Charles wouldn't be able to meet me in Rome—"

"What has been happening? Why are those police here?"

"Oh, Fitz," Sarah cried and pushed her head further into his shoulder. "I wanted you so much. I . . ." Magically the misty torpor that had crept upon her cleared away.

"Je-*sus*," Fanny exploded musically on two notes— Fanny, who disapproved of anything that could be called swearing. In spite of singing in the most passionate love scenes in opera, she didn't approve of emotion in private life. "If there's any more of all this kissing and carrying on! Norm, bring me some whiskey." She reached for tall glasses; she opened the sugar jar; she grasped a lemon and a sharp paring knife.

"I think," Fitz said, "I'd better hear the whole story."

"Yes." Corinna, without a word, by sheer force of will, led the way to the library.

Norm went out the back, toward the woods, to meet the police. A sharp odor of lemons, whiskey, sugar and cinnamon came from the kitchen. Corinna settled herself in her big chair with a pretense of calm, which was not very successful, and said, "So Charles made it possible for you to come home."

"Charles," Fitz said, "just has clout. I don't know how

he did it, but it was done. Arranging for my quick return, I mean. Well, now?''

"Yes." Corinna looked at Sarah. "Do you want to tell him or shall I, or—''

Fanny marched in, a glimpse of dirty jeans and muddy sneakers below her pale-blue dressing gown, her blond braids swinging, a tray with steaming glasses in her strong hands.

She had heard Corinna, and Fanny was not of a nature to quibble. "Forte has been murdered. We thought it best to keep it a secret—that's all.''

"A secret!" Fitz stared at her. "You can't mean—Why, Fanny, Corinna, you can't mean—''

Fanny set the tray down. "We decided not to report it to the police. Here, drink this.'' She shoved a glass at Corinna, who took it, winced at the heat from the glass and put it down hard on the table beside her.

Fanny continued, "The police are here now because somebody attacked Sarah tonight. In the woods.''

Eleven

Fitz looked from one to the other, incredulously. He had already stationed himself at the chair Sarah had dropped into. "Sarah." His voice was strained, unbelieving. "What has been going on? Is this—I mean, is Fanny—"

"Of course I'm telling the truth." Fanny handed him a glass. "Look out! It's hot."

"You'd better tell it all, Fanny." Corinna touched the steaming glass beside her again and quickly withdrew her hand. "The police will be here at the house, certainly. After they have taken a look through the woods. So tell him, Fanny. Everything."

Fanny told it. As Sarah listened, she thought: She missed nothing except—yes, except the brake that had been tampered with in her car. And a footstep in the night—but that could have been nothing, certainly nothing alarming, or Solly would not have relaxed and gone to sleep again.

Fitz seemed to be drinking in every word. But his face was a blank. Only his eyes showed his deep concern.

Finally Fanny said, "So that's all. Forte's body is somewhere. Only Gus and Rosart know where. But Gus told Sarah that the police wouldn't find him now. Corinna and I and Rosart and—well, all of us except Norm and Sarah agreed to"—for the first time she hesitated, probably at a fiery spark in Fitz's gaze—"to postpone the discovery."

"And just when do you think it may be convenient to discover poor old Forte?" Fitz asked with an edge to his voice.

Corinna leaned forward, her hands clasped together. "Fitz, you must know that we all suspect that Forte had something to do with . . . with spying, terrorist activities."

"Terrorists? You can't mean that!"

"We don't know. We only know Forte," said Corinna flatly.

"But there must be some other reason, some personal—" Fitz brushed his hands over his face. "I can't believe that Forte would have an opportunity to do anything of the kind. Besides, I have to say this! Forte really was not extra . . . extra . . ."

"Smart," said Fanny with her instinct for hitting the nail on the head. "All the same, Fitz, everyone knew he had relatives in the Foreign Service. He could have got involved in something—"

"Something that would react unfavorably upon Charles? And me? And Norm?"

"Yes," Corinna said. "That's it, Fitz! Remember, I've heard talk from Charles for years. I know that the most dreadful things can happen when a public servant is suspected of . . . of a connection with anything Forte might have done."

"But I can't believe—Good God"—Fitz seemed only then to realize the entire situation—"don't you see that you've all made yourselves accessories?"

"Yes, we did," said Corinna dryly. "And when you've had a moment to think it over, you'll agree that it was the only thing to do."

Fitz shook his head as if emerging from deep water.

"But see here, have you any reasonable indication that Forte was involved in anything adverse to national interest?"

"Only my—our knowledge of Forte and the family's vulnerability."

"I see, yes. But I can't seem to get this. You say somebody tried to—I mean attacked Sarah. Tonight."

"That's why the police are searching the woods," Corinna replied with obviously hard-held patience.

"Yes. But you must admit it is rather difficult for me to take this all in—just right away. Good God, Corinna, they'll be able to tell when he died. How could you have thought of concealing his"—he swallowed—"his death. Suicide? Accident?"

"Murder. Fanny has explained that. And you did leave your gun in Gus's care. He did find it on the lawn. It had been fired. But we knew you couldn't have killed Forte."

Fitz took a long breath and went to sit down on a big hassock, linking his hands between his knees. "It's hard to— Just give me time. Sarah, do you have any idea who attacked you?"

At last Sarah's shock and dizziness were entirely gone. "I don't know. I had on Fanny's raincoat. Whoever it was got hold of the sleeves and . . ." Her voice began to shake a little.

Fitz stood up and came to her. "You're all right now. I'll not let anything happen to you. But *why* should anyone try to . . . to hurt you?" He couldn't bring himself to say strangle.

Sarah shook her head. "No reason. Nothing." Later she would tell him about the brake in her car. Not then; he had enough to try to disentangle.

Norm came in from the front door, and cried loudly, as if warning them, "Corinna, the police want to talk to you! All of us!"

"Certainly," said Corinna, gulped down her now-cool toddy, sat up straight and faced the door.

Norm came in, met Corinna's eyes and shook his head,

meaning, Sarah knew, they didn't find Forte. She wondered fleetingly what Fitz would do or say or what course he had arrived at; probably nothing just then. All of it had been thrown at him too hastily—no, he would say nothing now of Forte.

Corinna's dark eyes, steely and determined, fixed upon Fitz, as if she wanted to say, Keep quiet: Norm tells me that they haven't found Forte.

Two policemen followed Norm, removed their caps and greeted Corinna pleasantly. "Mrs. Favor—"

"Oh, Barney Cloom! I remember you." said Corinna pleasantly.

One of the police, a young man, ducked politely. "Yes, Mrs. Favor. I guess I've grown some."

"Yes." Corinna gave him her most charming smile. "I see you joined our police force."

The other man, older than Barney but equally polite, said, "Sorry you had this bother, Mrs. Favor. We didn't find anybody at all."

"And we searched, Mrs. Favor," said Barney. "We really searched."

"Just you two?" Corinna asked. "It's a large area."

"Oh, no, the other three men went on back to the village. Now we'll make inquiries. Filling stations, trains, taxi stands, everywhere. But so far we just couldn't find even—well, even a footprint. Not that there would be much of a print in those leaves," Barney said.

The other took up the inquiry, turning to Fanny. "You the young lady who had the scare?"

"Her," Fanny said laconically, nodding at Sarah.

Both policemen turned to her. Fitz said, "Miss Favor—"

"Oh, I know," Barney said. "We used to skate on the Simmons pond. How are you, Sarah?"

Sarah swallowed hard. "I was frightened."

"You might tell us all about it."

"There's not much to tell. Norm—"

Norm nodded. "I told, them but they want to hear it from you."

"Well, then, someone had tied the dog—"

"Yes, we know," the older policeman said briskly. "Your cousin here"—he jerked his neat head and ruddy face toward Norm—"told us all that. He came and Gus came—everybody around here knows Gus. We believe him, too. He showed us the rope. By the way, Mrs. Favor"—he now turned to Corinna—"you know that Gus has a perfect arsenal of guns in his place? All clean and shining."

It was like Corinna to know his name. She said, "Captain Wood, whoever attacked this girl didn't use a gun."

Sarah knew instinctively that Corinna's lips were stiff.

"Some of those guns are mine," Fitz said. "I gave my revolver to Gus to take care of. Also my rifle and shotguns."

"Mine, too," Norm said. "That is, only a rifle and a shotgun. I don't have a revolver."

There was a short silence on the part of both the policemen, as if they had run out of questions. They hadn't.

"There were some lights in that cottage—the one Gus used to use—"

"Rosart's," Fanny said flatly.

"Oh, yes. Sure." The young policeman turned to Captain Wood. "He's a poet."

This did not seem to strike the other policeman with any particular respect. "I tried to talk to him and he said to go away. He used some language. Not," he said with disapproval, "poet talk."

Barney blushed a vivid pink. "There's no harm in Rosart. He would never attack anybody. I've known him a long time—"

"Lately?" There was a slight tinge of acid in Captain Wood's voice.

Barney turned an even deeper pink. "Well, no. You see, he went away to school. And the university," he said thoughtfully, "for years and years, and got a bunch of degrees. And then—" He brightened. "I read in the *Village Crier*. He was given some very special award. Today," he finished with triumph.

"All right. Where was he when this attack took place?"

"Getting married," Sarah said.

"Well, not at that very time." Fanny intervened with her passion for facts. "Actually, he was at some garage, getting a new battery for his car."

There was another silence. Fitz's face was without any expression at all, except, possibly, a kind of concentrated awareness.

Then Barney said, "We can check on the garages. But would he have any reason to try to—well, would he?"

He addressed Sarah, who shook her head. "None. Nothing. Rosart wouldn't hurt a fly."

There was still another silence. Finally Captain Wood said, as if to himself, "I hear that lots of murderers say that. I mean, people say it about them."

"Rosart *wouldn't* hurt a fly!" Barney said indignantly. "And I don't see any reason for making these people uncomfortable. Honestly—"

"Honestly," Captain Wood said sternly, "you can mind your own business. Or rather our business." But then he spoke to Corinna. "Thank you, Mrs. Favor. We'll keep a lookout. If you have any more trouble, just let us know." He turned to Sarah. "Now, young lady, I'm sure you were frightened and you thought—"

"I *knew!*" Sarah said curtly.

"Well, yes, of course," he replied soothingly. "But it is possible, isn't it, that the hood of that raincoat—we looked at it—just fell over your face and you got entangled with the sleeves?"

"Somebody entangled me. I mean, held the sleeves so I was scared." Sarah thought she shouted it, but apparently she didn't, for both policemen merely looked sorry and indulgent.

"Well, we'll watch out for anybody who's got no business around here. You call us if anything bothers you and we'll be here." He now was speaking to Corinna, who nodded stiffly.

Norm went to the front door with them.

"They don't believe me," Sarah said.

After a moment Corinna said, "Perhaps that's better, on the whole. They'll not be poking their noses around soon again. I hope."

The heavy front door closed; all of them heard the rasp as Norm shot the bolt across it. He returned. "Well, Fitz—any plan?"

Fitz shook his head wearily. "Sure, the murder should have been reported at once. I can see why Corinna didn't want it reported. But still, it's simply preposterous that you didn't call the police right away!"

Sarah answered him. "That's what we said. Norm and I. But then we began to think what it just might do to Charles. And to you and Norm. I did write to you this morning."

"But there's no proof—not even a sound suggestion—that anything Forte was involved in was something that might affect any of us."

Corinna leaned forward. "I thought of it only because I have an idea of the kind of thing that would react very adversely upon all three of you. But especially Charles and his distinguished career." She thought for a moment and added, "We've all seen it. Guilt by association. Can't be proved one way or the other. It isn't fair to Charles to publicize this unless it's perfectly certain that Forte was not doing anything that . . ." Her voice faltered again.

"We haven't really investigated Forte's recent activities," Norm said quietly. "We can't be sure until . . ."

"Yes. We'll try to do that." Fitz looked at his watch. "If we could talk to Charles. Not a good plan to try to reach him now. Especially after all the ruckus there."

Suddenly, unexpectedly he yawned hugely, sighed, and said in a mumble, "Jet lag."

Corinna rose to that at once. "You've had two trips in the past twenty-four hours. They must have put you straight on the first available plane back."

"I guess so," Fitz said. "I'll have another drink, Fanny."

Sarah said with a firmness which rather surprised her, "One more. Make it strong, Fanny. And then take it up to bed with you, Fitz. Your room is ready—that is, it's cleaned."

"Aired, too," Fanny said. "I saw to that. See to the whole house every day. Good exercise. Here you are, Fitz."

The drink was very dark.

Fitz took it, sipped, gave a little start as the strength of it stung his throat and said, "Come with me, Sarah. I want to talk to you."

Solly had been sprawled full length near Sarah's chair. He rose as Sarah did and trotted along beside her. Fitz's suitcase and briefcase stood at the door; he took the briefcase and Norm the suitcase. Solly walked seriously beside Sarah up the stairs. Gitz gave him an automatic but good-natured pat. "Good old fellow. Got any squirrels lately?"

"Skunks," Sarah said briefly. Norm behind them said in a low voice, "You haven't heard it all, Fitz."

"All right." Fitz paused and listened as they reached the top of the stairs. Already Corinna, in her pleasant yet very precise way, was on the telephone in the hall below them, canceling her proposed trip to Rome.

Fitz led the way into his big corner room opposite Corinna's—the two most desirable rooms in the house. Sarah had gone into the room often whenever he was away—it seemed to bring Fitz nearer. She knew the worn old rug with the frayed corner where Solly had cut his teeth; she knew the big brown leather armchair where Fitz had read—and read and read. Corinna always said complacently that all Favors were readers. There was the big writing table, a row of French, German and Russian grammars, the ashtray with a bronze dog on top (a bulldog, which would have offended Solly if he had only known about it).

Fitz motioned Sarah to the armchair and sat down on the bed, stretching out his long legs. He was suitably dressed for a budding diplomat except for the sweater he wore under his jacket, which now, with a glance of apology at Sarah, he removed and tossed on the bed. "All right. Now, Norm, what really has been doing on?"

"You should rest," Sarah said. "You said you were tired."

"I said that because to tell you the truth I was getting more and more confused. Corinna can be very evasive—at least when she doesn't want to get down to brass tacks. You really have no idea who was in the woods tonight, Sarah?"

"I told you. I don't know. Maybe I'm wrong and it was only Fanny's raincoat!" But the memory of the pressure on her throat was too strong. She put her hands up in a pained gesture, and Fitz's eyes darkened.

"Still hurts?"

"A little sore."

"Oh, don't be heroic. Let me see."

He crossed to her, lifted her chin and looked at her throat. His face was white, the muscles around his mouth very hard and firm. All Favor, she thought vaguely; it was the way Corinna looked when she was moved. He said to Norm, *"Why didn't you see to her? Why did you let this happen?"*

"He couldn't have helped it," Sarah said.

"I got there in time, but I really didn't think such a thing— Yes, I thought to have watched her more carefully," Norm finished miserably. "After the brakes on her car—"

For an instant Fitz caressed Sarah's face; then he rose

and went back to sit on the bed. "What about the brakes? Go on, Norm."

"Nobody knows but Sarah and me—except the somebody who actually did it. And somebody did tamper with them. Andy said so. You know Andy at the garage?"

"Go on."

"He said they definitely had been tampered with. The brakes on Sarah's little car. She almost crashed. I was right behind her. I saw what happened." Norm, the imperturbable, got out a handkerchief and wiped his face. "Honestly, Fitz, when I saw her going like hell down that slope toward the bridge, I didn't know what I'd find when I got there—"

"For God's sake, begin at the beginning."

Sarah just sat and listened.

Fitz wouldn't look at her as Norm talked. Finally he rose again, went to the pipe rack over the fireplace, selected one pipe, put it back, tried another, then finally turned to Sarah. "Why would anybody try to injure you? There's got to be some reason."

"She doesn't know a thing she hasn't told us." Norm took a straight chair and sat astride it, chin and arms resting on the back. "Tonight I simply didn't see anybody I could possibly identify. As a matter of fact, I'm not sure I actually saw a person. I just had a notion that a kind of black something moved very swiftly out of sight when I reached—stumbled over Sarah. It could have been a shadow. Then Gus came along. We got to the house and called the police."

"I take it that by then if anybody was in the woods who shouldn't have been, he had time to get away."

Norm shrugged. "But he's got to be somewhere."

"Yes." Fitz sighed. "Yes, that argues somebody who knows the place—and knows us. Rosart said he was at a garage tonight at that time."

Norm nodded. "It can be checked, of course. But

honestly, I don't see why Rosart would sneak back here and try to . . . to hurt Sarah.''

"What about this girl he married?"

Sarah sat up. "Nannie Pie? Good heavens, Fitz!"

The barest flicker of a grin touched Fitz's lips. "All right. I'm only trying to piece things out. Now then, Norm, the afternoon Forte was shot—"

"Yesterday," said Sarah, not quite believing it.

Fitz didn't quite believe it, either. "Good God! Only something over twenty-four hours, and all this! Did you see anybody strange around the place when you came back from your hunting trip, Norm?"

"Not a soul. Ham Wilder brought me back, dumped me at the driveway. He was on his way to Lemport to pick up some things from his home. He's been posted to China—"

"I know. Go on."

"So I lugged my stuff up to Rosart's cottage and left it on the porch. Then I heard Sarah scream and I ran to the house."

"See anybody at all?"

"No-no. Now wait—" Norm scowled down at his hands. "Now I think of it, I think there was somebody—I just had a glimpse of somebody in blue jeans beyond the garage. Thought it was Gus, if I thought at all."

"Fanny—" Sarah began, thinking of the jeans under the dressing gown, and answered herself. "No. Fanny was singing when I got home. I heard her. Then Rosart came by way of the kitchen and he had some cake in his hand, and Fanny came in, very cross because she had planned to have the cake for our dinner."

"What was she wearing?"

"Why, I—well, I think blue jeans. Honestly, Fitz, it was all so dreadful. I can't remember what anybody was wearing. I only remember Rosart dropping the cake on the carpet, and thinking Corinna wouldn't like it."

Fitz stared down at his pipe, which he had not filled. "Then you all decided not to report to the police. Not even call a doctor! I simply cannot believe you all could be such fools! Norm, I don't see how you could stand by and let this go on—''

"I didn't! Have you ever tried tangling with Rosart, singlehanded? And then both Rosart and Gus were standing there in the doorway, looking ready to mop up the floor with me. And I've no doubt they could have," said Norm flatly.

A corner of Fitz's mouth twitched. "No. I wouldn't tackle either of them. Not if I could help it. But there's been time since."

"Time to think about it," Norm said slowly. "I began to get the notion that Corinna just might be right. And then I knew Sarah wrote you all about it. She mailed the letter this morning. We decided that it had to be your decision—yours and Charles's—because it involved your interests so directly."

Sarah said, "Listen, Fitz. Forte was dead. There was no use in calling a doctor. I was sure. Corinna asked if I had felt his pulse, and I hadn't but—oh, Fitz, I knew. He couldn't have been alive and . . . and looked like that."

"There now! Oh, hell!" Fitz looked absently at his pipe. "What I'm getting at, didn't any of you *insist* about the police?"

"Of course, Sarah and I did. We thought they were—" Norm checked himself.

"Loony?" said Fitz. "Yes. But you decided later they really were sane."

Norm nodded. "Well, yes. I think so. At least, all at once I understood why Corinna had taken that stand. I wasn't as quick on the uptake as she was. She thinks like lightning."

"I know. And also," Fitz said rather dryly, "your father, Sarah, has educated her over the years about quite a number of aspects of a Foreign Service officer's life and career."

Sarah stared at him. "Why, you knew about my father and Corinna all the time!"

"I never said anything to her, of course, but their—I don't want to call it an affair; it's more dignified than that, but—"

"Oh, I know now! Corinna told me. You know how very reticent she has always been about herself, but since Forte was killed, she's talked to me. Even how it happened that she took on the care of Forte."

"Forte, yes. Look here." Fitz studied his pipe and said, it seemed to Sarah, rather carefully, "I take it that so far you have found nothing to prove, or even suggest, that Forte really was in some dubious activity."

"Not yet," Norm said. "I haven't had time to search his things. Rosart had dropped them outside the cottage to make room for Nannie Pie. A duffel bag and a big suitcase. I'll go through them soon."

"Funny, but I wonder if Forte ever saw his father during all these years."

Twelve

Sarah thought back to Corinna's candid talk with her. "Corinna said she didn't know where Forte's father is, even if he's alive. She and my father have been trying to find him so Corinna can ask for a divorce. She says she deserted him. So she can't get a divorce on the grounds of desertion."

"I expect they mean to pay him off," Fitz said. "Seems likely. From the very little I've heard, a bit at a time over the years, I don't believe that Forte's father is a very admirable person. His mother—I never heard a word about her."

"Forte's own father wouldn't have shot him," Norm said.

Fitz thought that over. "As I said, we don't even know that he has seen Forte at all. Certainly we don't know if, or what, he could have led Forte into doing. That's all surmise. Now look here. Sarah came into the house and heard Fanny singing."

"Yes. 'The Bell Song' up in the old playroom."

Both men, results of Corinna's wide view of education

133

("You can't know everything about everything but you can know a little about many things"), looked surprised.

"I know, I know," Sarah said. "It's not her range. I thought it was unusual for her to try it, even as an exercise. But that's what I heard. You can't mistake that song."

"Well, no. But Fanny is so sensible as a rule." Fitz rose and returned his unfilled pipe to the rack. "Norm, search through Forte's baggage. Tomorrow we'll talk to Gus. Fanny said he found my gun on the lawn."

Norm nodded. "Sure. Brought it in, showed it to us. Said he'd found it outside. But he wouldn't let us call the police, hand the gun over to them. Anything. You know how he feels about Corinna."

"To be fair," Fitz said, "his living has depended upon Corinna for many years. Lately, of course, with wages so high, he could earn more by taking on other jobs, but his first loyalty is to Corinna." Fitz lifted his peaked black Favor eyebrows. "And the money she earns. That money has meant a great deal to all of us."

"She loves us," Sarah said in a low voice.

"I know." Fitz shot her a swiftly perceiving glance. "Yes, she does love us. We have been like a family to her. She has earned our gratitude and loyalty. But...but murder!"

Norm shook his head. "I can see Corinna's view. It took me a while to understand it. But then I could see that any facts that digging into Forte's life brought out could possibly be very damn painful to Charles. Good God, Fitz, you didn't see that mob raging around his embassy."

Fitz said wearily. "I can imagine it all too well. Has Gus gone to bed?"

"Gus!" Sarah almost laughed. You know Gus. He's been in bed and asleep for hours. You couldn't possibly get him up and sensible at this time of night."

"All right. Well then, Norm."

Norm disentangled himself from the chair. Solly, beside

Sarah, lifted his long nose and uttered something disgruntled in his throat.

"I'll take a look at Forte's things now. Want to help, Fitz?"

Corinna knocked on the door and opened it at once. "Jet lag?" she asked sweetly.

Fitz said as sweetly, "Yes, darling Corinna. Jet lag. So you run along to bed and forget us."

"Really, Fitz!" Corinna's eyes flashed. Fitz went to her, put his arms around her and gave her a warm hug. "It's all right. We had to talk. But we can't do any more tonight."

"Fitz!" She clung to him. "You do think I was right not to get the police. Not for the moment!"

Fitz didn't reply for a second. Then he said, "Where did Gus and Rosart—"

She put both small, firm white hands on Fitz's shoulders. "I don't know where, and I'm not going to ask! I don't want to know. Good night."

She whisked away, rustling in her silk, toward her own room.

"If only she weren't so damn dear," Fitz said.

"And so damn smart," Norm said. "She's got us all licked any time. What are you going to do, Fitz? Throw Corinna and all of us to the wolves? We were in the wrong and we did break the law, but—"

"I don't know. I can't see any way out that doesn't bring all of you into some ugly conflict with the law."

Sarah saw that Norm was not going to speak of her own questionable position regarding Forte. She said quickly, "You see, Fitz, I found Forte. And the taxi driver knew that we had— Well, we didn't exactly quarrel, Forte and I, but he did try to get into the cab and I did, well—"

"Push him out," Fitz said with a slight and quickly vanishing grin. "Yes, I remember. But still—"

"I know, I know!" Norm said. "At the time I realized that the taxi driver could have come forward and made things unpleasant for Sarah. And then, it was like a conjurer's trick. Corinna worked it, and I can see why Rosart and Fanny agreed—and Gus, of course, would do what he thought Corinna wanted. But I ought to have stopped it. There were always phones and—''

"Oh, I see," Fitz said wearily. "But it doesn't excuse— I don't know what I'm going to do, Norm! Something's got to be done and the sooner the better. Of course I don't want all the publicity, but—'' He broke off. "The first thing we've got do do is find Forte's body.''

Norm nodded. "No proof whatever until we can induce Gus or Rosart to tell us what they did and where—that is, the police will have to see Forte.''

"I know as well as you, Norm, that Fanny and Corinna will stick to their positions. They won't tell flat lies, not if I know Corinna, but by the time she thinks up some good, convincing way to reply to any questions from the police, the police will begin to think we don't know what we're talking about.''

Norm lifted an eyebrow. "So tonight you and I have a few hours to plan, do we, Fitz?''

"I don't know what we can plan, but you're right, I can't throw any of them to the wolves.''

Norm sighed heavily. "If only we weren't all so close, so like a family. I'll go search Forte's bags now. Coming, Fitz?''

"In a minute. But I really am getting fuzzy-headed. And I still can't believe— Come here, Sarah.''

Norm discreetly disappeared. But Fitz's goodnight to Sarah was very brief. He simply walked her to her room, patted Solly on the head, said, "Bark like anything, old fellow, if there's anything to bark at. Try to sleep, Sarah.'' He did kiss her, but too swiftly, and then went down the hall toward Norm's room.

Sarah's life had been tranquil and pleasant for all her twenty years; now she could scarcely believe that so much had happened to her in such a short time. She was sure she would never sleep.

Corinna must have been sure of that, too, for a shiny red capsule, a sleeping pill of some kind, lay on her bedside table.

She didn't need it; she didn't need anything; even her throat felt less painful. But she fell into sleep as if, in fact, she was drugged.

Fanny had her say to Fitz at breakfast, and Sarah heard it. "I was a great fool." She served up a fine plate of eggs, bacon and sausages. The fragrance of coffee filled the room, and Solly, outside, smelling the food, gave an imploring bark.

"A fool?" Fitz said good-naturedly. "Not you, Fanny. You've got very good sense."

"Not always. You see, right after Forte was found—you understand we were all in shock—well, I remembered something the press man for the opera had said once in my hearing, something very flattering and admiring about a singer who had had a lover and a tragedy, really, in her life. And I don't know why, but I remembered it." Fanny sat down opposite him, planted her elbows on the table and, her lovely face and light-blue eyes very earnest, said, "So I thought I'd pretend that Forte had been my lover. Now don't say anything. It was very foolish and there wasn't a word of truth in it, and I don't know why—that is, I do know why, but it was very silly and I'm sorry. Do you want more coffee?"

Fanny spoke with such an air of bland common sense that Fitz stared, choked on his coffee and said, spluttering, "Oh, come on, Fanny. You know perfectly well why you said all that."

"Why, of course, I was foolish—"

"You flew to Corinna's support. You may not have known why she was desperately playing for time, but you made a commotion, I take it, and you gave everybody pause to think about it. Whatever. More coffee, please."

Fanny reached for his cup, her thoughts still far away. "Yes, I could see that Corinna had something very urgent in her mind so—what I said was the only thing I could think of just then. An impulse. I regretted it at once. But we were all so upset." Fanny took Fitz's cup and went to the stove. "Murder is all right," she said coolly, "on the stage. I really don't like it in the parlor."

Norm said from the doorway, "Corinna wouldn't like you to use the word parlor. Not"—he dropped into a chair at the table—"not that it matters."

"Why wouldn't she like it?" Fanny set a full cup down at Fitz's elbow.

Norm sighed. "Oh, never mind. Give me some of that, Fanny."

They were having breakfast at the huge table in the kitchen, which had become a custom since the latest and, indeed, the last cook had departed. That was when Corinna decided that Fanny could use some of her time to employ her second gift for cooking. As far as Corinna was concerned, someone always carried a breakfast tray up to her bedroom. The rest of the meals were eaten in the big dining room, although Fanny took a firm but fair stand that while she would cook, they must serve themselves.

In the winters, when Fanny was singing, she used the *pied-à-terre* which Corinna still maintained in the Gramercy Park area. Corinna had used it mainly when they were young, as a stopping place for a washroom and neatening up of clothes and hair before the young Favors went to the opera, a museum, a theatre. And she had also, certainly, used it for more rewarding and pleasant purposes. Charles Favor knew the tiny apartment as well or better than any of them.

"What's the matter with you, Norm?" Fanny asked, pouring coffee.

"Me?" Norm lifted his head. "Oh, it's not me. It's Corinna."

"Corinna?" Fitz said quickly. "What's wrong with her?"

"Nothing. That is, I don't know. She said that she'd had an unpleasant phone call. She looked terrible."

"Who phoned her?" Fanny got more eggs.

"She wouldn't say." Norm hesitated and said again, "But she looked terrible. I asked who phoned, and she said it didn't matter and thanked me for taking up her breakfast."

"An obscene caller," Fanny said.

Norm shook his head. "No, I don't think so. Something else."

Rosart walked through the back entry. He went right to the refrigerator and opened the door, obviously intent upon food. Scowling, Fanny tugged at his arm. "Listen, Rosart. You're married now. You can get your own ... oranges," she said as one escaped Rosart and bounded across the floor. She picked it up with one muscular swoop. "You can have breakfast things—today. But you've got to stop looting. Buy your own groceries."

Rosart said sheepishly, "Everything costs like everything."

"All the more reason. All right, though. Take some. This morning."

Rosart departed, letting in Solly, who bounded over to Fanny, at the moment the dispenser of food. She reached for dog biscuits.

Fitz said slowly, "I'll ask Corinna what has upset her, but if she doesn't want to tell me—" They all knew how to finish his sentence. He rose. "First, I want to take a look at the guns—or rather, my revolver, and talk to Gus."

Fanny said with her usual cool, matter-of-fact manner, "Can't talk to Gus. This is his day at the Simmonses'. He'll not be back till late afternoon."

"I can go there, then."

"No," Fanny said. "That is, naturally, you can go there. But if Gus doesn't want you to find him, you'll not find him."

"I'll find him," Fitz said shortly.

"Go ahead. But it's a big place." Fanny turned some

bacon, which was sizzling in a pan. "The Simmonses have gone south. Early, but they've gone. So you and Norm were searching Forte's things last night. I heard you. I saw you, too. Opened the door a little and looked in. Did you find anything interesting?"

Fitz put down his coffee cup. "Only clothes."

Norm said, "He must have been somewhere in a warm country before he came home last summer. He was here about a month, wasn't he, Fanny?"

She tossed her heavy yellow braids back, thought and said, "Only a week, this time. Too long."

"He had only some lightweight worsteds, a mass of ties—I thought I recognized one or two of mine," Fitz said. "But there was nothing useful—no receipts from hotels, envelopes for plane tickets, anything. Not even a letter."

"One thing is certain, he was out of money," Fanny said.

"How do you know?" Fitz asked.

"He came home only when he was out of money. All of you know that. But he didn't come to me. He knew I wouldn't have any money to speak of until this winter. He probably intended to work on Corinna. Probably did."

Fitz sighed. "Let's get back to what you said before, Fanny. Why do you think I won't be able to find Gus at the Simmons place?"

"Why, because he'll figure out that you'll insist on knowing what was done about Forte. And he doesn't want to tell until Corinna gives him the word."

There was a short silence except for Solly's crunching a dog biscuit. Then Fitz said, "But Rosart knows."

"Then get him to tell you." Fanny almost laughed.

Norm rose. "Come on, Fitz. We'll try to get in Gus's rooms. I don't think he keeps his place locked."

"He can't have kept it locked if someone got into it, took my gun and . . . and then shot Forte with it."

"Solly," Sarah said, "can't you eat without all that noise? Oh, all right. Here's more biscuits."

"That's another peculiar thing," Fitz said. "If a stranger came into the woods yesterday and got into Gus's apartment and took my gun, why didn't Solly do something about it? He's supposed to be a watchdog."

"He *is* a watchdog," Sarah said warmly. "But yesterday he was skunk hunting. He goes out of his head when he's chasing a rabbit or a skunk." She thought for a moment. "But he never catches one. Not even a squirrel. He's a good dog."

At the door Fitz turned back to Sarah. "I'll take a look at Gus's apartment and then we'll go to—I expect the nearest place would be White Plains. Or Greenwich. Anyway, we'll get an application for our marriage license started. I believe it takes about three days. I'll find out."

"Oh, Fitz, can you stay that long? Is that what you mean?"

"Why, of course. Don't worry. I suggested the possibility to your father, and he said he was positive he could arrange it. And I'm sure he can!"

He went off after Norm.

Three days. Sarah said, suddenly, almost in a wail, "But there's no time to get all the clothes I was going to buy. And I've got to investigate ways and regulations about shipping Solly—"

Corinna said, "Good morning, girls," and came into the room. On this surprising day she carried down her own breakfast tray, which, when Sarah took it from her, didn't look as if Corinna had had an appetite for anything but orange juice and coffee.

Corinna said flatly, "There's a man at the door. I saw him coming up the drive."

"I'll go—" Fanny started to roll down the sleeves of her fresh white blouse, startlingly clean above the same dirty jeans and sneakers she had worn the previous night.

"No, let him in. It's my . . . my husband." Corinna said stonily.

"You mean—" Fanny began.

"It can't be!" Sarah cried.

"It is. He phoned me this morning, early." Corinna leaned against the door jamb. "He wants to talk to Forte."

"Oh." Fanny rolled up her sleeve again as if preparing to cope in a realistic way with anybody who threatened Corinna's peace of mind.

"No, no, I tell you! Don't try to stop him. I've got to see him. I've got to work out an arrangement with him. Dear God, we've been trying to find him for so many years! Open the door for him, Fanny. Tell him to wait. I'll be there in a moment."

"All right. But—" Fanny jerked around to Sarah. "Get Fitz. Hurry."

Corinna quietly sank down into a chair and absently, in almost a hypnotized way, began to push at her hair.

Sarah ran out the door, toward the garage. She didn't stop to snatch a sweater or coat from the row of hooks in the back entry, and no sooner was she outside than she wished that she had, for the weather had turned completely. It was no longer blue and gold and crisp; it was damp and chill, with the clouds so gray and low that they seemed almost close enough to touch and a mean little wind that ruffled her hair and clothes. She pushed through the door to the stairs leading to Gus's apartment and shouted, "Fitz . . . Fitz . . ."

He appeared at once.

"It's Corinna. I mean, no, it's Forte's father!"

"Here!"

"Yes, at the house. Hurry! Corinna looks like death. Oh, hurry."

He took her arm and shouted up to Norm, saying he'd be back. When they reached the kitchen Corinna looked at

Fitz with firm determination. She was still pale, but resolute.

"Don't let him get away, Fitz. He's got to agree to a divorce. I don't care how much it costs. But he's got to agree and give us some address, someplace where he can be found."

"All right. You don't have to see him if you don't want to."

"Oh, yes, I'll see him. I must see him. I must be perfectly sure it's Len."

It *was* Len Briggs. He was standing in the living room, just before the sofa, so near, so terribly near, where Forte had been shot. The long room was dark with the dark day. No one had turned on a light. But even in the dimness Sarah could sense, vaguely, a vestige of the charm and daring or whatever it was that had attracted a young and romantic Corinna so long ago. Now he looked like Forte; older, seedier, yet with a certain flashy style that was both cheap and new, but still dreadfully like Forte.

The same sleek black head, the same rather sly, laughing look, almost like a sneer; the small black mustache, the same thin face, thin body, wiry look of being ready to escape at any moment. He looked at Corinna for a long moment and then said, his thin lips smiling and showing yellow teeth, "Dear wife. You haven't changed much. Except for your white hair. All these years . . ."

Corinna had gathered up courage. She said promptly, "Where have you been?"

"Now, dear wife, wouldn't you like to know?"

"And you are going to tell me."

Fitz's mouth had hardened. He interrupted—quite pleasantly, however. "Suppose we sit down and talk this over, Mr. . . . Mr. . . ."

"Briggs," Corinna said, biting off the name.

Len Briggs gave Fitz a long, considering, yet oddly sly look. "All right. Thank you, I'm sure. In my wife's home . . ." He sank down in the sofa.

"It's my house," Fitz said, still with a remote politeness. "I'm afraid you're not welcome here. Tell us your reason for coming."

"I want to talk to my son. Forte, I think you call him. Of course, my wife changed his name from Len. She couldn't bear to let him use my name."

Corinna, now seated tensely on a straight chair, flashed, "Naturally, I didn't want any poor child to have your name."

"You mean you didn't want to think of me every time you spoke to the boy."

"Oh, I couldn't help thinking of you!" For the first time in Sarah's knowledge of her, Corinna was bitter. "Every time I looked at him, even when he was very young, I couldn't help thinking of you. He looked—looks so like you."

Nearly a slip there, Sarah thought in a sudden panic. But Len Briggs did not appear to notice it. He said, showing his yellowish teeth again, "He said he'd be here. I came to meet him—at a place we had agreed upon."

"You've been seeing him," Fitz said, still pleasantly but very coolly.

Len Briggs gave him a long look; then nodded. "Why not? My own son—"

"Your son!" Corinna almost shouted. "A child you wouldn't keep, wouldn't have anything to do with. You refused to take him. You left him to me—you knew I wouldn't want the child to go to an orphanage."

"They wouldn't take him in an orphanage." Len Briggs was insufferably smug. "He had a father. And a stepmother. With plenty of money," he added, smiling.

Corinna said, "You took care to keep out of the way, hiding all this time. You wouldn't see Forte when he needed you. But where—when did you begin to see him?"

"Now, my dear, that really is none of your business, is it? Len—call him Forte, if you insist—is over twenty-one.

His own man. Can do as he pleases. Now then, where is he?''

Fitz said, "He's not here."

His flat statement, Sarah thought, rather took the wind out of Len Briggs's sails. He blinked, eyed Fitz, finally said, again, "Then—where he is?"

Gus at that instant appeared in the doorway. He was in a towering rage, and saw only Corinna. "Mrs. Favor, just let me tell you—" Something in the atmosphere seemed to strike Gus. He gave a swift glance around the room, saw Briggs, stared, turned around, gripped the back of a chair and collapsed with a resounding crash like a lightning-struck tree.

Thirteen

For an appalled second nobody moved. Then Fitz sprang to Gus. Fanny shoved Corinna, who had jumped to her feet, out of the way, and went to help Fitz, but Gus needed no help. He was on all fours, already struggling to his feet, his face gray.

Fitz said gently, "It's all right, Gus. It's Forte's father."

Gus said nothing, gripped Fitz's arm, pulled himself erect and then simply walked out of the room, unsteadily but under his own steam.

Corinna, worried, said, "Could it have been a heart attack? But Gus has never showed any symptoms. He's very strong and—"

Fitz put a firm hand on her wrist. "It wasn't a heart attack. Just a . . . a momentary dizziness perhaps."

But it wasn't a momentary dizziness, Sarah knew. Forte's father, in the shadowy room that dark day, had resembled his son too nearly. Gus had probably thought, just for an instant, that Forte himself had returned. Gus was a Scot; he had a certain deep and abiding instinct for the supernatural. If he'd had sufficient warning, he would undoubtedly have booted Forte's father off the place. But taken unaware, with the fact of Forte's death in his consciousness—yes, it was a faint. But he had recovered quickly, and had also left the room very quickly. He had been in a towering rage when he entered. Later perhaps they would know the reason for that.

Mr. Briggs raised his eyebrows and straightened his natty jacket. "Dear me! Who was that?"

Fitz said coldly, "He's the gardener. Now then, Mr. Briggs, Forte is not here. I'd be interested to know why you planned to meet here."

Briggs touched his tie, thought for a moment and showed his teeth again. "As I said before, that's really none of your business."

"Why, yes," Fitz said, "I think it is."

"Any reason why I shouldn't want to see my son?"

"Certainly," Fitz replied. "Aunt Corinna has paid all his expenses; she's taken care of him since he was a boy."

Len Briggs seemed more than a little surprised. "But I sent you money, Cora. I sent you check after check. Not much, perhaps, but all I could."

"You didn't," said Corinna.

"I have the canceled checks." Briggs leaned back, smugly. "You can't get around those."

Corinna was honestly astonished and angry. "You sent no checks to me for his care. Never—"

"But I did. Of course, I addressed them to Forte Favor. I really do have them canceled, endorsed by you."

"Endorsed—" Corinna's small nostrils looked pinched and white, and she spoke with quiet fury. "I never endorsed one of your checks!" Then she paused and said, seeming both sad and deflated, "Oh! Forte—"

Fanny said, "Forte forged your signature. Right, Corinna?"

"I'm afraid it's possible. Yes."

It was like Forte, and all of them knew it. Even his father must have guessed. But he rallied. "Forgery or not, I have the checks, Cora. I have sent you money during at least ten or fifteen of the past years. So you can't get a divorce for non-support.''

Corinna sat back in her chair. Sarah knew her expression of remoteness; it meant that she was not remote at all, she was thinking hard.

Fitz said, ''You have no claim upon Corinna. We don't know where Forte is. So you can get out before I kick you out.'' It was said smoothly, quietly, but Sarah knew that Fitz meant what he said.

''Try it.'' Briggs smiled. ''This looks like a nice place. Even luxurious. I think I'll stay here—with my wife—until my son returns. If her fancy-pants lover shows up, he'll just have to leave.''

Fitz started across the room, and Sarah saw his doubled-up hand. ''Oh, no, Fitz!'' she cried. ''Oh, no—''

Corinna said, ''Let him stay, Fitz.''

Fitz turned around to face her, angry, astonished. ''This rat—''

''Let him stay,'' Corinna said.

Fitz was between her and Briggs; after a swift glance to make sure of that, Corinna formed a word with her lips. Fitz stared. The word was ''police.''

Fitz paused abruptly. Behind him Briggs chuckled. ''Can't put me out, can you? Say—'' Suddenly he rose as if a new thought had struck him. ''Look here. Where *is* Forte? You all act so— What's the secret here?'' He paused, and as if he had tentacles, seemed to sense the uneasiness in the air. ''There's something peculiar going on—you're hiding something. Something about my son. Look here, why did that gardener fall over as if somebody had hit him when he saw me? Because my son resembles me? Listen, you're all into something that I don't like. Get out of my way, I'm going to the police!''

Fitz, then, quite neatly landed a blow on Briggs's jaw.

Fanny took it in stride, swept to Briggs and eased him into the sofa. As Sarah stared, she even put a cushion under his head.

Corinna said dully, "We can't let him go. The police, the—everything. We'll have to keep him here."

"You do realize that you're still his wife. If he stays here under your roof, no court in the world will believe that you didn't cash those checks and that you didn't consent to a reconciliation."

"Oh, yes, I know all that. He's suspicious. He'll not give up. He'll go to the police and— Oh, Fitz, I don't know what to do. If only Charles were here!"

Her "fancy-pants" lover, Sarah thought incredulously. But then—a divorce court wouldn't like that either. She wondered, again, how she could have been so naive all those years. She had always believed that her father had made his frequent visits to see her. Yet all the others—Fitz, Norm, Fanny, even Forte—had known, or guessed, the truth. She wanted to go to Corinna, take her in her arms. Instead, she said flatly, "If you're going to keep him here, you'd better take him somewhere before he's conscious again!"

"I think he's coming to." Fanny leaned over and peered at Briggs's face.

Norm came running into the room. "What's the matter with Gus? He's out there walking up and down, kicking gravel and swearing! Did you ever hear a Scot when he gets mad? The way he's swearing would curdle—" He saw the figure on the sofa and stopped dead still.

Like Gus, he looked for a moment as if he had been sandbagged. "But that"—he pointed a shaking hand at Mr. Briggs—"that—"

Sarah reached out and snapped on the lights. Fitz said, "It's not. It's his father."

"His—" Norm sank down on a chair and thrust his arm across his forehead. "What's he doing here?"

"He came to see Forte," Sarah said.

"But he . . . that is . . . what did you tell him? What did he say?"

Fitz replied, "Said he had to see Forte. Said we were hiding something. Said he was going to the police."

Norm rubbed his hands over his eyes. "But then Gus—"

"Gus saw him. Had the same impression you had, Norm." Fitz moved over to the figure on the sofa, still unconscious but now stirring lightly.

Sarah cried, "Oh, hurry, get rid of him."

Fitz said curtly, "Help me, Norm. We'll have to do something with him until, well— Come on." He didn't say until what; he couldn't have said that, for none of them seemed to know what to do except Corinna, who said sharply, "There's a key to the maid's room, on the second floor, by the back stairs."

"But we can't keep him—" Sarah began.

"We can't let him go."

"But, Corinna—"

"Necessity knows no law." Corinna was marble-white again and marble-firm.

"All right," Fitz said shortly. "But we can't keep him there indefinitely."

"Oh, I realize that, but we've got to have time to—"

"To what?" Norm asked.

"I don't know. I just know that we can't let him go to the police. Not now. Oh, Fitz, Norm. Take him away. He's beginning to move."

He was indeed returning to consciousness, for he opened his eyes and shot a snake-swift look at Fitz, and when Fitz grasped at one of his arms and Norm the other, he twisted away from them, slid to his feet and cast a venomous look at Corinna. "Don't touch me, you young fools! And you, Cora, you'll regret this. I came here this morning in good faith to see my son. And you treat me like—"

"Come on," Fitz said. "Don't talk."

Fitz and Norm were both strong, but there was a struggle; Forte's father was as eely and wiry as Forte had been. At some time in the scuffle a lamp was knocked over. Sarah picked it up and set it on the table again. The struggle continued all the way up the stairs, with streams of vivid language which probably even Gus could not have given vent to.

Then there was a sudden silence. The three women were quiet, too. Corinna finally took a long breath and leaned back in her chair, her white hair a halo around her lovely but still stony face.

"I hope they didn't hit him again," Sarah said.

"Serve him right." Fanny briskly straightened the cushions on the sofa.

"Time," said Corinna. "We've got to have time for—"

"But if my father can't come soon enough— That's what you're waiting for, isn't it, Corinna?" Sarah didn't even feel daring when she asked it.

Corinna looked at her helplessly, but not quite hopelessly. "Yes. I suppose so."

"They're coming back."

They could hear Norm and Fitz running down the stairs. Then they were in the room—Fitz's black hair ruffled, Norm's face red.

"Did you lock him in?" Corinna asked sternly.

"Yes," Norm said.

"Here's the key." Fitz gave it to Corinna. "Now then, darling Corinna, let's have the whole truth."

"The whole—"

"You've given us some of it, little by little, I gather. Now I want it all."

"What—"

"Oh, come clean." Fitz gave an impatient shrug. "Why did you think that Forte had something to do with some enemy agents? Anything like that? You had to have a reason. Not just a hunch. You acted immediately to keep his death a secret. You were that sure that it would involve Charles—and me and Norm. So what is the reason?"

Corinna sighed, flexing her white hands almost as if in pain, and said, "I didn't know. Not for sure."

"I suppose Forte didn't ask you for money," Fitz said wearily.

"Yes. I mean, no, he didn't. That was the first time he had ever come home and not asked for money—"

"Wait a minute, darling Corinna. Was he . . . well, blackmailing you?" He needn't have hesitated, for Corinna said flatly, "Of course not. All of you knew about Charles and me. That is, everybody but Sarah. Somehow, neither of us wanted Sarah to know anything about our—about us." She gave Sarah a rather apologetic glance. "You do understand, don't you?"

"I don't know; I guess so."

Fitz came to her rescue. "Naturally, you thought that Charles Favor had come to see you, his daughter. His visits, I expect, were somewhat brief—"

Corinna interrupted. "Of course they were brief. Frequent as he could make them, but brief." She sighed. "There was always my little apartment in the city. Of course, when Fanny was there . . ."

Fanny gave a melodious, genuinely amused laugh. "Oh, I knew why, now and then, you sent me to that hotel. You would say that your apartment was being painted or something was out of order. Several times you said I must try some place nearer my studio!"

Fanny had first attended the Juilliard School, then, somehow, Corinna had got in touch with an old but one-time great opera singer and had induced her to take Fanny as a pupil. Not, as Sarah remembered, that it took much inducement, for the singer had listened once to Fanny and said, "You can't take this girl away from me. Now, my dear Fanny, you must learn to breathe."

It was an incident belonging to the Favor legend. She had heard it many times.

Corinna said calmly, "No, it really didn't seem—oh, quite proper to talk to Sarah about us. She was so young at the beginning. And then—I've only begun to realize that you're out of your teens, Sarah."

"I'm getting married," Sarah began defensively, and Fitz looked at his watch.

"That's right, Sarah! License! Corinna, let's get this over. You say Forte didn't ask you for money."

"No, he didn't. It was so different. And—well, I couldn't help wondering about it. And then, you see, he was staying at Rosart's cottage, but he would stroll over here whenever he wanted to and then he would . . . just ramble on. But there were a few things he said that—Oh, I took it as drunken nonsense at first, but when he talked about coming back in a Rolls-Royce and all the millions he was about to have—"

"Millions!" Sarah said. "Forte?"

"Exactly! So I suspected that Forte had got himself involved in something shady."

"There was a stunned silence.

"Millions," Norm said thoughtfully. "But Forte just wasn't bright enough—"

"Oh, I know." Corinna bit her lip, but went on. "There was no honest way Forte could come into any sizable sum of money, so—Well, we've talked about this before—this crazy world, with its assassinations, kidnappings, hostages, mobs, riots, terrorists, violence." She rose. "It didn't matter so much about you, Norm—or you, Fitz. You're both at the beginning of your careers. You can change your courses or live down anything questionable. And I knew that whatever Forte was involved in had to be illegal, and that anything exposed as being illegal—*anything*—would reflect mainly upon Charles. He's put his life—and a large part of mine, actually—into his career. And I will not let you damage Charles."

And she *wouldn't* let anything damage Charles. She was adamant. She was dearly loved. Not one of them could oppose her.

Fitz at last sighed. Norm said lamely, "But we don't want to damage Charles. Or ourselves, as a matter of fact."

"But we can't be *sure* about Forte," Fitz said thoughtfully.

Corinna's dark eyes flashed at him. "You can be sure that whatever he was talking about was serious and would eventually be revealed. I know—we all know—how vulnerable a Foreign Service officer can be. I also knew that if Forte could hurt any of you, in any way, he would. He hated all of you. It was jealousy because you were—oh, bigger, stronger, Norm and Fitz. And Fanny is so gifted and intelligent. You knew Forte. He would secretly brood over something and then find some mean little revenge."

Norm sighed. "But, Corinna, didn't you come straight out and ask him what he was planning?"

"Ask Forte to tell the truth?" It was reply enough.

Fitz adjusted his watch and frowned. "It's nearly noon. Corinna, his father made it clear that he had been seeing Forte—"

"And that Forte had been forging checks made out to me, checks from his father. That is, if his father was telling the truth."

Fitz nodded. "If I'm right, those checks would be evidence in a divorce case. Wouldn't they?"

"Evidence that Forte's father was contributing to my support? I suppose so. Yes." Corinna looked suddenly old and frightened again.

Fitz said, "Apparently they had agreed to meet somewhere. When Forte didn't meet him, his father came here—but that means, must mean, that they were in—"

"Cahoots," Fanny said firmly.

Fitz went on. "Yes. But we have no idea what."

"No. Except he talked so much about money. And he mentioned . . . just *mentioned* Ligunia. Something that had happened there. I didn't pay much attention. But after Forte was shot I began to wonder. Fitz, why were you posted so suddenly to Ligunia? What happened to that Hicks boy—Bill?"

A mask—easy, polite and calm—slid over Fitz's face. "A busted leg. Why?"

Corinna shook her head. "Oh, I really don't know. I couldn't get a word out of Forte that I could believe. There's another thing you must understand, all of you. If you do insist upon police, they won't believe you."

"But, Corinna—" That was Fitz.

"You and Norm are both indebted to Charles, remember that. And I won't let you hurt him. The police will believe *me*, whatever I tell them. I'm known here. I've done things for the town. And you can't show them Forte's—the corpus delicti," said Corinna with almost a flash of triumph.

Fitz and Norm exchanged swift glances. Corinna said, "Yes, Gus, what is it?" Gus wavered in the doorway, then came sturdily and yet defiantly into the room. "Didn't mean to get so upset," he said sourly. "Seeing that man there—the room was so dark and he had his face away from the window and—"

"You needn't apologize, Gus." Corinna was now collected and pleasant, as was her custom.

Gus said, "It was seeing him and—"

Corinna broke in. "Yes, we know—"

"What you don't know, Mrs. Favor, is that Fitz's gun has disappeared."

Fitz whirled toward him. "What do you mean? When did it disappear?"

Gus eyed him crankily. "If I knew that, I'd know a lot. I don't know when it disappeared. I only know it's not with the other guns now. And it didn't walk away." He paused and cocked a long ear toward the stairs. "What's that?"

Sarah listened; everybody listened; there was a distant sound of shouts and thumping, like somebody kicking at a door. Solly stood up and growled softly.

Corinna said. "It's all right, Gus. It's Mr. Briggs. We shut him in there because he insisted upon seeing"—she did hesitate there, but went on—"seeing Forte and said that he would go to the police, so we—well, we didn't know what else to do."

Gus nodded soberly. "But he wouldn't find anything. The police can look all they want to. Better let him go."

Corinna looked questioningly at Norm, then at Fitz, but it was Fanny who decided. "Not yet, Gus. He's in a dangerous mood. We'll keep him here till he cools down."

Gus's tufty eyebrows lowered over his big nose. He turned pointedly to Corinna. "If *you* say so, Mrs. Favor. But what I want to know is who took Fitz's revolver and," Gus added, "*why*?"

Fitz sighed. "We'll try to find it, Gus."

"Better," Gus said and disappeared.

Corinna said slowly, "If only Charles were here—"

"Well, he's not," Sarah said shortly.

"What can we do about Briggs?" Norm asked.

"Keep him here for a day or two." Again Fanny had the answer. "I'll fix food for him. One of you can slide it into that room. Now I really must get to work." Majestic in spite of blue jeans and sneakers, she strode out into the hall.

Corinna looked worried. "She's right. She hasn't had any time to practice lately. She's got to keep at it."

Fitz said, very quietly, "How much does Rosart know of all this?"

"Hardly anything," Corinna said conclusively. "He was only in at the beginning and he's been absorbed in Nannie Pie ever since."

Suddenly Sarah recalled the very unwelcome notion suggested by Fanny. "Somebody tied up Solly last night, remember." Hearing his name, Solly put his long nose on her knee, his eyes dark and worried. She continued. "Rosart took steak from the refrigerator. Solly knows Rosart. He wouldn't have objected if Rosart tied him to the tree. He'd have taken the steak without question."

All three simply stared at her. Fitz said after a moment, "But why—why would Rosart want to hurt—or even frighten—you!"

Sarah felt guilty, miserable, but also prodded by the

need to find the truth. "He moves as quietly and swiftly as . . . as a Red Indian. I remember thinking that when I knew someone was in the woods last night. But—oh, no!" A revulsion of feeling and a stab of conscience conquered her simultaneously. "But it couldn't have been Rosart!"

"Nobody quite knows what anybody else can do. If he puts his mind to it." Corinna rose. "I'm going to walk down to the mailbox. It's time for the postman. Fanny must have time to work. Will you see to lunch for us, Sarah?"

"Oh. Yes. Yes, certainly." Distracted, Sarah thought rather wildly of what was or was not in the refrigerator.

Fitz said, "But we're going to White Plains."

"Yes! Well, I'll just set out sandwiches or something."

The shouts and pounding upstairs had stopped suddenly, as if from sheer weariness on Briggs's part.

"We can't keep that man forever," Sarah said into space and hurried out.

But Briggs had not ceased his efforts from weariness. He had crept down the back stairs, and was standing in the kitchen when Sarah walked in.

Fourteen

"Don't be scared," he whispered. "I won't hurt you."

"*Wait . . . wait . . .*"

"*Don't scream!*"

"But you can't— How did you—"

"I discovered the door wasn't locked. See you," said Briggs jauntily and sped out through the back entry. He was so like Forte—sliding like an eel out of everybody's way whenever he had done something that invited, indeed required, some measure of retribution—that for a second Sarah felt as Gus had felt: That is Forte.

By the time she had gathered her strength to run after him, meanwhile shouting for Fitz and Norm, there was no nattily clad, pin-striped form in sight.

Solly answered her first, leaping out the door and barking wildly, but then stopping and looking around for something to bark at. Norm and Fitz shot past her and into the driveway. Gus came thudding along from somewhere, with a look on his face that made Sarah flinch; he grasped the situation quickly, but not quickly enough—the engine of the rattletrap car that stood near Rosart's cottage had already started up with a wild roar. The engine caught and the car went down the driveway as if it had wings, and noisy wings at that, for everything in the car creaked and squealed. As it passed them, Forte's father, so like Forte that it was deeply shocking every time, leaned out and waved at them. Even though it was obvious that it would be useless to chase after him, Gus was already in the garage and could be heard turning on the engine of Corinna's big car.

Gus was now in a blind and murderous rage.

He never took out Corinna's car without her permission. But he was clearly prepared to deal with Forte's father in an all too certain manner. "Don't let him go," Sarah shouted at Norm and Fitz. Fitz ran into the garage. Voices rose as he remonstrated with Gus. In a moment both Gus and Fitz came outside. Gus's face was worse than any thundercloud Sarah had ever seen, not a face to come upon in the dark of night. Fitz was saying, "No use trying to follow him."

Distantly, from the house, Sarah could hear Fanny; even pedestrian practicing sounded beautiful when Fanny sang.

Corinna was standing in the door of the entry, silent, her face white.

Norm said, "He'll go to the police."

"I doubt it, and even so, there's nothing we can do about it." Fitz thought for a moment. Then he turned back to Sarah's car, parked in the driveway. "Come on, Sarah. We'll have lunch in White Plains."

"But Corinna told me to—"

"Let them take care of themselves," said Fitz and took her by the elbow. "Get in. I'll drive."

She got in the car. Norm stared at them, and then turned to Gus, whose expression was still the kind to frighten children. Sarah had a glimpse of Nannie Pie and Rosart, emerging from the woods, hand in hand.

The car turned onto the main road.

"Why do you think he'll not go to the police?" Sarah asked as they rounded the first curve.

"Because he smells a rat. And first wants to find out for himself just what has been going on."

"But the police—"

Fitz glanced at her. "Pull yourself together, honey. If Corinna is right about him, whatever business he and Forte might have undertaken could attract considerable interest on the part of the police. That's my guess, anyway. No, I don't think he'll go to the police."

"But you agreed to keep him at the house."

"It seemed the thing to do at the time." He laughed shortly. "What I'd like to know is who let him out."

"He said he discovered the door was unlocked. But we were all together in the living room!"

"Not Fanny."

"But I could hear her."

"Maybe," said Fitz after a while. "There's an old Victrola in the playroom."

"You mean she could have put on a record! But why? Oh, Fitz, do you think that's what she did the day Forte was killed—what I heard when I got home?"

"Norm said he thought he saw somebody near the garage after he heard you scream. He said in blue jeans. Fanny's favorite apparel."

"I suppose she could have put on any old record to make us think she was working. After all, I could barely hear it. But I'm sure it was 'The Bell Song.'"

"She might have thought she'd play any music just to sound busy. Then she could get her exercise without being bothered—something like that. Fanny is very direct."

"That doesn't seem so very direct."

Fitz looked at her, smiling. "Remember, Corinna was expected home. She would be tired and not likely to pay much attention to anything but the fact that Fanny was singing. She does drive her."

"Fanny drives herself. But—yes, that could be the reason for it. I'll ask Fanny."

"I don't think it matters. Unless Fanny had helped

herself to my revolver in Gus's room. And I can't see her running into the house and taking a shot at Forte just after you arrived. No, there's something out of kilter about that.'' He frowned, thinking and driving; the car was so small that his long legs had to be doubled up uncomfortably.

The path to a marriage license was suddenly and unexpectedly smooth. Fitz had health certificates which were barely three days old; that was because he was being sent to Ligunia. In the summer Sarah, herself, had had the customary going over by the doctor, which Corinna insisted upon for all the Favors. The doctor's nurse obligingly promised to send over the reports. The county clerk was a boyhood friend of Fitz and did not stand on his dignity. As a matter of fact, he didn't seem inclined to stand on the law too rigidly either. "Everything looks all right to me. You'll have to see Judge—''

He vanished through a door in the wired-in and railed-off desk space, leaving them both in hhe waiting room, with its golden-oak chairs, its smell of floor-cleaning compounds.

"Looks like we may make it,'' Fitz said.

The county clerk came back, all smiles. "I think it may be okay. You'll want to talk to the J.P.?''

The justice of the peace was older; he knew Corinna. He knew all of them. He beamed, adjusted spectacles, rubbed his chin, frowned, beamed again and said at last, "Sometimes rules are made to be broken.''

"When?'' Fitz asked.

"Well, now—''

"I've got to leave soon.''

"Yes, I understand. I saw your papers. I think we can make an exception. Come back to see me tomorrow.''

They thanked the justice of the peace. They thanked the county clerk, who offered congratulations (ahead of time but welcome).

"So,'' Fitz said, "that must mean— Oh, for God's sake, how did he get here?''

Solly was sitting upright in the car, tongue lolling out of his mouth.

"Oh, he just does. All right, Solly."

Solly acknowledged them with a cold, poking nose at Sarah's neck as she got in the car. "He's probably hungry."

"So am I. Do you mind if we just eat somewhere, anywhere, in a hurry."

"No, it's all right."

"There should be that nice little restaurant— Oh, good," he said after a moment, "it's still there. Stay here, Solly."

It was not a leisurely pre-wedding luncheon. Fitz said, finally, "I'm not much good at conversation today, am I?"

"You're worried. So am I—plenty of reasons."

"Worried?" He tested the word. "Mainly uneasy. I keep feeling that something is happening. Something all wrong—at home."

But he remembered to ask for a hamburger, wrapped in wax paper, which he took to Solly, who accepted it as if it were his due.

"You drive, will you, Sarah? It's too short for my legs."

"Fitz, I love this little car. Can I bring it with me to Ligunia?"

"I'll find out. There'll be a car for you there, you know—chauffeurs, the works."

They were turning toward home when Fitz said thoughtfully, "Fanny is a powerful woman. Not as powerful as Corinna, but still—she'd do anything to protect Corinna."

"But really, Fitz," Sarah said hotly. "Fanny couldn't have shot Forte."

Yet in spite of herself she thought of the soiled blue jeans and the muddy sneakers she had seen below Fanny's proper pale-blue dressing gown the night hands had tried to throttle her. Even now, with Fitz beside her, the memory was terrifying.

She said, too firmly perhaps, "Fanny wouldn't have followed me into the woods and . . . and . . ."

"I don't really think so either," Fitz agreed equably. "But somebody did. Why would anybody at all try to hurt you? First something wrong with your car and then the attack in the woods."

"After he fixed the brakes, Andy said that someone didn't like me. He thought Forte could have done it."

"Tell me again every single thing that happened after you got home from the airport."

"I told you—"

"Tell me again, everything. The chauffeur brought you home. You got out of the car and went across the terrace. You opened the door and went into the hall. Go on—"

"All right. Nobody was around. I could hear Fanny singing—"

"Or a record playing."

"Yes. Anyway, what else? First, I thought something was burning."

"Burning!" Fitz sat up. *"What!"*

"It really wasn't like a fireplace, or a cigarette or something on the stove or a candle or— It was just a whiff of something unpleasant, something like smoke, but it wasn't smoke."

After a moment Fitz said, "Go on."

"It wasn't the smell of wilting chrysanthemums either. I checked. I didn't see anybody, but I didn't look in the living room or the library. Then I went upstairs. I got to my room—"

"Which is directly over the living room. Then right away you heard the shot."

"Not right away. I had dropped my coat and handbag. I remember I was brushing my hair. Then there was the shot. So I ran downstairs and found Forte and screamed and—"

"Wait. The living-room windows were not open?"

"No. I felt sick. Dizzy, something. I ran over and opened the windows—I wanted fresh air—and then I screamed."

"All right," Fitz said shortly, "go on."

"That's all, really. First Norm came, then Rosart. He had stopped in the kitchen and cut a piece of the cake Fanny had made for our dinner. Then Fanny appeared. And Gus came in with your gun and said he had found it on the lawn. And—oh, yes, Gus made Fanny go and get something to cover Forte and he herded us into the library and then the argument began and Corinna arrived—and the argument went on. We were all talking. Norm said we must call the police. Corinna said no. Rosart and Gus just looked at each other. In the middle of the . . . the . . ."

"Fracas," Fitz suggested tersely.

"Yes. Gus and Rosart just very quietly left the room, and then they took Forte away. I don't know where."

"I'll find out. Look, there's Norm over there by the mailbox."

She turned into the driveway and stopped beside the big mailbox as Norm stood up to greet them. He had been sitting on the stone wall that ran alongside the road.

It was a dry wall and rather broken down here and there in spite of Gus's efforts to keep it propped up by means of slyly inserted iron spikes. The story was that it had been built during the Civil War by Confederate prisoners. This was questioned by Fitz and Norm until Rosart told them that there had indeed been a prisoner-of-war camp somewhere in the area and Confederate prisoners had been employed in erecting some of the many fieldstone walls in that vicinity. Fitz had said that, if true, it was better than going hungry and being shot at. Rosart had said loftily that Fitz wouldn't understand.

Norm was hunched up in an old jacket of Fitz's, probably taken from the hooks in the back entry. He looked chilly and sober. He came up to them as Sarah stopped the car. "Where have you been?"

Fitz replied, "Getting our wedding license—at least I hope so—and then having lunch."

Norm's usually solid and imperturbable face seemed

rather shrunken and serious. Sarah thought, He doesn't like the fact of our getting a marriage license; perhaps he really does love me. No, that couldn't be; she was entertaining a completely conceited notion based on a bare few words of Norm's.

She put a hand lightly over his as it lay on the car beside her. He looked down at it so soberly that Fitz said, "What's the matter with you, Norm? You look like hell."

He removed his hand. "I don't like this place. It's got on my nerves. Anyway, I haven't seen or heard anything of Forte's father. He seems to have vanished, and there's no telling where he is or what he's doing. Enough to make anybody feel like the devil. It's all right for you. You'll be gone—far away. But I'll be in Washington. And my leave isn't up for four days. And Corinna and Fanny, or Rosart or even Gus, will keep after me to straighten everything out—and I can't."

Fitz said, "You aren't the only one with problems, Norm. Get in, we'll drive you back to the house. I'm going to track down Gus."

"Move over, Solly." Norm climbed in the back seat.

There were no lights in the house and it loomed up in a ghostly way—white, but shielded by the heavy autumn fog which had risen. The woods around were gray and blue, with darker patches of pines.

"Gus did try to tell us that someone had taken your gun," Norm said gloomily as Sarah stopped the car at the terrace steps.

"I know. I want to talk to him."

"You'll have to find him first."

"He's at the Simmons place," Sarah said, and added, "At least I think so."

"He's not around here." Norm got out of the car. "I looked for him." He glanced around at the fog wreaths which seemed to move and swirl a little. "To tell you the truth, I keep feeling that Forte's father got hold of that gun and he's creeping around, waiting to get off a good shot."

"At you?" Fitz got out of the car. Solly bounded after Sarah as she started toward the house.

"At somebody." Norm's shoulders moved uneasily under the leather jacket.

Fitz said, "We're going to try the Simmons place. Want to come along, Norm?"

"All right. No," he reversed himself sharply. "No use in leaving the place with nobody but Fanny and Corinna."

"You think her husband"—Fitz wrinkled up his forehead as he referred with distaste to Forte's father—"you think Briggs would try to take a shot at Corinna?"

"He's likely to try to talk to her, at least. Find out whatever he can about Forte," Norm said. "Yes, that's what I think."

Fitz took a long breath. "Get Rosart over here. He's big enough to scare anybody."

"Rosart?" said Norm—and nothing else, which was quite enough explanation. In football, yes, a formidable opponent. But in tackling somebody in cold blood, no. Not Rosart.

"All right. Come on, Sarah."

Norm went dejectedly, his shoulders hunched under the jacket, into the house.

"We'll take the path," Fitz said.

The public road at the foot of their long driveway met, after about a quarter of a mile, the Simmons driveway, which went up a slight rise to their house. But long ago the young Favors, with their neighbors' consent, had worn a path through the Favor woods and into the Simmons woods; it reached the Simmons pond on which they skated. Now the woods with its carpet of damp autumn leaves seemed strange; the rhododendrons along the path, the briars and raspberry canes stealthily thrust out as if to grasp at Sarah's skirt. The trees themselves didn't seem like the familiar ones all of them knew, but more like menacing strangers.

Fitz said, as he tried to hold low branches away from

Sarah's face, "Forte's father can't be hiding anywhere so near the house. Besides, Solly would know if there was a stranger around."

Solly had bounded ahead, looking in the distance like a pale, long-legged ghost.

"On the other hand, Solly didn't seem to know if a stranger came in and killed Forte," Fitz said.

"Skunk," said Sarah, reminding him.

The path was well marked now that Gus had taken over the care of the Simmons estate. Sarah noticed the marks of Gus's wheelbarrow now and then but could see little beyond the crowding foliage until they came out at the pond. Here, too, however, shrubs covered the marshy banks. "We skated there so many times," she said softly.

Fitz turned to her. "Dear," he said and took her in his arms. "You won't be homesick, you know. I'll not let you be homesick. You'll like Ligunia. It's supposed to have everything. Good climate. Good consulate enclave—even luxurious homes for the hired help like me."

It also had been the scene of an attempt to kill Bill Hicks. Sarah did not mention that, but Fitz guessed what she was thinking.

"I told you, Sarah. Things there will be cleared up. Soon, I hope."

She couldn't resist a little dart of mischief. "At the airport you said I couldn't come. Now you want to get married right away."

"I've changed my mind. The fact is—I am beginning to think you'll be safer there than here."

"Fitz," she said abruptly, "I thought of Bill Hicks when I found Forte."

Fitz stared at her. "Why?"

"Because—well, you had told me about Bill Hicks only that evening. I came home and heard the shot that killed Forte. I mean—not a gunshot in the woods, but a . . . a shot at a person. Oh, I'm not making sense. It simply seemed too much of a coincidence."

His mouth tightened. But he said only, "I don't like coincidences either. Especially if— Right now, let's try to find Gus."

But they didn't move. He held her close for a moment, so close and hard that she could feel his heart thudding and knew that her own breath was coming short and fast. "I do love you," he said. "More than that, I like you."

"Yes," she whispered, which seemed to be the answer he wanted, for he released her and they went on to where Solly was standing, waving his tail and looking his feckless and happy self. "I think he's found Gus," Sarah said.

They followed the well-trodden path past the pond, past the jumbled remains of a fieldstone wall that had been erected many years before to surround a cemetery. This old cemetery put a slight stamp of authenticity upon the legend that Confederate prisoners had built the dry wall around the Favor place; for when the young Favors had explored it and tried to decipher the moss-grown or fallen gravestones, some of them did reveal names and in some cases a military title. Sarah had always felt a sorrowing regret that, in all probability, none of the families of the men resting here had known for certain of their last retreat.

Gus was in the greenhouse.

It wasn't kept up in its original condition, but the Simmons good-naturedly allowed Gus to use it not only for their potting shed but for anything Gus wished to tend for Corinna.

They paused at the door; Solly frolicked into the greenhouse, gave Gus's leg a sniff of greeting and went off again into the fog.

Gus, however, was not potting anything. He was simply sitting on a carpenter's sawhorse, his elbows on his knees, his face dour.

"So it's you," he said crankily. "High time. Didn't you hear me say your gun had been stolen?"

Fitz sat down beside him. "Yes. First, though, Gus, you'll have to tell me what you did with Forte."

Gus seemed deep in thought, his lower lip sticking out stubbornly, finally he said, "Nope. Not yet. First I want to find out who took that gun?"

"Well, I didn't," Fitz said. "When did you discover it was gone?"

"Just before I went up to the house. Don't ask me when it was taken because I don't know. I was working over here. I'm going to get a lock for my place. Too handy for anybody that wants anything. Such as a gun. Especially," said Gus glumly, "if the gun is loaded."

"Gus! You mean you loaded that revolver?"

"Sure. Oh, when you gave it to me to keep for you it wasn't loaded. You had seen to that. But I had your box of shells, too. So I thought I'd load it."

"But *why?*"

"No sense in keeping a gun around, a revolver, anyway, without loading it. Some mean things happen nowadays. Away from town. Out in the woods like this. Certainly I loaded it."

"But what about the box of shells?"

"Anybody could have got at that, too. Not now. I've hidden it. Too late," said Gus.

"Too— Oh, Forte—"

Gus nodded once. "Maybe. When I found the revolver, though, outside the windows, there were four shells left in it. Two gone. So is the gun. With four more shells in it."

Fifteen

The two men stared silently at each other; it seemed to Sarah that in fact they were exchanging thoughts.

Off in the distance Solly gave a yelp.

"Wait," she cried. "I'd better catch Solly before he gets after another skunk."

Nobody said, Wait for what? She ran out of the damp-smelling greenhouse. Panes here and there were broken, but still it served as a shelter for tender young plants which would emerge neatly in the wooden flats ranged around on benches.

The fog had deepened; it felt almost like rain, touching her face lightly. She saw Solly at a distance; he had bounced over the remnants of the wall around the Confederate graveyard and was up on a slight rise, digging furiously in the soil.

If he had found a woodchuck hole and if mama or papa woodchuck was at home, vicious, protruding teeth would sink into Solly's nose and fasten there. She stepped over the broken-down wall and started toward him, calling, walking carefully around the headstones. Solly was digging with such determination that soil and sod flew back from his front paws.

He paid no attention at all to her call.

"Solly!" she cried in exasperation, and reached him just as he uncovered something in the grave which was definitely not a woodchuck. She caught a glimpse of what looked like a new plank.

"Solly—" She sank down on her knees and grasped the dog's collar.

He wriggled and squirmed, but she held on, got a good grip on him and forced him back through the cemetery, avoiding other fallen headstones, to the greenhouse.

Solly gave strong protest, combined yells and wriggles. Fitz reached out automatically to take his collar. Sarah said, "I've found him! Oh, Gus, I know!"

Gus eyed Solly. "You're no good, you Solly. No good."

Fitz was standing. "You don't mean—"

"Yes. Yes, I'm sure. Gus buried him."

"Eh, well, and so I did. Decent, too. Did it yesterday when you were all at that award affair. Made a coffin for him and buried him and said a word of prayer over him. All proper."

"My God," said Fitz and sank down on the bench.

"Wasn't easy," Gus said. "Had to cart him up here in a wheelbarrow. Dug into that old grave. That wasn't hard. It had sunken. And the rest—all proper. I told you."

Fitz moistened his lips. "Who else knows about this?"

"Nobody."

"Not even Rosart?"

"Him?" Gus's face expressed a kind of indulgent scorn. "He's got his head in the clouds half the time. He'd tell and not know he was telling."

"I don't think so." Fitz seemed to be recovering his scattered wits. He said slowly, "You know there'll be trouble about this, Gus."

"I don't know any such thing. Nobody's ever going to

know about it. Except for this no-good dog of yours, nobody would ever have known.''

Fitz rallied slightly. "But, Gus, it's a criminal offense.''

"Not criminal to bury a man. Decently,'' he added, as if that put a seal of approval on it, made it respectable and proper legally.

"But, Gus, you must understand. All of us are accessories after the fact.''

"Nobody needs to know about it. Look here''—Gus was indignant—"do you think I was going to let even Forte lie out in the woods or somewhere all winter—at least until Mrs. Favor wanted the thing to be reported! Now, that *would* be wicked. No, I couldn't do that.''

Fitz opened his mouth, seemed to debate with himself, then simply stared at Gus.

Gus patted Solly. "Besides, you and Norm and Mr. Favor, your father''—he explained to Sarah as if she might not know his name—"everyone of you is—or could be—in a bad position, anyway.''

"Well, naturally—with a murder, a concealed murder—''

"Not what I mean. I read, I listen to the news. I know what's going on all over the world. Like a germ, a fungus. Contagious! All those riots and kidnappings and . . . and assassinations. Dangerous kind of job, if you ask me.''

Fitz swallowed hard. "Do you mean that's why you—''

"I knew Mrs. Favor was thinking of that. I knew she was right. Just keep quiet about the whole thing. Nothing else to do. Murder in the family! Why, the newspapers—''

"All right, Gus. All right.'' Fitz rose.

"You're not going to report this to the police. Be sensible, Fitz. You've always been sensible. That is''—Gus seemed to think back to youthful misdeeds—"maybe not always. But since you settled down with a job, yes. And going to marry Sarah—I mean Miss Sarah—now, that's sensible too.''

"That's not why— Oh, never mind, Gus.''

"Well, then, what are you going to do?''

Fitz shoved both hands across his eyes. "I'm damned if I know."

Gus showed an unexpected sarcasm. "You'll be damned if you do. Go to the police, I mean. Now."

Fitz stared at Gus for a long time. In for a penny, in for a pound, thought Sarah. There was a chilling truth about that.

Good old Gus! He did what he felt was best, and it couldn't have been easy. The picture of Gus, head bent, saying a good Scottish prayer over Forte seemed, in its peculiar way, more moving than a conventional burial might have been.

Gus hadn't liked Forte; he had had many a problem with him. Once when Forte had put pebbles into the power mower Corinna had bought, Gus had thoroughly lost his temper and given Forte the trouncing he deserved. Sarah herself was not under Corinna's care at that time but she had heard of it, for it was an epic tale in the Favor house, probably told by Corinna to induce the rest of them to show respect and obey Gus—especially when she was not at home.

And, of course, whoever said that Gus was loyal to Corinna and would carry out her every wish was perfectly right. It was not wholly a matter of Corinna's being his employer; it was something inherent in Gus's strong Scottish blood, like a first principle of behavior.

Fitz made up his mind. "All right. For now. I don't know what we can do later. We'd better get back to the house, Sarah."

"Tie the dog with this rope. I'll fix up the grave again so nobody will guess." He handed over a rope about ten feet in length, and added dourly, "It's the rope that tied Solly to the tree."

It was raining; the gentle sprinkle had turned into a slanting heavy downpour.

"Come on, Sarah—" Fitz took the rope, looped it around Solly's collar, and the three of them made a dash into the rain, toward the woods and house. Sarah knew that Gus was standing in the doorway of the greenhouse, watching them.

"No reasoning with that old bird." Fitz said as he tugged at the rope.

But there was no need to urge Solly to accompany them. He hated rain, and had already pulled loose from the rope and was ahead of them.

The trees shut off some of the force of the storm.

"What about your gun?" Sarah gasped.

"Gus says he doesn't know what happened to it. Said it just vanished. Point is, it's gone. And still loaded. Look out for that branch—"

She ducked under a swinging elm branch, which showered water on her head.

They came out at the garage. There were lights now in Rosart's cottage. Fitz paused, thought for a second and said, "Let's go and see Rosart."

Nannie Pie opened the door for them and pulled them into the house. She was in blue jeans and a turtleneck sweater, and was rosily, neatly clean. Her eyes sparkled; even her hair sparkled brightly. The strains of the Beethoven Fifth Piano Concerto poured triumphantly from Rosart's enormous stereo. A fire was blazing cheerfully in the tiny fireplace, which Rosart, whose mechanical ability encompassed some knowledge of carpentry and masonry, had built. He came to meet them. "You look like a drowned rat," he said flatteringly to Sarah.

"Rosart!" Nannie Pie was indignant. "You poor thing, Sarah. I'll get a towel."

Sarah tried to shrug water from herself and her clothes. Solly had swiftly squeezed past them and was now shaking vigorously before the fire.

No use trying to stop him; no use putting him outdoors either, Sarah knew; he would merely howl at the door until he was let in again.

Rosart said, looking pleased behind his beard, "How do you like the room?"

"It's very, very nice." Sarah pushed her wet hair back. Nannie Pie returned with a towel and in a motherly manner began to dry Sarah's hair.

The room was nice. Rosart had outdone himself. The chairs, the tables, the red curtains, and the handsome rug which Sarah remembered as being in one of the guest rooms of the big house and given to Rosart by Corinna (a Sarouk, all blues and reds, which Corinna had decided was much too garish to be used in the bedroom)—all was warmly attractive. Rosart had painted the walls a pleasant primrose-yellow; the bright colors of the rug seemed to glow in contrast. There were laden bookcases (built, Sarah knew, by Rosart), a magazine rack, a sturdy table in one corner on which lay yellow notepads and pencils—probably in the event of some immortal verse striking Rosart. There was a battered old typewriter on which he had written his dissertation. He had insisted upon reading long portions of it to all of them; the only thing Sarah remembered of it was the fact that Pablo Casals, Dali and Ortega y Gasset all came from the same vicinity of Barcelona—and what that had to do with poetry, she never discovered.

Nannie Pie might have been married for years. She said to Rosart, "Drinks, don't you think? Keep off the chill—"

Already she had overcome Rosart's antipathy to liquor. He shrugged his massive shoulders, grinned lovingly at Nannie Pie behind his beard, (at least his teeth shone whitely), and shambled off toward the tiny kitchen. Nannie Pie turned off the stereo and smiled apologetically at them. "I'm sure you'd like to talk."

At Nannie Pie's gesture, Fitz said, "Thank you," just as Rosart (trained early by Corinna in the proper way to present drinks to guests) returned with a small tray, a silver one, which Sarah recognized; Corinna had either given him the tray or he had simply appropriated it.

He poured drinks for all of them; they only had bourbon,

he said, and Nannie Pie said they hoped that would be all right. "We're going to stock up a little when we have time," Nannie Pie went on calmly and accepted the glass Rosart offered her. "What in the world were you two doing in the woods? Didn't you notice it was about to pour?"

Fitz said gently yet abruptly, "Rosart, you knew what Gus did about Forte."

Rosart did not show any surprise. "Well, I guessed. I had helped him carry Forte out as far as the garage. Then he told me to leave things to him. So I did. But naturally, I could guess what he intended to do."

Fitz blinked. "You didn't try to stop him?"

Rosart's eyes opened wide. "Why?" he asked simply.

"There *is* a law." Fitz sipped at his drink, watching Rosart over the rim of the glass.

Rosart said lightly, "Man-made law."

"Man-made law does operate." Fitz's face had its tight, half-angry, fully determined look.

"Yes." Rosart seemed to consider it for the first time, for he added, "Doesn't mean laws are fair. Or right."

"They're the best we can do."

"Up to now," Rosart said.

"Now look here!" Fitz was holding his temper in. "We needn't have a discourse on the history of civilization. You know as well as I do that Forte's murder should have been reported."

Clearly, Nannie Pie now knew as much of the affair as any of them—or, a cruel little voice said in Sarah's mind, as much as Rosart wished to tell her. Yet Rosart was kind, Rosart sincerely detested cruelty to anything at all. "Oh, yes," he said agreeably.

Fitz turned the glass in his hands. "How long have you known what Gus did with Forte?"

"Let me see. I suppose right away it seemed to me a logical place to put him. As a matter of fact, a damn sight better than all this artificiality and carrying-on. Just a quiet place in the woods with all those men who had gone before him. "Yes"—even Rosart's huge black beard seemed to soften—"I thought it almost like a Viking funeral. Not as spectacular, of course, but—"

"Certainly not spectacular." Fitz now had an edge to his voice. "Can't you get it through your head—or at least through that hellish great beard of yours—that what you and Gus did has put all of us in danger. It's a felony, punishable by—well, I don't know exactly, but it's a serious crime. Can't you understand—"

"Now keep calm, Fitz. Nothing is going to happen. Another drink?"

"Can't I knock sense into you?" Fitz almost shouted.

Nannie Pie said, very gently, "Really, I wouldn't try, if I were you. Rosart—"

"Oh, I'm not going to fight him. He'd finish me off with one blow." Fitz added bitterly, "Why God made him such a fool—"

"Now, Fitz." Rosatt spoke as though his feelings had not been in the slightest degree ruffled by Fitz's outburst. "If you'll just take it easy, everything will settle itself. You'll see."

"Not with Forte's father coming around, threatening, taking off with your car—"

"Oh! Is that who that man was! I thought he looked like Forte!" Rosart leaned over to pick up the rope still dangling from Solly's collar. "I got to the door just as he dashed away. Really gave me kind of a shock. Looks so like Forte." He didn't seem at all disturbed by the theft of his car.

"Listen! He said he was going to the police—"

"Well, obviously, he hasn't. What's this rope?"

"To hold Solly." Fitz said. "You know that Solly was tied up last night."

"Solly? Why?"

"So somebody could get Sarah into the woods and strangle her," Fitz said. "You know about that, too. It happened while you say you were at the garage getting the car fixed up. Several garages.''

Now Rosart did blink above his black mask. ''If you mean I tried to kill Sarah, I didn't.'' Then he said calmly, ''I can't see why anybody would try to kill her. What have you been up to, Sarah?''

''This,'' Fitz said too quietly, ''is simply too much! Nannie Pie, you'll have to talk some sense into this great bear!''

''How'd Sarah get away?'' Rosart asked, with at last a flicker of interest. ''I didn't wait to hear.''

Sarah swallowed the rest of her drink before she spoke. ''Norm and Gus found me. And Norm saw something—a shadow—something moving back in the woods and . . .'' Her voice wavered.

''There, there, Sarah!'' said Nannie Pie in that charming, motherly way. ''Of course, it happened while we were in White Plains. I'm so sorry! How dreadful—but how lucky you were.'' She paused there, and pushed back the red ribbon around her shining brown hair. ''But I can't understand why! Sarah, who?''

''Don't need to understand,'' Rosart began. '' 'There are more things in heaven and earth—' ''

''Shut up! You—a poet!'' Fitz almost yelled.

''It was all right for Shakespeare,'' Rosart said mildly. ''Of course, at that time it was original, not an overworked quotation.''

''You are not Shakespeare!'' Fitz said hotly and rather childishly.

Rosart's white teeth showed. ''But I'm good,'' he said. ''Even Corinna admits that.''

''She's very proud of you,'' Sarah said quickly, hoping to divert the exasperation she saw boiling up in Fitz.

''Well—yes, in a way.'' Rosart sighed. ''Do you know, a few weeks ago I said that I wrote for posterity. And do you know what Corinna said to me? She claimed that she wrote for *prosperity*.''

"What did you say to that?" Fitz asked, momentarily but honestly curious.

Rosart's big shoulders lifted. "What could I say! It's perfectly true, in a way. She does supply all of us from the proceeds of what she writes. Now don't jump at me, Fitz."

"No, don't," said Nannie Pie hurriedly. The tidy housewife, Sarah thought on a tangent, not wishing to have a body, Fitz, flattened out in her living room.

Fitz put his glass down on a table with such force that Nannie Pie frowned. "Thank you, Nannie Pie, for the drink. And"—he shot a hostile glance at Rosart, but didn't quite snarl—"for the hospitality."

"By the way," Rosart said amiably, "does anybody know what Forte was doing in the garage the afternoon he was shot?"

"What's that! Did you see him?" Fitz couldn't stand over Rosart, Rosart was too big, but Fitz gave that impression.

Rosart took it calmly. "Oh, sure. We'd had a bit of a row, you know. I told him he had to get out of my house and stay out. Then I went into the woods to walk and think about my speech—"

"What did Forte do?" Fitz seemed to be holding himself in with difficulty.

"Well, really, I don't know. He fiddled around Sarah's little car for a while. Then he went up those stairs to Gus's place, but that's all I saw. I wasn't even interested in what Forte was doing—"

Fitz was about to explode.

Sarah said quickly, "Rosart, did Forte know anything about the brakes on my car?"

"Why, I suppose so. They're not too complicated."

"And you saw him going up to Gus's rooms?" Fitz said.

"Sure. But I didn't hang around. I'd had enough of Forte."

"Since you saw so much, did you also happen," Fitz

asked with icy control, "to notice if he took my revolver from Gus's place?"

Rosart considered, then shook his head. "Nope. Can't say I do. I just saw him and then—" At last his good-natured affability vanished. "Then next time I saw him he was, well, dead. That's all."

"Oh," Fitz said after a long moment. "That's all, is it? Well, it might interest you to know that we think he fixed the brakes on Sarah's car so she nearly smashed up."

"No! Why do you think that? How do you know?" Rosart did, now, seem shocked.

Fitz sighed. "I don't know. Andy, at the garage, thinks so. It's a reasonable guess. Come on, Sarah."

Solly got up awkwardly, as if he had suddenly developed terrific rheumatic problems; the fact was he hated to be lured out into the rain, for he hated getting his feet wet.

"Well, come again," said both Nannie Pie and Rosart pleasantly, each smiling in a friendly way.

The door closed behind them, shutting off warmth and color. The rain slanted fiercely against their faces.

"Fitz! Do you really think that Forte tampered with my brakes?" Sarah cried against the wind.

Fitz was a long time answering. Finally he said, "Sounds like Forte. He was furious because you had shoved him out of the taxi. Probably never occurred to him that a smash-up might kill you. He just wanted to get even. Yes, it's likely. Andy is very smart about those things. But right now I'm more concerned about my gun."

She trudged on, rain cold on her face. "I agree. Your gun. That's the most important thing now—we must find out what happened to it."

"Forte could have taken it from Gus's room. It's the kind of thing he would do. But I wonder what he intended to do with it. Besides make himself a nuisance to Gus. Or me, if he knew it was my gun, as he probably did. Oh, yes, all of it sounds like Forte was the one who was apparently shot with it."

They came out of the woods.

Fitz sighed. "I'm wondering if Rosart let Forte's father out of that room."

"Rosart! I never thought of that!"

"Somebody let him out. Rosart believes in kindness, no matter what. He always lets animals out of traps—"

"But that's good."

"Well, it wasn't good to let Briggs out of that room. Trouble is—Corinna had the key. Nobody left the living room, except Fanny. And we're almost sure we heard her practicing. That leaves Rosart or Gus to open that door—"

"Another key?" Sarah blinked against the heavy raindrops.

"Yes. There must be dozens of old keys around the place. Rosart could have found one—or he's a good mechanic, he could know how to pick a lock with a toothpick," said Fitz crossly. "And he hates to have anything shut up."

"I thought he was honestly surprised to hear that it was Forte's father who stole the car."

"I thought so, too. But with that damn beard, how can anybody tell what he thinks? Of course, I ought to report a stolen car, if you can call that old rattletrap a car. But that would mean reporting Briggs. And start a hunt for him, and then we know what will happen!"

She said softly, "You don't want to—Norm said it— throw us to the wolves. But, Fitz, now that we know where Forte—"

"I know. I know! But— Oh, hell, it'll be so rough on you—on all of us. Me, too, don't forget. I heard of all this last night. There's been plenty of time to report to the police. I'm as culpable as any of you. I do understand the way it happened, but the police won't. No, I have to report it, even if I don't want to."

Solly had dashed ahead and stopped at the back door, giving his usual dramatic imitation of an orphan of the storm.

A light sprang up in the kitchen window and cast a

rectangle of pale gold on the grass and upon them, the rain slanting and glittering through it. Fitz stopped and again took Sarah in his arms. "Have you got a lock on your bedroom door? Otherwise, I'll have to sleep with you tonight."

Sarah laughed, her cheek against his wet coat. "Corinna would love that. Illicit romance in her own household."

Fitz put her away. "Corinna would be shocked to her backbone," he said severely. "What wicked thoughts you do have!"

Somebody opened the door for Solly; more light dimly outlined his figure, suddenly galvanized and lithe, springing into the shelter of the house.

"You out there?" Norm called.

"Sure. We're coming."

They got into the entry, their wet clothes dripping. Waves of sound all but submerged the house. Fanny was doing scales again—or hadn't stopped. From above there was the light, brisk sound of Corinna's typewriter. From the library, music, Mozart this time, Sarah thought, but in the confusion she couldn't be sure, and Solly began to bark for his food bowl.

It was by then full dark.

Fanny still singing, but very softly, came in. "I suppose you all want food. I had to work, so I only made some sandwiches."

"Fanny," Fitz said. "The night Forte was shot—I mean that evening—were you singing?"

She lifted plates and set them down on the table. "No. I was exercising."

"Well, but Sarah heard you singing—'The Bell Song'."

Fanny shrugged, but did look slightly embarrassed. "I knew Corinna would be coming home soon. But I didn't know when. I wanted to jog—and of course, you know how Corinna acts as if we let up on any kind of job, especially my singing. So, well, the fact is I just put on any old record I happened to find. 'The Bell Song,'" said

Fanny in real horror. "I wouldn't think of working on that!"

"But . . . but that was what I heard," Sarah said. She believed Fanny.

So, apparently, did the others.

Fitz sighed. "You couldn't have been jogging in the woods or around the garage."

"Of course not. I got outside and decided it was getting too near dusk to run on the highway. Dangerous. So I only walked in the woods. Hard walking, but good for me. Develops the—"

Norm and Fitz broke in together. "Did you see anyone?"

Fanny paused to give each a long look. "You mean did I see anybody standing around waiting for a chance to kill Forte. No, I didn't. Now then, here are the sandwiches."

She strode back into the hall.

Fitz said slowly, "I do wish she had seen somebody—something—but I think she was telling the truth."

"So do I." Norm took Sarah's coat and shook it. "Where have you been?"

"Calling on Rosart," Fitz said shortly. "By the way, do you know what Gus did with Forte?"

"I guessed. Knowing Gus. The old Confederate cemetery, wasn't it?"

"Everybody but me knows everything," Fitz said morosely.

There was a plate of sandwiches and an enormous bowl of salad on the table.

"I'll make fresh coffee," Norm said. "When are we going to go to the police?" He set the coffeepot over the burner.

"I'll be damned," Fitz said slowly, "if I know."

Fanny's singing resumed, Corinna's typewriter continued; so did the music from the library, until the three of them went there and turned the television to the news, got local weather conditions, which indeed they were already aware of, and switched from one program to another, watching none of them, until Corinna appeared in the doorway. "You do know that it's late," she said. "Goodnight."

"Perhaps I'd better lock up the kitchen." Norm vanished.

Fitz saw to the front door and the French windows in the living room. Sarah wondered if she would ever be able to look into the living room without seeing that tragic figure on the floor behind the sofa. Fitz went upstairs with her. "I'll not give Corinna the thrill of a heavy romance," he said and tried the lock on the door. "Works all right. Lock it, but leave the key in the lock— Oh, there you are, Solly."

Solly leaped along the hall, pushed past Sarah and in one bound established himself on the chaise longue with an air of resolution.

Sometime or other, Fanny had stopped singing and probably gone to bed, after tightly closing every window in her room. She'll suffocate someday, Corinna had predicted direly.

Fitz said, "I'll be around somewhere. Yell if you—well, yell."

Sarah locked the door obediently and obediently left the key in the lock. Suddenly the house had become strangely new to her, alien in an indescribable way.

Corinna had left another sleeping capsule on the bedside table. This time it was yellow.

Sixteen

The rain pattered against the windowpanes. Solly settled down and began to snore.

Sarah thumped her pillows and tried to relax, but she could not fall asleep. She saw far too many pictures: Forte behind the sofa; his father, jauntily dashing down the back stairs and into the ancient car and rattling away. Where could he be now?

In view of Rosart's belated observations, it seemed more than likely that Andy was right and it was Forte who had tampered with the brakes on her car. It was perfectly consistent with Forte's pettily angry reaction to the fall from the taxi. It was like Forte, too, to explore Gus's rooms, find Fitz's gun and take it away.

But Forte himself was shot with it.

She turned over and tried to sleep.

But Rosart and Nannie Pie, too, hovered on the edge of her consciousness, so happy, so right for one another. Yet—yet Rosart had always been unpredictable. Had he been as truthful and candid as he had seemed?

But Rosart would never have tried to hurt me, Sarah thought. She turned on the bedside light again. She didn't like those sudden, lonely fears. She just might take the capsule.

It was odd that Corinna had changed them. The first one had been red; this one was yellow. But there were probably many, many kinds of drugs.

Yet, thinking it over, she was reasonably sure that Corinna did not like to take sedatives. She seemed to remember her stern admonitions about the use of such things.

She sat up straight and stared in ugly suspicion at the yellow capsule. It looked perfectly safe—and who would have placed it there if not Corinna? Fanny was almost a zealot in her pursuit of health and independence from medicines; once, indeed, when she had been rehearsing in an out-of-town opera house, the rather violent action required her being dragged across the stage. The stage crew had not put down a ground cloth, and though Fanny had slid along with great dramatic effect, she ended up with long blue-black splinters all along one of her handsome thighs. She had refused to see a doctor, and to nobody's astonishment had treated herself with eyebrow tweezers, hot water, soap and Vaseline. It was another small piece of the patchwork quilt of Favor legend.

So Fanny had not donated the sleeping capsule.

Sarah said aloud, "I'll show this to Fitz," and slid out of bed.

Solly opened one eye as she thrust herself into her dressing gown. Clasping the capsule in one hand, she unlocked the door and started to tiptoe along the hall to the stairs. She was halfway down when she heard the murmur of men's voices; she stopped to listen, and one of the voices was Fitz's! He was saying, "I tell you I don't know what we can do. That is, I know what we must do, but Corinna—"

"I know," Norm said. "It will be hell for all of us!" There was a thump and stir and resultant crackle as if one of them had put fresh logs on the fire. Then Norm said clearly, "But now that we *know* where Forte is, we do have proof, whatever Corinna says."

"It's still hard for me to believe that Forte was into any kind of subversive activity."

Norm apparently settled back into a chair. "I can't see him as a terrorist, either. Yet it seems like an odd coincidence after that business with Bill Hicks."

"You knew about that?"

"Oh, sure. I talked to the pretty girl at the Ligunia desk telephone. Everybody knows it, but nobody seems to want to talk about it."

"Have they found out who shot at him?"

"If so, she didn't know—or didn't tell me. The lid has been clamped down very tight. Fitz, this sounds preposterous, but do you think there's a possibility that Forte *could* have been involved in anything about Ligunia?"

"You and I are the only links Forte had with Ligunia. But other than that, I honestly can't see what Forte could have done to get himself connected even in the smallest way. Also, there has never before been the slightest hint of terrorist activity there. It's obvious that somebody wanted to remove Forte, sure. But Forte—well, we both know he just didn't have sense enough to be of much use to anybody."

"You don't think that somebody might have used him without Forte's knowledge that he *was* being used?"

After a moment Fitz said slowly, "No, I can't accept that. I can see why he would tamper with the brakes on Sarah's car—"

"Andy did say Forte must have done that."

"Rosart saw him at the car! Didn't think to mention it," Fitz said angrily. "And he hadn't thought, either, to mention seeing Forte entering Gus's room afterward, when the subject of a gun arose."

Norm said, "It was dreadful watching that little car

going faster and faster and— Well, thank heavens Sarah managed it perfectly. But, Fitz, that gun—''

"Yes," Fitz said heavily. "If Forte himself took the gun, why was he shot with it? Or *was* he shot with my gun? Only an autopsy would get the bullet for the police so it could be identified."

Both men were silent for a moment, then Norm said, "Forte did brag to Corinna about the money he expected to get, but as Corinna used to say—regretfully but factually— 'The truth isn't in him.' ''

"Money," Fitz said slowly. "Even if he wanted to impress the family—Rosart, Fanny, Corinna, Sarah— But, no, none of them would have been impressed. They knew Forte too well."

Norm said shortly, "Somebody knew him too well for Forte's own good. Fitz, you aren't going to like this, but I talked over the phone today to old Parling—you know, Corinna's lawyer. Nobody heard me. Corinna was working. Typewriter going. Fanny singing."

"Did you tell him—''

"No. And I don't think he has an inkling. I told him that a point had come up in something I was doing. I made it vague, so it sounded as if I was interested only in some point of law."

"Well—''

"I asked what would be the penalty for an accessory after the fact."

"Jail, I should think. And a big fine—or both."

"He made a great to-do, fussing over every word. But what I gathered was that an accessory after or before the fact is one who has taken part in the crime or has shielded or assisted another person in committing a felony. So all of us did in a way shield the murderer. He had things to say about a material witness, too. Said police sometimes had a hard time protecting a material witness. Altogether'' —Norm's face was stern—"we are in a very equivocal position."

"Not equivocal at all. Seems altogether too certain," Fitz said gloomily. "Will he tell Corinna that you talked to him?"

"I don't think so. He didn't seem very interested, as a matter of fact. Seemed to think I was merely asking academic questions. He kidded me a little about my education in a quiet way, but he seemed to feel rather pleased about my lack of knowledge of the basics of criminal law."

There was a long pause. Solly had come quietly down the steps and nudged his long nose under Sarah's arm. Eavesdropping was not nice but it was interesting, she decided. Norm sighed so heavily that she could hear it over the crackle of the fire. "We have to do it, Fitz. I know it's late, they'll say—truly, too late. But now we can guide them to Forte."

It was Fitz, she thought, who rose and started to pace the floor, for his voice came at intervals, closer and then farther away. "You thought you saw somebody out around the garage or the woods somewhere as you ran to the house after you heard Sarah scream."

"Well, yes. In blue jeans and—"

"Fanny wears blue jeans and sneakers. Very dirty sneakers," said Fitz disapprovingly. "But she told us what she was doing when Forte was shot—said she was out walking."

"I believe her."

"And she said she just thrust the first record she came to on the machine, so if Corinna came home while she was out, she'd hear music and might not pounce on Fanny for not practicing."

"Funny! People always think of blondes as being cuddly little creatures—"

Fitz laughed heartily. "Anybody thinking that of Fanny would make a big mistake!"

"She did claim that she and Forte were in love—"

"Oh, Norm! You saw through that! She knew that

Corinna wanted an excuse to keep the police out of this. Fanny simply played for time to give Corinna time to think up something. Fanny—''

"Yes, I know," Norm said broodingly. "Fanny is so beautiful, really. All golden curls and big blue eyes and a perfect face—''

"Splendidly regular, icily calm—" Fitz continued in the same vein.

Someone whispered in Sarah's ear, '''Faultlessly faultless, icily regular, splendidly null!' ''

Sarah knew instantly that Corinna had joined her; only she would be unable to resist correction.

Corinna, in a pink silk housecoat, was sitting on the step above her. She put a finger to her lips. Then she whispered, "Eavesdropping?"

"Interesting," Sarah whispered frankly.

The voices in the library were going on.

"Well, yes." That was Norm. "But I don't believe she ever gives a thought to a man in real life. Unless he can sing.''

"It's too bad, really," Fitz said thoughtfully. "She is beautiful, no question of that. What an Isolde she'd be!"

"Wrong range. But she's got a great future whatever she sings. But let's get back to Forte. Did Rosart know where he had been last summer? On his trips, I mean.''

Fitz said crossly, "I forgot to ask him! But we'll find out. Although Rosart may not know. He seems to have seen just as little of Forte as he could.''.

"Rosart knows quite a lot more than he admits knowing.''

"He's not really secretive. He wouldn't have intentionally concealed anything he knew about Forte.''

"With that beard," Norm said morosely, "he can conceal anything. I didn't mean that he would purposely protect Forte. He just wouldn't be interested.''

Corinna made a slight rustle above Sarah as she leaned her elbows on her silk-covered knees, intent on listening.

Solly had prudently withdrawn; Corinna was not above using her slipper on his sensitive nose if he got in her way.

Presently Fitz said, "I agree. He isn't interested in anything outside his own special world. And yet I ought to have pressed him. Well, I'll see him tomorrow."

"Look here, Fitz. You do realize that that damn gun of yours, which seems to have disappeared again, is our biggest worry now."

"What do you think!" Fitz sounded angry. "I also realize that that man Briggs is still out there somewhere, and he's going to make things very unpleasant for all of us before he gets through. We ought to call the police, even if it's just to put out a warning for a missing car—"

"And bring Briggs back into the picture very prominently—with all he knows?"

"Or suspects. Norm, how do you think he got out of that room? We locked him in. You handed me the key and I gave it to Corinna. She still had it when Briggs got away."

"Gus?" Norm suggested.

Fitz did not seem to consider this worth answering. "That guy didn't crawl out through the keyhole."

There was a faint, fragrant whisper in Sarah's ear—"They'll not go to the police tonight—" then a soft rustle attested to Corinna's departure.

Sarah had completely forgotten the capsule in her hand, which had grown soft from the heat of her palm. It didn't seem so important any more, and she decided not to interrupt the conversation. She also decided to follow Corinna's example and go back to bed. She felt reasonably sure that Norm and Fitz had said everything significant they were likely to say, for she heard one of them give a vast yawn. But they were still talking as she started up the stairs.

Fitz said, "Tomorrow. We'll see about things then."

"What are we going to do?"

"I wish everybody wouldn't ask me that!"

"All right, all right. But I'm for reporting the whole damn thing. And don't try to stop me."

"I'll not try to stop you. But believe me, Corinna will." Then, in a brooding voice, Fitz said, "I hope we can find Corinna's husband. "What a name to go with Cora! Cora Briggs."

Sarah slid inside her room. Solly, waiting at the door, crowded past her and yawned.

She dropped the now dilapidated capsule in the waste basket. She would ask Corinna about it the next morning. She hadn't thought of it while they were on the stairway. They had both been too fully intent upon their eavesdropping.

She, too, hoped they would find Forte's father soon. She turned out the light, and had an uneasy feeling that he was somewhere in the woods, even in the garage, or somewhere watching them.

However, he had obviously not yet gone to the police.

She was pretending that she was asleep, and thinking that surely in a few more moments it would be true, when a slight current of air touched her face. She sat up. The door into the hall was slightly ajar, so the night light always left burning at the top of the stairs shed a faint beam of light into her room. Then the door closed quietly and Fitz whispered, "Don't scream. It's only me." He came close to the bed. "Here—touch me." She felt his hand, warm and strong in the darkness, and sank back. "I didn't mean to frighten you."

"No I . . . I was awake. What's wrong?"

"Nothing. That is, yes. You didn't lock the door. I told you to lock it."

"No, I didn't. I forgot. Fitz, I was on the stairs a while ago. I heard you and Norm talking, so I just listened and—"

"Hear anything of interest?"

"Norm said the penalty—"

"Sure. Not a very attractive prospect, is it? Norm didn't seem to get out of Corinna's lawyer just what penalties we might expect, but it can't be very happy for anybody. But especially—" He drew in a long breath.

"Me," Sarah said. "I found him. And I shoved him out of the taxi and the driver knows it—"

"Don't," Fitz said shortly. "That doesn't mean you shot him. Or even quarreled with him."

"The police will consider it—"

"Let them! That means nothing."

"Fitz, you know that I'll be the first suspect."

"I know no such thing! Anyway, I was thinking of your father. Corinna was right about that, you know. Norm and I—we're young, we haven't any remarkable positions to protect or to be proud of. But your father—why, Sarah, he's a big wheel and don't you forget it."

"I know."

"History has shown us, tragically, that the bigger they are, the harder they can fall."

"Corinna was sitting on the steps, too. She heard—"

"She's now talking to Charles. In her room. But I could hear her voice and I heard her say Charles. You know—somehow, one does shout when it's such a faraway phone call. Anyway, I'm sure he was trying to explain that he couldn't meet her in Rome or anywhere else for the time being, and I think she kept trying to reassure him and still could not come down to brass tacks and tell him why. All these electronic listening devices!" he said sourly. "Now then, goodnight, my love. Dear me, I can't say Sarah Pie, can I? Sarry Pie?" He said experimentally. "No, it doesn't work. Go to sleep."

"Oh, Fitz, either Corinna or Fanny put a sleeping capsule on my table. Last night, too."

"*Put what?*"

"A sleeping pill."

"*Did you take it?*"

"No. It's in the wastebasket."

"Where's your light?"

He snapped on the bedside lamp and went to scramble

in the wastebasket. Solly eyed him and rose, stretching lankily, to see what he was doing.

Fitz drew out the limp capsule. He looked at it for a long time, his face white in the glow from the nearby lamp. Finally he said, "Did you take the first one last night?"

"No. I had been so terrified—and then you came and I was so thankful and *really* tired, I went to sleep peacefully. Knowing you were here," she said flatly.

Fitz gave her a troubled look. "Was it yellow, too?"

"No, it was red."

"As I remember, Fanny is a health fiend. She wouldn't take a pill unless someone shoved it down her throat, and then she'd spit it out." He was frowning, his face shockingly white, his black eyebrows drawn into sharp peaks as he turned the flaccid capsule over and over in his fingers. "I don't think it a good idea to taste it," he said at last.

"Taste it! Fitz!"

"Oh, it's probably some old thing Corinna has had around. I'll ask her tomorrow. If she doesn't know anything about it— Rosart? No. Norm? No. And I honestly don't think Corinna's husband would have the nerve to come into the house and—" He went to her little writing desk and drew an envelope out of a slot. "I'll just put this away. Maybe go to the drugstore tomorrow and check it out."

"Fitz, *nobody*—"

"Somebody tried to strangle you."

Suddenly a bewildering thought struck her. Why hadn't it occurred to her before? She sat up. "I was wearing a red coat that belonged to Fanny."

He dropped the envelope in his pocket. "Yes, I've already puzzled over that. But I can't think of anybody who would want to throttle Fanny, either. Unless she practiced too long and hard."

"You aren't being serious!"

A change came over his face. "I'm serious, all right.

And I'm going to sleep here tonight. Out of my way, Solly.''

There really was nothing she could do about it, even if she wanted to, Sarah thought vaguely as he locked the door and shoved Solly off the chaise longue. Solly didn't like it, but relaxed philosophically on the rug.

Fitz, rather annoyingly, appeared to go instantly to sleep. After a while, watching his Favor nose and firmly closed eyes sink down deeped and deeper into the cushions, she reached out and turned off the bedside light. She thought happily, but sleepily, that they would soon be married. Perhaps even tomorrow. If the judge gave the required permission. At that point she felt so cared-for and thankful for it, she slept.

She woke to another cloudy, dreary day, and after a moment remembered Fitz and looked around. Fitz had gone; Solly had gone. There was, as always, the distant and attractive fragrance of breakfast coffee.

So everybody was downstairs. Nothing at all had happened during the night.

When, showered and dressed, she ran down the stairs, Fanny, Fitz, Norm and Gus were in the kitchen. Corinna, as usual, was probably having breakfast from a tray somebody had obligingly taken to her.

But she was mistaken. She realized that as soon as she saw Gus's face. Something had happened, maybe not during the night, but—

"—in the pond," he was saying dourly. "Saw it this morning. Don't know how long it's been there."

Fitz was standing at the head of the table. There was a short silence. Then he said, "And you're sure nobody was in it."

Seventeen

Gus's heavy gray eyebrows went up and then, crankily, down again. "Think I was going to wade out there and find out? Deep—that lake. Some places. Besides," said Gus, looking suddenly rather old. "I got rheumatism. Bad this kind of weather."

It was the first time she had ever heard Gus admit to having any human ailment. That shocked Sarah almost as much as the chill notion that she was going to hear something she didn't want to hear.

Fitz said, "So you don't know whether he's in the car or not."

"Nope," said Gus. "But we've got to talk to Mrs. Favor before we do anything reckless."

Norm was leaning on his elbows at the table. "Not exactly reckless to call the police," he said, but in a low voice. Gus was clearly in no mood to be trifled with.

Fitz saw Sarah, gave her a quick nod and said to Norm, "We'd better look."

"Not," said Gus predictably, "unless Mrs. Favor says so."

"Gus, you can't stop us, you know."

A gleam came into Gus's eyes. "You don't know where the car is."

"In the lake. That's what you said."

"Now, Fitz, use your head. I didn't say *where* in the lake. That lake is wide—you know that. Long. Of course, if you want to get whole crowds of police out here dragging the lake and starting all kinds of talk— Well, Mrs. Favor won't like it."

"But, Gus—" Norm began.

"Fitz said, "How did you happen to see it if you think we can't?"

Gus waited a moment, eyes busy and shining under his bushy eyebrows. "Guess maybe I knew where to look. Anyway, I thought it over last night and decided to tell you what happened to the car. "So"—he cast a baleful look around at all of them—"so you wouldn't report a stolen car to the police and start all sorts of talk and— Well, that's all I have to say."

And it was all he would say. He turned around and walked out.

Sarah shuddered as she visualized the car, the car Briggs had stolen, sunk in the pond. And perhaps, just perhaps, Briggs with it!

Clearly, Norm and Fitz were seeing the same picture.

Norm said thoughtfully, "Do you think Gus—"

Fitz shook his head. "Murder? He's not *that* devoted to anybody!"

Norm rose. "Well, we might as well try to find the car."

"We'll need rakes. Even then—"

"Oh, for goodness sake!" Fanny waved a spoon in the air. "Do you really think you can drag that lake? Out of your heads—" she went back to stirring something.

Sarah said absently, "What was that thing Gus was carrying in his hand?"

Both Norm and Fitz simply stared at her. Fanny, however, answered. "That old baseball bat that's been standing out there in the entry for—oh, years and years. Since you two stopped knocking baseballs into the windows."

"Gus," said Fitz "is scared. He's sure Briggs is in that car. So he's carrying that old baseball bat to—well, arm himself, I suppose. And I'll bet he knows what happened to my gun. If I could make him tell—"

"Maybe he doesn't know."

Fitz said, "Let's eat. Then we'll do what we can about the car, Norm. If that man Briggs—"

"You think he's in the car," Fanny said and set down a plate of handsomely browned pancakes. "If he is, he deserved it. I think—" she added doubtfully. "A mean man, that's a fact, but still—" Her eyes widened. "Why, Fitz, you and Norm are thinking he may have been shot, or something, and the car run into the lake and—Corinna's not going to like that."

Corinna said from the doorway, "What is Corinna not going to like?"

Fitz told her. "The old car is in the Simmons lake. Gus told us. He refuses to say exactly where it is. I'm afraid it'll take the police to find it."

Corinna's hand clutched the frame of the door, but after a second or two she regained her poise. "Not just yet. Probably—well, there are a number of ways that old car could have run itself into the lake."

Fanny suddenly gave a fine operatic groan. Everyone turned as if on a string to look at her. She was standing at the trash can, holding the cover in one hand and eggshells in the other.

"What on earth, Fanny—" Fitz began.

"That Rosart! This hasn't been emptied! He can't remember anything that requires a little work. Fitz, Norm—you've got to take this out and empty it. I *will not* have it in the kitchen another day. Another minute!"

They went like schoolboys. There were in fact two receptacles. One was for cans and papers, to be deposited in a pit and sent for recycling. The other went to Gus's compost heap back of the garage.

Fitz grasped one can, Norm the other; they went out the back entry. One of them was swearing, but quietly.

Corinna said coldly, "I wish to talk to you, Sarah."

Sarah knew that tone in her voice. Now what have I done, she thought. But, unexpectedly hungry, she took several more bites of pancake, swallowing as she followed Corinna toward the library. Once there, Corinna said, "Get that down. No use trying to talk with your mouth full. Now then—" She sat down in her favorite wing chair. "I saw Fitz coming out of your room. Early this morning. I take it he spent the night with you."

"He did. But it's not what you think."

"Never mind what I think. I'll not have it. That's all."

"But, Corinna—" She wished she had the courage to mention glass houses, as Fanny had done.

Corinna said sharply, "You're going to say that you'll be married soon. But you are not married yet, so—"

Again Sarah bit back the indignant comment she was about to make.

"You're thinking of your father and me. That's different."

Sarah thought for a moment, then said soberly, meaning only what she said, with no intention of being ironic, "I suppose it's always different—"

Corinna didn't like that, either. "No impertinence, if you please."

"I didn't mean to be impertinent. I was only thinking—well, it's true, isn't it? Every love affair is different from any other—"

"Depends," said Corinna shortly. "Sometimes they're far too much alike. Now then—"

"Wait, Corinna. That reminds me. There was a capsule on my bedside table. Did you put it there?"

"A . . . capsule?" Corinna leaned back, looking puzzled and distressed.

"Yellow. And the night before there was a red one."

Corinna opened her lips, closed them again—and grasped the arms of the chair. "I had some capsules for sleep. That time I sprained my wrist. But I don't like to take them. There were two bottles in my medicine cabinet. One red," she said, "and one yellow." She thought for a moment, then shook her head. "I have no idea how many there were left—I remember that I took only a few. But"—her face was bleak—"anybody could have taken them, Sarah. I didn't put them in your room."

"Somebody was on the stairs—that first night after Forte was shot."

"Are you sure of that, Sarah?"

"Yes. That is, I heard the creak and then—well, then just nothing."

"Didn't that dog of yours bark?"

"No. He sat up and listened. But then he just went to sleep again."

Corinna frowned. "Probably it was Fanny raiding the refrigerator. She does that. Obviously it was nothing—nobody, I mean."

"So nothing happened," Sarah said flatly. "Corinna, remember, I was wearing Fanny's red raincoat when—"

"Yes, I did think of that. Did you tell anyone that you thought perhaps someone had attacked you, believing you to be Fanny?"

"I told only Fitz. He didn't think it likely that anyone would try to . . . to strangle Fanny."

The flicker of a rather sardonic smile touched Corinna's lips. "Nobody in his right mind would try to tackle Fanny. However, stranger things have happened. Fanny doesn't bother much about tact. I suppose it could be that she insulted some other singer or even a conductor, or— Well, perhaps there is somebody who's jealous of her. Doesn't want her to do Amneris." She paused, sighed and said, "But I'm sure nobody would try to kill Fanny for those reasons. About these capsules, Sarah. What did you do with them?"

"Fitz has the yellow one. He's going to take it to the druggist and find out what's in it."

Corinna became thoughtful, swinging one knee over the other. Somehow, Corinna's slacks were always trimly cut and gracefully tailored, and were that morning pressed knife-edged neat. "I don't know," she said at last. "I think Fitz is right to find out what's in that capsule. What happened to the red one?"

"I threw it in the wastebasket."

"Get it out—"

"I can't. Fitz looked. It was gone."

"Oh." Corinna's foot stopped swinging. "Somebody removed it, obviously." She made a leap into speculation. "Len Briggs might have come back to the house. Yes, perhaps he did—trying to find something—"

"Norm and Fitz think he's in the car in the lake."

"But that's only an assumption. He's wily as an eel. He got out of that room, didn't he? I still can't imagine how. I had the key in my hand."

"Just opened the door, he said. There must be another key."

"You mean Gus could have another key and let him out. I thought of that. Yet—" She stopped, for there were voices in the hall. "Somebody's at the phone—" Corinna began when the door opened and Fanny rushed in. "Rosart's calling the doctor and he won't come! Corinna, you'll have to talk to him."

Corinna rose. *"Rosart?"*

"No, no. The doctor. He says we've got to take Fitz to the hospital, and Rosart says the doctor has got to come here—"

Sarah didn't stay to hear more. Since Fanny had planted her stalwart body in the doorway, Sarah remembered later that she had given Fanny a thrust in the stomach with her elbow which—a miracle—sent Fanny staggering backward. Rosart was at the telephone. "But, Doctor, he's been shot—he's got to have you—he says no hospital. Of course he's still conscious, but he can't talk to you, Doctor—''

Corinna had followed Sarah swiftly. Sarah was at the dining-room door when she heard Corinna. "Doctor, this is Corinna Favor, we really do need you—''

Norm was holding Fitz upright in a chair. Fitz was blue-white, blood dripping down his shoulder, his arm— Sarah couldn't see anything but Fitz's face. He was saying, "All right, all right! No harm done, I think.''

"Fitz—oh, Fitz—''

"Don't touch him, Sarah!'' Norm said sharply. "You'll just make it bleed more. Has Rosart got the doctor?''

"No—yes—that is, Corinna—Fitz, what happened?''

"Stop it!'' Norm shook her arm authoritatively. "He's in no condition to talk. If you want to help, get some towels. Hurry!''

Fitz looked at Sarah. "I tell you it's all right—'' His words were cut off by a gasp.

Sarah was terrified. She put a hand on Fitz's shoulder and felt the sticky red ooze; panic-stricken, she turned away and ran toward the stairs and up to the linen closet.

Corinna had hung up the telephone and was hurrying down the hall. Fanny and Rosart passed Sarah as if neither one saw her.

Towels! Yes, big towels. Huge bath towels. Would they check that dreadful ooze? She seized an armful and rushed down the stairs. Nannie Pie had come from somewhere; sensibly she had brought kitchen towels and was holding a pad of them on Fitz's shoulder. She took it away to permit Sarah to apply a heavier towel.

But the doctor *was* coming. They must listen for his car. Fanny thudded off to the kitchen, muttering about hot tea with sugar for shock. Rosart mumbled below his beard and Corinna held Fitz's wrist tight—too tight, for she couldn't find the pulse. Norm corrected her. "Here—let me—''

It was all they could do: hold one towel after another to Fitz's shoulder. Nannie Pie helped Sarah.

"But what happened?" Corinna cried, leaning on the table like an old, old woman. "How did it happen?"

Norm, his fingers still on Fitz's wrist, said, "I don't know. I simply don't know. We were together."

"Taking out the trash cans," Fanny said.

"Yes. You told us to. And then—I don't know who shot him or why or—"

"But you were there," Fanny said.

"No, I wasn't." Norm frowned down at Fitz's wrist, seemed to be listening, feeling for the pulse, and said absently, "I had the orange peels and eggshells and all that, and I went to dump them onto Gus's compost heap. Last I saw, Fitz was bending over the other can, the one for the things that could be recycled—"

"Cans," said Fanny. "Papers. Magazines—"

Norm nodded. "I thought I'd just go and take a look at the lake. All that talk of Gus's about the car. Anyway, I had barely got into the woods toward the lake when I heard a shot. I was scared—"

Rosart broke in. "I was scared, too. I heard the shot and ran out toward the back of the garage. There was Fitz, doubled up over the trash heap—papers and junk in his hands." He touched his sagging pockets. "I got all those, just junk. Norm came running from the woods. So we got him to the house—"

"Who shot him?" Corinna said stiffly, almost accusingly.

Norm shook his head. "I tell you I don't know. I didn't see anyone—anywhere. I only heard the shot. Hold on now, Fitz—" Fitz had given a weak murmur. "The doctor's coming. He'll be here in a few minutes."

It was—literally—not many minutes, although it seemed a long time, before the doctor came running in, his little bag swinging.

After his arrival, the nightmarish scene returned to sanity, became more orderly.

"Now, just a whiff of ether." The doctor looked at Sarah. "Think you can manage?"

"Tell me what to do."

"Just hold this so he breathes it. I'll tell you when to let up."

The sickly-sweet smell crept over them all. Sarah held the pad and the tiny cone. In a moment or two Fitz gave a stifled groan and slumped down.

"Good," said the doctor cheerfully. "Now I can get at it—"

It was a bullet, which the doctor dug out of Fitz's shoulder and placed on the table as casually as he would have put down a spoon. Sarah continued to assist the doctor.

Eventually Fitz was bandaged up and a sling was adjusted to hold his arm; he opened his eyes. "Here," said the doctor, extracting a capsule from his bag. "Take this. It's only a sedative. You"—he turned to Sarah—"are a born nurse. Glad to have you—anytime you want a job."

"Married," Fitz said groggily. "Married . . . Mine . . ."

The doctor's eyes twinkled. "We should get him to the hospital."

"*No!*" said Fitz.

The doctor hesitated briefly, then nodded at Norm and Rosart. "Will you get him to bed?"

Rosart and Norm together lifted Fitz, who gave a faint murmur, tried to struggle and fell back. Nannie Pie, white-faced, followed them.

The doctor turned briskly to Corinna. "We've got to get him to the hospital later, you know. I can't tell how close to the bone that shot went. I need some x-rays. May have splintered the bone. Besides, I don't intend to run any risk of infection. But right now, we'll let him rest."

Corinna was sitting at the end of the table, looking like a very pretty doll who had regrettably lost her stuffing. Fanny muttered. "Got to clean up this mess. Help me, Sarah."

Fitz's jacket and sweater were streaked with red; red towels everywhere. Sarah numbly started to roll up the jacket and sweater. Fanny said, "No hot water now, Sarah. Only cold water to take out the bloodstains." She glanced at Corinna. "You'll be wanting brandy or something. Well, you're going to have sweetened tea. Do you more good than alcohol. Drink—drink—drink—" Fanny all but chanted. "Nothing but drink all day long." She vanished toward the kitchen.

The doctor, not surprisingly, stared at Corinna. "Does she mean he was drunk? At this time of the day?"

Corinna did have the strength to shake her head. "No. It's just that Fanny disapproves of any kind of drinking. She does take something occasionally, but on the whole—"

"I see. A food faddist."

"Well, not exactly."

Fanny came back with a cup of steaming tea and put it down beside Corinna. "Drink that."

The doctor got out a small black notebook. "Now then, Mrs. Favor, I have to report this, you know. A gunshot wound. Do you have any idea how the accident happened?"

Sarah glanced at Corinna, who now looked like a very pretty doll who miraculously had got back some stuffing. Of course, she thought, it was the word accident. What was she going to say to account for this?

Fanny said sharply, "Hurry up, Sarah. The stains will set."

She was still in a daze of fear and confusion. She took Fitz's jacket and sweater to the laundry, put them down on the table and fled up the back stairs.

Rosart and Norm had got Fitz into pajamas and settled in bed. His eyes were open, but he still looked deathly pale. Nannie Pie, at his side, said, "You can talk later. You boys get out."

Probably nobody in his life had ever told Rosart, peremptorily, to get out. But Nannie Pie displayed no hesitation. Rosart gave her a surprised look but seemed to decide he'd better obey, and got out. Norm looked at Fitz, mumbled, "You'll be all right, Fitz. The doctor says so."

"*Out!*" said Nannie Pie.

Norm also was not proof against the adamant figure; he backed out, almost apologetically.

"That's better. Fitz has got to be quiet. Now I'll leave him to you. "Nannie Pie vanished.

Sarah knelt down beside Fitz. He seemed to be aware of her, and put out his bandaged arm and said, again, "It's all right."

"But the sedative must have been a strong one. He was already mumbling. He gave a sigh and closed his eyes. In only a short time the doctor came lightly into the room. "Doing all right?" he asked Sarah.

"I don't know! Oh, I don't know."

"Well, now I'll just give him an antibiotic. Hold his arm."

She held his arm and watched as the doctor filled the needle and thrust it into Fitz's arm.

"That's fine." The doctor straightened, replaced small objects axnd closed his black bag, then said slowly, "'There's always a danger of infection in these accidental wounds."

Accidental, Sarah thought. She said, "Did Corinna know what—I mean, how it happened?"

"No. That is, she wasn't sure. She said somebody—one of your cousins—had found him, outdoors somewhere. She thought nobody had heard the sound of a shot. Dear Mrs. Favor, it was a great shock to her."

And undoubtedly, Corinna had lifted her lovely eyes in a plea for protection and knightly aid from the big, strong man. Not that the doctor was especially big, but he was a man, Sarah reflected briefly. The doctor brightened. "But then your cousin—I mean that lovely girl with the blue eyes and golden hair—a beautiful woman," said the doctor on a tangent and rather dreamily. "Strong. Healthy. Well, she came in and said that there were sometimes illegal hunters in the woods, and obviously a stray shot had caught your—I mean this cousin."

He looked down at Fitz and nodded. "I'll be back this afternoon."

Sarah said stiffly, "You have the bullet you dug out of his shoulder."

"Oh, yes. In my pocket." He reached into a pocket, searched, opened his medicine bag, searched, went through his pockets again, and finally said, "That's strange. I thought I had it."

Eighteen

Oh, yes, Sarah thought. You put it on the table. And it disappeared.

The doctor said crossly. "I suppose your beautiful cousin—Miss Fanny, isn't it? The singer? I suppose she gathered it up when she took the towels and cotton pads away."

Until that instant the vague but welcome notion of an outsider, someone who could come and go in the house and yet was not one of the family, had almost established itself in her mind. But only the family—only—was in the room when the bullet vanished.

She crossed an enormous chasm—with the strange feeling that she ought to have done so long ago.

Yet in a way she had partially crossed it during the first hour or so after Forte's murder; she had painstakingly called the short roll of the family members—and, with what she had felt was reason, refused to accept even a conjecture that any one of them was a killer. Now she was forced to acknowledge an ugly and unwelcome fact. Someone in the family was a murderer.

There are times when a decision announces that it has

been made—that it cannot be denied. This was one of those times. Sarah said, "No, someone took it. It's gone—in the woods, anywhere. Someone—"

The doctor stared at her. She cast one glance at Fitz, who might have tried to stop her, might not have approved. She thought swiftly, Whether or not, this is what I must do before . . . before someone shoots again, and this time kills him.

"You must call the police, Doctor—"

"Police! But this is only a gunshot accident! There's no hurry." He made a rather flurried motion toward Fitz, who couldn't see, couldn't hear, didn't know.

"Not that one—I can't let it go on when there is danger"—the word caught in her throat; she tried again—"danger to him. Or to me or to anyone else. Murder—"

"My dear Miss Favor—"

"Yes. Here! In the house! They took Forte away. He's buried in the old Confederate cemetery on the Simmons place. They—we—all agreed not to report the murder to the police, but it was murder. And now—" The doctor's mouth was open; he was shocked and disbelieving. She said, "And now there's a car in the lake, on the Simmons place. We think there may be a man named Briggs in the car—"

"You really mean this!"

He seemed to see in her face that she did mean it. He said, almost gasping, "Where is the nearest phone?"

She must have motioned toward Corinna's room, for he dashed out the door, dashed back again to snatch his bag, as if someone might wrest it away, and then out again.

I hope I've done the right thing; I had to do it; they'll all hate me. She was mumbling to herself. Fitz seemed to hear something—he stirred a little, unconsciously, thoroughly drugged now.

She heard the doctor's voice, high-pitched with concern, with excitement, but with belief. At least he was calling the police; he hadn't let Corinna prevent him. He hadn't even waited to talk to Corinna, or anyone else.

So, now, what would they do?

She closed the bedroom door. She drew a chair up to the bed and sat there stonily; once in a while she touched Fitz's wrist and searched for a pulse, and was relieved when she felt the steady rhythm. She wondered how soon the police would arrive, how soon they would get the car out of the lake and what they would find in it, how soon everyone would be told of her treachery— Treachery? They could call it that. She wondered, but only vaguely, just what each one would say—how they would explain, how they would cover themselves.

Yet in fact, once they knew that the police knew—no, none of them would seek excuses. There was too much inherent courage in the family to allow for that.

There had been no other course she could have taken. The course *they* had all taken had nearly cost Fitz his life.

And there was always Fitz's gun, which Gus had said had disappeared again. Guns don't walk.

She put her hand on Fitz's wrist lightly, and kept it there.

The commotion was beginning downstairs.

First the police car—two cars, surely. Voices. The doctor's, Corinna's, then Fanny's and Norm's and—yes, Rosart's voice suddenly joined in the mingled sounds that wafted their way upstairs.

She heard someone say the lake, yes, the lake; that was clear. She heard a door slam; she heard Gus then, shouting at somebody, probably one of the police, she thought wryly, and Solly, outside somewhere, barking furiously. An automobile started up again and raced down the driveway. So they were going to look for the car—and possibly (probably) find Briggs's body. They were going to find Forte's burial place.

Nobody came near Sarah while that search went on. She

was now certain that the family was thinking of her as a renegade, a traitor.

Fitz didn't stir.

The sounds downstairs dulled, retired to another part of the house. Perhaps Norm and Rosart and Gus had gone with the police, to show them the way, to point out the exact spots.

It was a long, long time before the door opened cautiously and Nannie Pie poked in a scared white face. "Can I come in?" she whispered.

Sarah nodded and said, also whispering, "What are they doing?"

Nannie Pie brought a tray; she put it down on Fitz's writing table.

"They found Briggs in the car. And they found the grave where Gus told them and—I brought you some hot soup. How is he?"

They both looked at Fitz's face, relaxed and quiet.

Nannie Pie nodded. "Good thing he's missing all this." She took a long, wavering breath.

"Is everyone very, very—"

Nannie Pie guessed. "Upset? Oh, yes. But I don't think anybody blames you. They seem—I don't know how to say it—relieved?"

"Oh. Well, what are the police doing?"

"Questioning. Everybody. There are more policemen—I think they're state police. I think they're going to question you."

"Oh, of course."

Rosart stuck his head in the door; his eyes were blazing above his great beard. "I put them in the trash can! How was I to know there was anything important? Come on, Nannie Pie—"

"Wait, Rosart. What did you put in the trash can?"

He eyed Sarah sharply. "Why, Forte's junk," he said, as if it were the most sensible thing in the world. "All the stuff he had in a drawer in that room he used. I had to clean it up, hadn't I, before Nannie Pie got here?''

"What papers?" Sarah asked stiffly.

"Oh, just junk. I threw it away, I told you. But Fitz found them. All that junk in his hands. I shoved them in my pocket. Now they've got it all out on the dining-room table, along with stuff they took out of Briggs's pocket. Did Nannie Pie tell you?''

Sarah must have nodded. Rosart went on. ''They're drying things out with Fanny's hair dryer so they can read them. One of them said not to take the time for the police laboratory just now. Gus found the gun.''

Her heart leaped. ''Fitz's gun?''

"Sure. Guess where it was. Simply tied up in a tree not far from the garage. Four shells gone, Gus said. That meant two for Forte and one for Briggs and one for Fitz this morning—''

She plucked out one inconsistent fact. ''*Two* shots for Forte?''

Fitz muttered and stirred. Nannie Pie whispered, ''That's what somebody said. We'd better get out, Rosart. Now. Come on.''

They tiptoed away, Nannie Pie like a small tug, leading the way for an enormous steamship.

It was late in the afternoon when Sarah thought of the soup. It was cold and had no taste, but she drank it slowly, watching Fitz, who didn't move or try to speak again.

It was much later when the door opened very quietly and Corinna came in, softly. ''Is he all right?''

"I think so. Sleeping . . .''

"I'll stay with him. The police want you downstairs.''

"Corinna, I *had* to tell the doctor to send for them—''

"Oh, I know. You were right, child. We couldn't have held out—we shouldn't have tried to. It nearly killed Fitz. Go on.''

"What will they do to us?''

Corinna managed a rather bleak smile. ''I don't know. I

ried to explain but— Don't look like that. They can't hang us.''

Sarah swallowed hard. Corinna's understanding and, surely, her forgiveness were almost more than she could accept.

"I'm sorry. I had to—"

"Oh, I know. I know. What do I do for Fitz? Medicine or . . ."

"Just sit there. Watch him. That's all. I'll be back soon," Sarah said, then wondered when she would return and in what circumstances. But she was no more culpable than the rest of the family.

It was poor reassurance.

The police—represented by the two from the village, who had searched the woods, and another man, a stranger, in state police uniform—were waiting for her in the library.

The young policeman, Barney Cloom, ushered her in and closed the library door. She told her story.

She told it over. She told it over again. Barney had a recording machine; he gave her an apologetic look as he explained that it was to record the entire interview and of course she wouldn't mind.

It wouldn't matter if she did mind, Sarah thought, and said it was all right.

She lost count of the times she had gone over everything she could remember—from the time she had returned to the house after seeing Fitz off, to this morning, when the shot had come from somewhere and Fitz could so easily have been killed by it.

There was at last a slight pause. Barney stared at the carpet; the state policeman adjusted his belt, as if it were a little tight. The older village policeman, Captain Wood, said at last, "Did you—that is, Forte—have anything to do with Ligunia?"

"Ligunia!" Up to then none of them had mentioned Ligunia. She said, "Why, I . . . I don't think so! I'm not sure. All of us knew, of course, that Fitz was posted to

Ligunia. But Forte said—well, he called Fitz our hero, as if—Oh, he could have meant—''

Captain Wood said quickly, ''As if he knew there had been trouble there. Now then, I rather think you have been told not to speak of anything about Ligunia or Fitz's assignment there. I have to tell you that we must know everything, I mean everything you know or have been told. This is murder,'' he said grimly. ''Two murders. One attempt to strangle you. One attempt to kill Fitz. Now then . . .''

His attitude said: Make up your mind. Tell the truth, the whole truth and nothing but the truth. The phrases almost spoke in her ears.

All right, then. Fitz couldn't speak for himself. ''The man there, Bill Hicks, whose place Fitz was to take, was shot.''

Captain Wood and the state policeman nodded encouragingly. Barney turned scarlet and muttered, low, ''Miranda . . .''

Captain Wood turned on him. ''I'm not trying to trap her into anything like a confession! But perhaps it would be best to destroy the record. Come to think of it''—he made up his mind and turned again to Barney—''turn that thing off. We'll have to keep our mouths shut about this unless—or until—it's all right to talk of it. Understand?''

Young Barney nodded. ''Yes, sir,'' he said smartly. The state policeman's eyes were bulging, but he, too, nodded.

''All right, then. Now, Miss Favor, tell us all you know—or rather, tell us whatever young Fitz Favor told you.''

''He made me promise.'' She felt tears in her eyes. ''And I promised. But it seems different. He was nearly killed—''

''Go on. Don't take note of this, Barney. We can keep what we need in our heads.''

Whatever she had promised Fitz, she had to break that promise now, because it had been nullified by his own narrow escape from death.

So she talked.

All three men listened so closely that when one of them hifted in his chair, it was like a sharp creak in the silence f the room.

Corinna, of course, was upstairs with Fitz. Probably the thers were huddled around the kitchen table, the dining oom, anywhere—all together. Certainly none of them ould hear through the solid mahogany panels of the ibrary door. It was like a sober confessional to officers of he law only.

When she finished, there was still silence. Finally Captain Wood said, "Your aunt's—I mean Mrs. Favor's— usband, this Briggs, we found—among other things in his ocket—a passport. It had been used on a trip to Ligunia. n August."

"Briggs?"

"He also had been in Georgia. The receipted bill from n Atlanta hotel was in his pocket too." He paused. "The nan—that is, his son . . ."

Barney muttered, "Forte."

"Yes, Forte. Among the papers your . . ."

Again Barney supplied the name. "Rosart. The poet."

"Yes. Among the papers he dumped in the trash can vas a receipt from the same Atlanta hotel for a few days at he same dates, so apparently Forte met his father there. At east, he could have. However, it seems his father remained n Atlanta after Forte left."

Sarah fumbled through his statements. "But I don't ee . . . I don't understand . . ."

"Well," Captain Wood said more briskly "We don't, ither. Not yet. But there must have been a reason for 3riggs's remaining there, and later turning up here and nquiring for his son. They must have planned to meet. Now this shot—the one that killed Forte Favor—Briggs, vhatever his name was—"

"Doesn't matter," Barney murmured. "We all knew im. Didn't know much good of him, either—"

"That will do." Captain Wood spoke sternly. The state policeman said, "Miss Favor, will you please begin at the beginning again."

"But I did—"

"I mean from the time you reached home and came into the house—every detail. You didn't see Forte then. Did you?"

"No, no. I told you. I just went upstairs—"

"Didn't hear anyone?"

"I heard Fanny—that is, it wasn't Fanny. It was a record. But just for a moment I thought it was Fanny. Then I went upstairs—"

"Nothing else?"

"No. Well, I noticed a kind of odor of some kind. I thought a fire had been lighted or Fanny was cooking something. But it wasn't that kind of smell. I went upstairs, and hadn't been there long when I heard the shot."

Barney, Captain Wood and the state policeman exchanged a long look; without a word they went out into the hall and closed the door. She could hear only a murmur of voices. When they came back, Captain Wood took over the questioning. "There were four shells gone from the revolver Gus found hidden in a tree. Just hanging there by a piece of rope. Now, our medical examiner has taken a look at Forte's body. He can't be sure, but he thinks there was only one shot—and fatal. Of course, he can't even guess the exact time Forte was shot. But now we— I wonder if you'll be so kind as to go up to your room and open the windows and just wait."

"Why—why, no! That is, yes." Sarah got to her feet.

Barney turned toward her. "Shall I go with her? Sir," he remembered to add, looking at Captain Wood, who nodded.

What is it now? Sarah thought wearily. She went up the stairs, glanced toward Fitz's room, wishing she could return to him, but led the way, obediently, into her own room. She opened the windows and then stood there, thinking of such a hodgepodge of possibilities, reasons, motives that she could not select any one which seemed likely. "Listen," said Barney. But he stood with his back to the door as if to prevent her leaving.

The windows let in a mild, rather damp current of air. When the gunshot came, it blasted through the late-afternoon silence.

Her ears were shocked by the sudden sound. She put her hands over them, and then cried, "But it was on the terrace! Not in the living room at all! It was outside—"

Barney merely nodded, went in a leap to the window and shouted down, "All right. She heard. So did I! All right!"

"I don't understand." Sarah took her hands down. "I heard it that evening, but I thought it was in the living room."

"That," said Barney, looking as if he felt sorry for her, "could have been what you were supposed to think."

"But I— Oh," said Sarah. "Oh!"

"Well, what?" Captain Wood and the state policeman were already at the door; she hadn't known that they had opened it. Captain Wood nodded. "Looks that way," he said into space.

An acid whiff of gun smoke had drifted in through the open window. Sarah said, "*That's* what I smelled! When I came into the house. I thought it was chrysanthemums, but it wasn't. I thought of something cooking. But then I went upstairs. I didn't smell it then. I heard the shot here, but I didn't wait. I ran downstairs. But I never, never thought of gun smoke. It's the same." She was shocked but certain. "Why, then . . . then Forte . . ."

All three men nodded. Captain Wood said, "It's what we thought possible after we heard your version of Forte's murder. Of course, it's impossible now for anybody to say just when Forte was killed. But it looks as if he was dead before you reached home."

Barney said slowly, "That would mean one shot for Forte. Then one outside and into the air, below those windows. To suggest that he was killed after Sarah had got home."

"But why?"

Captain Wood replied, "Probably to confuse the time of the murder. In order to suggest that the murderer was not here at the time of the actual killing. You were supposed to think that Forte was shot just then—after you had returned home. And consequently—" He thought for a long moment, and then nodded. "Yes. If you were in danger of being charged with murder, simply because you were in the house—and then found Forte—wouldn't Fitz have tried to come home immediately to help you? Wouldn't he?"

"Not if he didn't know. And I had promised not to try to get in touch with him except by letter. I told you why."

"But you did write to him."

"Oh, yes. But it would have been days before he got the letter. It was my father who arranged for Fitz to come back. Corinna told him enough to let him know that there was some very serious problem here."

Barney said unexpectedly, "Please, sir. I don't think Sarah was in any real danger at all. Yes, there was the brake failure. That does sound like Forte. Mean, but didn't hurt her. And the business in the woods. She was frightened but she wasn't really hurt."

Sarah said slowly, "There were those capsules—"

"Oh, yes. We'll see about them. But—no," Captain Wood said. "It's likely Barney is right. Forte could have tampered with the brakes out of sheer cussedness. Seems likely, too, that he prowled around Gus's place and took that revolver. How he got himself shot with it is something else."

He paused, then said, "Yes, seems to me there was a deliberate intention to frighten you. So seriously that you would send for Fitz." Barney shuffled from one foot to the other, his face intent. The state policeman seemed to be gazing into space. There was another pause.

At last Captain Wood said to Sarah, "Did you tell anyone about the odor in the hall when you opened the front door?"

"Why, I . . . no. That is, yes. Oh, I don't remember!"

"Try to remember."

"Fitz. Norm. Perhaps someone else—I can't remember! What are you going to do?"

"Talk to Fitz," said Captain Wood. "Barney, which room?"

The world was whirling. Sarah went into the hall with the three men, each of whom seemed to feel it necessary to go on tiptoes. But when Barney tapped lightly and then opened the door to Fitz's room, Corinna said calmly, "Come in."

Fitz said, "What was that shot?"

Captain Wood drew a manila envelope from inside his tunic. He said, "We'll explain," opened the envelope and delved into papers within it.

Fitz was sitting up against pillows, color in his face and his eyes very bright and sensible. "Come here, Sarah—" He motioned with his uninjured arm, and she sat down on the edge of the bed. Captain Wood drew a crinkled and stiff paper from the envelope and gave it to Fitz. "Will you tell us just what this is?"

Fitz gave it one look. "It's a map of Ligunia."

"Yes, that's what we thought. But why would this Briggs carry such a thing in his pocket, along with the passport that he used to enter Ligunia and return here last summer?"

"Briggs! In Ligunia? I don't know. Bill Hicks, whose place I am to take, might know of Briggs's visit. Yes, he'd know. But that whole affair is to be kept very quiet until—"

"We know," Captain Wood said.

"I told them," Sarah said. "I told them everything, Fitz."

"All right." Fitz gave her a quick but approving look. "There isn't much use in trying to keep it secret now." He looked at the three men gravely. "I think they understand—"

"We understand some," Captain Wood said bluntly. "Not all. Tell me, what's that ridge there. Mountains?" He put a heavy finger on the map.

"They call them mountains. It's really a range of what we'd call hills."

With the air of a conjurer, Captain Wood drew out another piece of paper. Sarah could see that it was covered with rather scratchy writing. Fitz took it and looked; his mouth shut very tightly.

Barney said, "Looks to me like some kind of sales agreement. In French, but not very good French. My high school French—that's not too good, either. But that's the way it looks to me."

"That's the way it is," Fitz said.

"What is there of value in that bit of land?" Captain Wood asked.

Barney's whole face blazed with excitement. "Oil!"

Fitz shook his head. "No. Not oil. But possibly something very scarce. Very valuable." Then he lapsed into silence.

Nineteen

Captain Wood, Corinna, the state policeman, Barney, Sarah waited for Fitz's next words. Finally he lifted his eyes. "I said something scarce and valuable. A very precious metal. I have a list of all these things in my briefcase. But as I remember it, there were reports of some finds of molybdenum ore. Reported very vaguely—not as established facts, but reported."

"Mol—" Captain Wood began, but again Barney burst out. "I know! Molybdenum. Need it for nuclear research and—"

"Wait now, Barney. Would this sales agreement—if that's what it is," Captain Wood said, with an air of refusing to be influenced by any young squirt like Barney. "Would such an agreement, in the normal course of affairs, have come to your office, Fitz?"

"Why, yes. Probably. It's a Ligunian law. If one of our nationals—"

"You didn't turn the paper over."

Fitz turned it over. "Looks like the rest of the agreement. Signed by somebody—a Ligunian name. Nobody I know of there— But then, I wouldn't know—" He stopped abruptly. "Why, that's Briggs! Corinna, that's Briggs's signature! Do you know anything about this?"

"No." Corinna wouldn't even look at the signature on the paper.

Captain Wood nodded. "Now then, suppose this Briggs and his son, Forte, had got together enough money—"

"As things stood until recently, they wouldn't have had to get together much," Fitz said tensely. "Acres in those hills were formerly to be bought for peanuts."

"Not now—if anybody sitting at the desk this Bill Hicks occupied, and you were to occupy, saw the sales agreement."

Fitz said after a moment, "Yes. Yes, I'm afraid I begin to see. Molybdenum ore—Briggs and Forte. Sure, they had to get Bill Hicks out. Briggs was there. Briggs could have shot at Bill—must have, not to kill, only to remove him. But that's only a guess."

"Reasonable," said Captain Wood shortly.

"But then"—Fitz's face seemed to tighten—"then, I was sent to take Bill's place."

Nobody spoke for a moment, yet there was a strong feeling of understanding among them.

"Things went wrong," Captain Wood said soberly.

"A mistake," Fitz said, as if agreeing to an unspoken fact. "A turn they didn't plan on, or expect. A matter of a hole in their timing. Bill—yes, Bill was shot too soon. Perhaps the opportunity to shoot him arose, and I was assigned immediately. That stopped the whole scheme until they could get rid of me, get me sent back here—anything." He was growing tired: that or the drug the doctor had given him was resuming its power.

Fitz sank back on the pillows; his eyes closed. He seemed to struggle against fatigue, sat up—but sank back again. The state policeman said, in a low voice, as if he didn't want to rouse Fitz, "If the two Briggses were concerned in this—as they must have been—why should anybody shoot Forte? And then kill his father?"

Sarah said abruptly, "The old double cross."

Everyone in the room stared at her. Even Fitz's eyes fluttered open. She said, "That's what Norm said. He thought that Forte was involved in something illegal, and somebody, also involved, tried to . . . to double-cross someone—" She stopped to put her hand on Fitz's pulse. It had a regular beat.

Barney, red to the ears, said, but softly, "That's it! I knew Forte. He'd double-cross his own grandmother. And of course his father tried the same thing—only this time he threatened blackmail or disclosure or something! He knew what and whom to threaten, and so he was killed too, and the old car run into the lake and—" He paused, out of breath, then said defiantly. "That's what happened! I'm as sure of it as—"

"We aren't quite sure of anything," Captain Wood said. "But Fitz has got to be left to rest."

Fanny opened the door, splendidly beautiful in spite of shabby blue jeans and dirty sneakers. She put a finger dramatically to her lips. "Phone for you, Sarah. Your father . . ."

Corinna started up. Fanny whispered, "No, it's for Sarah."

Corinna said, low, "It must be important. Hurry, Sarah."

"Yes. Yes, I'm coming." She glanced at Fitz; his eyes were still closed. She went quickly out into the hall, but Fanny had already vanished.

Norm was standing at the foot of the stairs, a raincoat over his arm. He, too, put a finger to his lips, and as she ran down to meet him he said, low, "It's not your father. That was just an excuse I gave Fanny to get you out of that room. I've got to do something for Fitz. Here, put this coat around you."

The front door was open upon misty gray fog. She hadn't realized how late in the day it was. Corinna's car stood at the steps to the terrace. Norm took her arm and hurried her down and into the car.

"Fitz told me that whatever happened, to put his briefcase in the bank. He said you were to sign for it."

"Where is the briefcase?"

"Here in the car. I took it from his room. Fitz told me to. Come on—"

She was in the car, huddled in a raincoat; she knew how important that briefcase could be in the wrong hands.

"I had to act fast before anybody could stop us," Norm said. "It isn't a long drive."

But it was a long drive. It was already early dusk; it wasn't raining, but the fog wavered ahead of them.

After a while she said, puzzled, "This isn't the road to White Plains."

Norm was peering ahead. "I think I'd better turn on parking lights. Now, let me see—this is the turn—"

"But, Norm, where are we going?"

"The bank—I told you."

The word "bank" seemed to explode in her mind as the car sped along the winding road, going faster and faster. "But it's too late for the bank!" she said, suddenly terrified. "And this is the road to the Westchester airport."

There was no answer.

"Norm! Didn't you hear me?"

Norm's face was white. "My dear, you are a hostage. Nobody will follow us. Nobody will try to stop me. No shooting. They won't dare. They might kill you."

A hostage, her shocked mind shouted at her. She didn't have any breath at all; she had only a wildly thudding heart.

He braked the car; they were approaching the airport. Beams of light from it traveled upward into the misty dark sky.

"Stay here," he said. "I'll be watching—" He jumped out of the car, opened the back door and seized the briefcase. She still could not believe him, could not accept his words: "You are a hostage."

He leaned into the car; his face in the half-light was pale

and desperate. "I never meant to hurt you! Forte must have fixed the brakes. I didn't mean to kill Forte, either. We were supposed to meet in Atlanta. Make plans. But his father must have had a chance to shoot at Bill Hicks sooner than he expected. They got there ahead of me. His father had sent Forte back here to wait for me. Before we could do anything, Fitz had been posted to Ligunia. But Forte accused me of trying to double-cross them and get the ore myself. He waved that gun around—Forte was a fool, but a dangerous fool. I got it away from him. In the struggle the gun went off. I heard a car—yours—coming up the drive. I ran out the back way with the gun—well, I didn't realize, until Gus found it and told us, that it belonged to Fitz. I've got to see about the plane."

"Norm, wait! Forte's father—"

He half turned back. "I had to do that. I had to let him out of the house before he told everything. But he hung around the place—I knew he would. I stole the gun back from Gus just in case. Then Briggs caught me outside while you and Fitz had gone to White Plains. So I—well, there wasn't anything else to do. I had to protect myself. He guessed about Forte and—I thought I'd covered every-thing and then—my bad luck that that damned fool Rosart—well, it never occurred to me that he might have dumped Forte's papers into the trash. When Fitz and I took the cans out for Fanny, I recognized them at a glance—but what could I do without calling more attention to them? I had to try and stop Fitz from seeing them. I fired at him from the edge of the woods after I emptied my can, and then pretended to head for the lake. I was hoping in the excitement that I could get hold of the papers and get rid of them. And I would have, too, if that idiot Rosart hadn't interfered again. Stay there—I've got to make sure of the plane. I think there's one about this time. Don't try to get away, don't move. I'll be right back—"

He left her in the car. She watched his dark figure,

silhouetted against lights from the airport, running, the briefcase bumping against his legs.

Norm! said her stunned mind.

There would be telephones in the airport. She could hide behind other cars in the parking lot, she could circle cautiously around them, and maybe, just maybe, get into the airport. There were telephones—and there were also people!

She crept out of the car. She didn't close the door, for he might be able to hear that.

The autumn night was closing in rapidly. Lights from the airport and the runways shot out into the dusk. She could see dim figures of men moving about here and there. She couldn't see Norm's solid figure, the briefcase swinging beside him, so he must have entered the sprawling building. If she could find a car that was unlocked, she could hide—perhaps.

She tried the next car; its doors were firmly locked. She tried the next, watching for Norm to return.

The fifth car had been left with a door open. She tried it carefully, opened it, and a light sprang up inside. She had forgotten that. Before she could close the door again, Norm, behind her, said, "I told you not to move. Now then, you're going with me."

"Norm . . . Norm, you don't know what you're saying. I can't believe—"

"I heard them outside the house. That shot—I knew then I had to get away." He caught her arm savagely and jerked her with him—in the shadows of the parked cars but toward the runway area.

She tried to reason with him, and felt that her reasoning powers had gone. "Norm, you can't mean to make me go to . . . to wherever you are going!"

"Come on, there's a plane about to take off—"

And it was, thumping engines beating through the night.

"I won't! You can't make me. Norm, please—"

For answer he jerked at her arm again. She cried, "I'll tell them. I'll shout at them—"

"They'll try to stop me before I can get an overseas plane. So you'll stay with me until then— They'll not shoot, they'll be afraid of getting you—" He stopped.

A sharp fan of light caught them as if it had seeking fingers. She whirled around and saw, above the headlights' glare, the whirling red lights of a police car.

Norm dropped her arm. He ran—so fast that nobody could ever catch him, she thought, and she didn't care, for someone had jumped out of the police car, someone had his arm around her, someone shouted, "Here she is. She's all right!"

She sobbed against Fitz's shoulder, then realized that she was leaning on the bandages and shifted her head to the other side. Fitz held her firmly with one arm. "Did Norm tell you?"

"Yes. Some of it. He didn't hurt me, but he did scare me— Oh, Fitz, you shouldn't be here!"

She was dimly aware of other men in the half-gloom, running, shouting to one another, and beyond that tumult, a plane revved up loudly and then soared up and above them.

"Come back to the car—" Fitz and she were in the police car. Fitz was wearing one of Rosart's overcoats. It was large enough to wrap around her, too, which was a good thing, for she was suddenly very cold.

Rosart, Barney, Captain Wood and the state policeman came hurrying back and into the car. Another man, someone slim and very neat, crawled into the car and sat beside Sarah. He said, "You all right, Miss Favor?"

She let out her breath and moved closer to Fitz. "Yes. He's got your briefcase, Fitz."

The strange man said, in a congratulatory way, "Your guess was certainly right, Fitz. You said he'd make for the nearest airport." His name, or part of it, proved to be Jim, for Fitz said, "Good thing you came, Jim, as soon as I talked to you this morning. I think Norm must have heard me. The phone is in the hall. Careless of me. But I knew I had to report. I had to have advice. Things had got too far beyond me." He held Sarah closer.

Jim said, "You were right to phone. I took time only to talk to our boss. He said to get up here and—" He looked at Sarah. "I must have arrived a minute or two after you left."

Sarah thought she said, "What happened?" She must have said it, for Jim replied, "Fitz realized that you had gone—and then he yelled something about Norm. He was already getting into his pants, said he'd called the police and told them they had to come here and stop Norm." He paused and said, "One bad apple in the barrel. Too bad."

"How did you know?" She spoke into Fitz's cheek pressed down against ther face.

"Motive," he said. "I knew as soon as I saw the Ligunian sales agreement. It had to be Norm. Once they got rid of me, Norm would have been sent to Ligunia."

"But it was Forte who tampered with the brakes on my car! Forte threatened Norm with a gun— But, Fitz, Norm was the only one who kept insisting we should report Forte's murder to the police. He told me to mail my letter to you."

"He wanted to get Fitz back here," Jim said quietly.

Captain Wood jerked around in the front seat. "Did Norm have much to say?"

"Yes. Oh, yes—" She told them. There was a long silence. She added, "But Norm—in the woods. He didn't really mean to hurt me. And he was terribly upset when my brakes didn't work—"

Jim said, "He meant to frighten you enough so that you'd send for Fitz. That's my guess. A thoroughly frightened woman will do almost anything."

After a moment Sarah said slowly, "On the stairs—that first night after he shot Forte—I heard somebody. But then, if it was Norm, he'd remember the step that squeaks and . . . nothing happened."

Fitz's arm held her more tightly. "I don't really think he meant to harm you. Just tried everything to get me out of the way and take my place."

"Once he said he . . . he liked me," she whispered.

"He seems to have liked money better," Fitz said grimly.

Jim said, "We'll try to stop him at Kennedy and at Washington."

They reached the Favor house. All the lights were blazing out into the night.

Corinna, Nannie Pie, Rosart, Fanny, even Gus were at the door waiting for them.

Jim made it clear that he must use the telephone. Then all of them were in the big old library, Fitz stretched out in a lounge chair, Rosart lighting a fire. It was Fanny who asked the questions, her melodious voice clear in the quiet room: *"What happened? Why did he shoot Forte? And Forte's father—"*

Fitz glanced at Jim. He replied as neatly as if he were making a report, as doubtless he would. Barney listened avidly, even his ears red with excitement. Captain Wood and the state policeman stood like statues in the background. Jim said, "Seems likely that Norm was hooked into a scheme to get hold of some land in Ligunia. And seems likely that they slipped up. Bill Hicks was shot before Norm and Briggs had arranged to meet and plan. People do make mistakes sometimes when they get too . . . too smart for themselves," He leaned back, looking at the fire thoughtfully. "We believe Norm was supposed to come back to Washington and try to get the appointment to Ligunia. But they crossed themselves up on the meeting date and Fitz was posted to Ligunia instead. Somebody made a mistake. I think, myself, that Briggs saw a chance to shoot Bill Hicks and took it before the time they had decided upon. Not knowing this, Norm went on about his arrangements—a vacation, presumably a hunting trip to Maine as a cover, and then to Atlanta. But Briggs sent his son back here to watch out for Norm. He hadn't yet turned up, and they thought he was about to double-cross them. Probably in the end they would have double-crossed him— got the loot and threatened Norm with exposure.''

Fitz said slowly, ''Norm didn't really have an alibi for the time when Forte was shot. The man he said had dropped him here was posted to the Far East. It would have been difficult to get in touch with him immediately if Norm's alibi was ever questioned. When Briggs arrived here, it gave him a terrible shock. We all saw that, but didn't understand the real reason. Briggs was suddenly a very great danger. I ought to have known then. Norm— yes, Norm was desperately afraid of what Briggs might tell. He had to get him out of the house. So he only pretended to lock the door.''

''Ore,'' Fanny said. ''How did they know?''

Corinna answered, ''Len Briggs was a geologist.''

Jim was now putting his facts and his surmises together in an orderly fashion. ''Yes. Briggs was a geologist. Traveled, must have got into the fact that this stuff existed in Ligunia. Then, through his son, Briggs knew that both you, Fitz, and Norm had finished training and were at the Ligunia desk. Now, in the usual way of things, Norm, being senior, would have been sent to Ligunia to take the place of Bill Hicks. So Bill Hicks had to be gotten rid of. Probably Briggs meant only to provide for Norm's appointment. If Bill Hicks had to be sent home, father and son reasoned (at least the father reasoned; none of you seems too sure about Forte's intelligence) that Norm would be sent to take his place. Norm was in it for the money. He'd have gone along with them; when the sale of the land came across his desk he was expected to facilitate the whole thing. As,'' the man said simply, ''he could have. All sorts of trade and business affairs depend for facilitation upon the officer in charge. This was a purchase by an

American, so, under Ligunian law, it would have been the duty of the American consulate to approve it. That's the way things are. We—all Foreign Service officers—are in a way businessmen. We're expected to promote business affairs. But the Briggs-Norm planning went wrong. Luckily for us, they had agreed, I think, to meet in Atlanta and perfect the scheme. But Norm—while he was on his so-called vacation—phoned somebody in the department and found out that you, Fitz, had already got the appointment to Ligunia. So he hustled home without seeing Briggs at all and was met by Forte, waving that gun around and accusing Norm of trying to double-cross them both. Briggs's haste in taking a shot at Bill Hicks and Norm's sticking to his plan for a vacation, which would give him some needed time, in addition to Briggs's and Forte's suspicions—well, all that fouled things up. Of course, your man Gus says he suspected that Norm didn't go hunting, that he went somewhere where there were quail. Gus said he took the wrong gun for hunting in Maine.''

"You mean a shotgun?" Fitz said.

He nodded. "We don't know just what arrangements Briggs had made for the mining and sale of the ore. But we'll find out. Unless, in fact, he made no arrangements so far, which is possible. He might have preferred to keep the whole purchase a secret until he had completed the requisite formalities. But we'll find out," he said confidently.

He rose as if about to leave. Sarah said stiffly, "There were two capsules. On my bedside table. One red and one yellow and—"

Jim smoothed back his sleek hair. "I imagine they wouldn't have hurt you. All part of Norm's plan, I think, to scare you and cover up the fact that he'd already gotten what he wanted—Fitz's return. If he could keep Briggs from finding out about his son's death, maybe the deal would still have worked out."

"Yes," Fitz said. "I agree. I think he only meant to frighten her. Unless those capsules—"

"On the other hand," Jim interrupted, "the minute Sarah told him she smelled something odd before the shot occurred, he must have been worried sick that she might identify the odor at any time. We'll know definitely when we have the capsule analyzed."

"Norm never had money. He must have wanted it so desperately. All those years filled with secret resentment at being the poor Favor relation. What will happen to him?" Corinna asked sadly.

"I think he'll confess. That is, unless he has some very good friends somewhere who will protect him until he can reach a place where he will have full immunity from prosecution on our part. No law of extradition. As a matter of fact"—Jim put a friendly hand on Fitz's knee—"we're not going to make a big public story out of this. Would do nobody any good."

Captain Wood had been listening quietly. Now he said, "You might want to know, Fitz, that in our opinion nobody but the State's Attorney will hear about all this. Of course, we may have to send for you both to come back. There are such things as material witnesses—that is, of course, we can't overlook two murders. I think things will be made simple for all of you. Right, sir?" he asked Jim.

Jim nodded.

"You mean"—Sarah unexpectedly quoted Corinna—"they aren't going to hang any of us."

Captain Wood looked at her soberly. Jim said, "No," and smiled.

Fitz said, "Anything to keep me here, Captain?"

"Your shoulder—"

"Anything else?"

"I have to find out what the State's Attorney says."

"Whatever he says, we're going to be married. As soon as we can get a license and—"

"Oh," Barney cried, "I forgot! I answered the phone

this afternoon. Didn't make sense then—at least I didn't pay much attention. Anyway, it was the judge. He said to tell you everything is all right. You can get married any old time—''

"Now," Fitz said.

Solly, like a spring released, loped into the room and put his head on Sarah's knees. "How are we going to take him?" she asked Fitz.

Captain Wood had been knocked over a footstool by Solly's wild rush. "Your problem, Fitz," he said sourly. "Come on, Barney."

About the Author

MIGNON G. EBERHART's name has become a guarantee of excellence in the mystery and suspense field. Her work has been translated into sixteen languages, and has been serialized in many magazines and adapted for radio, television and motion pictures.

For many years Mrs. Eberhart traveled extensively abroad and in the United States. Now she lives in Greenwich, Connecticut.

In April 1971 the Mystery Writers of America gave Mrs. Eberhart their Grand Master Award, in recognition of her sustained excellence as a suspense writer, and in 1977 she served as president of that organization. She recently celebrated the fiftieth anniversary of the publication of her first novel, *The Patient in Room 18*.